AUTUMN EVER AFTER

J A ARMITAGE

1

Anais had been sitting at the window of the attic watching the autumn leaves fall for the last two hours. Hues of browns and oranges and reds twirled down creating a flame coloured patchwork blanket over the driveway. From her vantage point, she could see the tops of hundreds of trees, a riot of colour almost like a mosaic stretched out before her. The autumn view was spectacular, but Anais barely registered the beauty before her. Instead, she was counting the leaves dropping one by one. It was all she could do to keep calm. At the moment, her mind was numb as she watched the eighty-second leaf perform its twirling dance to join its brothers and sisters on the driveway below.

The reason for such a banal task is that she had once again found herself locked in a room. She had lost count at how many times she had been locked up in the previous year, but this time, it was much worse. This time, Jago, the man who had killed her parents, the man who had nearly killed her on more than one occasion, and the man who she had only ever known as her friend, Andrew, had been the one to lock her up. It wasn't really the fact that she was locked up that had caused her mind to shut down. She could escape easily, even though Andrew, aka Jago, had nailed boards to the other side of the door to prevent it. The attic contained plenty of heavy objects to use to knock the door down, and she knew that with a bit of force, she and her fellow prisoners, Sabine and Jennifer, could break through the door. The problem was that she knew how clever Andrew was, and it was what she would find on the other side of the door that was causing her fear. She knew Andrew well enough to know that he would have a contingency plan in place if they ever found out he was the evil Jago. She also knew that he would not let anything stop him from getting what he wanted. He had killed before and shown no remorse. That, coupled with the fact he was the most intelligent person Anais had ever known, made him extremely dangerous. Anais knew that he could kill her in a blink of an eye and not even break a sweat over it. That was why she just sat there watching the summer turn into autumn.

Sabine and Jennifer, on the other hand, had been slightly more productive. After calming down from the shock of seeing her captor, Sabine had led Jennifer on a mission to find an axe or sledgehammer. Anais had briefly wondered if she was planning to use it on the door or on Jago himself. She stifled a giggle at the thought of it, although it was not a laughing matter, and she knew that it was fear that was causing such a strange reaction. She also knew that it didn't matter anymore. There would be no escape, even if they did get through the door; Jago would not let them leave the house alive. Staying in the attic, in her opinion, was just a way of delaying the inevitable. Thoughts had gone through her head that he had already killed all the others in the house. She didn't think so, but she wasn't in any rush to get through the door to find out.

So far, the best they had come up with was a huge butcher's knife, which had been packed up in a box with some other kitchen utensils. Anais could hear them at the bottom of the stairs trying to hack through the wooden door. Suddenly there was a big crack and the girls ran up the stairs in fright.

Anais jumped up, her heart pounding.

"What was that?" asked Anais of a terrified looking Sabine.

"Jago's back. He's pulling the boards off from the other side."

Anais looked at Jennifer, who, up until now, had managed to keep her composure, but now, even she looked a little fearful.

Anais took the butcher's knife out of a trembling Sabine's hand and waited. The final nailed board came off and the attic door opened with a creak, causing Sabine to whimper. Anais held the knife in front of her as the sound of footsteps came up the stairs. Anais could not see who was coming, but by the sound of the heavy footfall, it was definitely a man. She gripped the knife tighter and steadied herself as the man came into view. She had only just registered who it was before Sabine flew past her and flung herself into his arms.

It was Alex. He had a confused grin on his face.

"What's going on?" He held onto the weeping Sabine and began to stroke her hair to calm her down.

"Anais? Seriously, what is going on? Dinner is ready.

Mama asked me to come and get you all. Andrew handed me a crowbar and told me you were all in the attic."

With this, Sabine whimpered even more and buried her head into his neck. He held her tightly.

"It's Jago," answered Anais.

"Jago? Where? The grin on Alex's face fell, to be replaced with a look of shock. He swivelled his head behind him as if expecting to find Jago in the attic."

"Andrew," said Anais, "Andrew is Jago."

The grin reappeared on Alex's face.

"Don't be silly. Andrew just told me where you are. He's already seated at the table waiting for you to come down so we can eat."

Anais looked him straight in the eye and repeated herself.

"Andrew is Jago."

Sabine muttered something that sounded like "He is!" before once again disappearing into Alex's neck.

"But?" Alex paused obviously not sure what to believe. "Eh?"

"He's downstairs in the dining room? Is everyone else there?" Anais asked him.

"Yes. We were just waiting for you. Seriously, though? What has happened? Have you guys banged your head or, or, or erm, eaten something funny?"

"Why do you think the door was nailed shut? Do you think we somehow managed to nail ourselves in from the other side of the door?"

Alex just looked at her blankly

Alex obviously did not believe her. She was not surprised. Andrew had fooled her completely and she had not known him for that long. She could only imagine the shock Alex must be feeling after knowing him six hundred years. Still, there was no point standing up here trying to convince him.

"Let's go and eat." She moved towards the attic stairs and made her way down with the others following behind.

"We are going to have to face him sooner or later. We may as well do it on a full stomach." She threw the butcher's knife to the floor, knowing that it would not help her in the slightest. Whatever Andrew/Jago had in store for them, a mere butcher's knife wouldn't be able to stop it.

Anais held her breath and opened the dining room door. With as much confidence as she could muster, she walked in and sat next to a confused looking Aethelu. She gripped Aethelu's hand harder than she had ever done before causing Aethelu to give a little squeal of pain.

"Where have you been?" Aethelu whispered to Anais, but Anais didn't answer. She had her eyes fixed on Andrew, who was watching her with an expression of macabre delight. Jennifer followed behind Anais but took a seat as far from Andrew as she could find. Anais could hear Sabine sobbing outside the room and Alex trying to cajole her into entering.

"Alex. Is everything alright?" Winnie shouted towards the door.

Everyone's eyes were focussed on the door, waiting for Alex and a wailing Sabine. All except for Anais, who was looking at Andrew, and Andrew, who was returning her gaze.

"Yes, Mama" Alex shouted back. "Just a minute."

Anais heard a quickly whispered discussion followed by Alex almost dragging a terrified Sabine through the door. They, too, took seats as far from Andrew as possible. Anais caught a questioning look from Rafe to his twin, which Alex answered with a shrug.

Andrew stood up to address everyone, which was a shock in itself to the majority there as Andrew was usually exceptionally shy, and only ever spoke one to one. Anais wondered what he was going to say.

"I think I can guess why Sabine is so upset and I'm afraid it's my fault. You see, I have rather a large announcement to make and I'm afraid Anais, Sabine and Jennifer found out before I was ready to tell you all, and I got a little angry and had words with them all. I apologise. I am hoping that they will let me tell you all myself; however, dinner smells wonderful, as always. Thank you, Winnie. So let us eat first before I tell you my wonderful news. He sat down and started helping himself to roast potatoes.

Most people looked a little confused at this except for August, who knew his cue to begin eating and started to fill up his plate with enormous heaps of food. Alex took Andrew's speech as the truth and also started to eat as if it explained why his girlfriend was so upset. Anais looked incredulously at Andrew as he popped a carrot into his mouth. He caught her stare and gave her a wink. It was so unlike him. Usually, he hid behind a curtain of hair. Now he looked proud, cocky even. It made Anais feel sick. Even though she knew what was coming, she forced herself to eat. It would do no good for the baby for her to starve herself. She knew that if she told everyone the truth, just as she had with Alex, no one would believe her. She would have to play this charade until after dinner when Andrew would announce it himself. She looked over at Sabine and Jennifer, who were sitting next to each other at the far end of the table. Jennifer was quietly eating her food and meeting no one's eyes. Sabine was also not looking up, but she was not eating. Her eyes were puffy from all the crying, but she also looked slightly angry. Anais could not blame her. She had told her boyfriend the truth about Andrew and not only had he not believed her, but he'd also forced her into this room against her will when she was obviously scared. It was unlike Alex to be so cruel, but she knew that it would never enter his head that Andrew could be Jago. Even as she watched, he put his arm around Sabine and kissed her head. He whispered something in her ear, which prompted no reaction from Sabine.

"What is it?" asked Aethelu under her breath. "Why is Sabine so upset?"

"I could tell you, but you wouldn't believe me if I did," Anais whispered back.

Aethelu gave her a quizzical look and then realised that Anais was not happy.

"Seriously, what's up? Are you ok? Is it something to do with the baby?"

"Andrew is Jago," Anais said it matter of factly. As predicted, Aethelu didn't believe her.

"Don't be silly." Aethelu playfully tapped Anais on the arm.

"He told me upstairs. Sabine recognised him. We have been locked in the attic for the last two hours. Where did you think we were?"

"Andrew told me you were tired and had gone for a nap. Mama decided to use whatever crockery she had in the kitchen. Are you feeling sick? I knew I should have checked on you."

"I'm not sick, I'm not tired. I've been in the attic with Sabine and Jennifer. Andrew nailed us in. We only got out when Alex crowbarred us out.

"But that makes no sense!" Aethelu forgot she was whispering and spoke this aloud. Everyone around the table turned to look at them.

Andrew had a strange smile on his face.

'He knows we are talking about him' thought Anais.

"I guess he'll tell you himself after dinner."

Aethelu looked slightly perturbed by the revelation that her long-time friend was, in fact, her greatest enemy. Actually, it was the fact Anais was telling her this that had her looking worried. She believed Anais as much as Alex had believed Sabine. Anais stole a look over at Alex. He seemed quite jovial as if it was all a big joke. Sabine was finally starting to eat, or at least push her food around her plate with a fork. Everyone else around the table was blissfully unaware that Jago was in their midst and were all enjoying being back together as a family. Aldrich had brought a few bottles of champagne to the table, which were disappearing rather quickly. Anais wondered if Andrew wanted them all drunk to tell them the news. It would probably be easier on him if they were all too drunk to get up and hit him. Anais looked around the table as Winnie served up a huge apple crumble, followed by August with a gigantic vat of vanilla custard. She watched as Andrew asked for extra custard and Winnie joked that his news must be something special if he wanted to build up his strength with extra helpings. Next to him, sat James and then there was Winnie's empty seat. Anais, herself, was followed by Aethelu, Aldrich, and Jennifer. Sabine sat at the furthest possible seat from Andrew and Alex sat next to her. Rafe sat next to his brother with August's empty seat next to him. Then she was back to Andrew, who was eating his crumble with a gleam in his eye. Anais could not believe that no one had noticed how different he was acting compared to his usual demeanour. Normally he hid away behind a curtain of silver-white hair and kept quiet unless someone addressed him. There were a few gaps where chairs usually filled by other family members had been taken away.

Aethelu grabbed Anais' hand to catch her attention.

"Look at me." This time, she kept her voice down so that only Anais could hear. Someone laughed at the far end of the table, over what, Anais didn't know. She turned to look at Aethelu.

"I love you and I know you would never lie to me," she looked her right in the eyes. "Are you sure? Is there any way at all you could be mistaken? Tiredness? Pregnancy hormones? You are positive that Andrew is Jago?"

"He is. He told me upstairs in the attic."

"Do you think that perhaps he was teasing you and went a bit too far? He always was a bit, I dunno, socially awkward."

"It's him. It's definitely him. You should have seen him in the attic. He was barely recognisable. His quiet demeanour was just an act. He killed my parents, and he almost killed us. Look at how he's eating apple crumble as if he doesn't have a care in the world. He knows he has to tell everyone and he's looking forward to it. Look at him."

Aethelu turned to look towards her oldest friend. He certainly looked like he didn't have a care in the world. He was currently scraping the last of the custard from his bowl with a spoon.

"Bastard!" screamed Aethelu making Anais and everyone else jump.

Aethelu picked up a glass full of champagne and threw it as hard as she could at Andrew. It smashed into his face causing a cut just above his eyebrow and splashing champagne all over him. He lifted his hand and wiped away a spot of blood that had appeared. Within seconds, the cut had vanished, thanks to The Light giving him amazing healing powers.

Aldrich grabbed hold of his daughter just as she was about to climb over the table to get to Andrew. He wrestled her back into her seat as the others watched in shock.

"Aethelu!" exclaimed Winnie. "What did you do that for? Andrew, love, are you ok?"

"Ask him," spat out Aethelu. She had already stopped squirming and fighting against Aldrich. Instead, she looked over at Andrew, anger spilling out of her from every pore.

Andrew stood, took a napkin and wiped the corner of his mouth.

"Well, I was hoping to get to this without incident, but I suppose it can only be expected. I'm afraid Aethelu has just had some devastating news, delivered to her by Anais, no doubt. You see, the reason that Aethelu is so upset is that she has just found out that I am Jago."

He waited for a response, but none came. Everyone had been rendered mute with shock. Eventually, Alex spoke.

"That's what Sabine said. Is this some kind of prank? Because, it's not funny."

"You should pay more attention to your girlfriend Alex. I assure you, it is no prank; however, before I continue, I think I should explain a few things. Firstly, if anybody tries to hurt me in any way or lock me up, I will not be able to get back to my room. You do not want this to happen. I have vials of Jagovirus set on a timer. If I do not program a key code in every four hours, they will break, unleashing it into the world. If you think that such small doses will be easily contained, think again. I have twenty vials hidden in different places around the house and grounds. Each vial contains the Jagovirus. If any of you come into contact with it, it will have an immediate effect. You will become paralysed. Soon after, your muscles will start to burn in excruciating pain. Then your respiratory system will give up and you will stop breathing. At that point, you have a little over two minutes left to live. Not a pleasant way to go at all. It is extremely contagious and acts within minutes. If just one vial is broken, it will infect the whole village within a week. From there its spread will be swift and devastating. It is a hundred percent effective, and, as you know, there is no cure."

Anais looked around the table as everyone processed this unbelievable information. It was evidently too much for most of them to process as they all sat there with their mouths open, looking at Andrew in disbelief.

Eventually, Aldrich stood up. "Nonsense, no infection or virus can work that quickly."

"You underestimate me, Aldrich. I have watched you for six-hundred years. I watched as you made The Light Elixir. I tried to be like you. I've been trying to emulate that recipe myself for so many years, but alas, I cannot get it right. However, the Jagovirus is perfect. It is so fast acting, it is almost immediate."

"Then if what you say is true and any of those vials do break in the house or grounds, it's highly unlikely that any virus will get to the village. It may infect us, but if it works how you say it does, we'll be dead long before any of us can get to The Manor's boundary."

"This is true. Its power will probably kill you long before you have a chance to infect anyone else. It is very a fast-acting infection. I did tinker with the idea of making it slower acting and having Mrs. Smithson catch it, but I thought that wouldn't be any fun. I have fired her, by the way. I didn't want her getting in the way. So, you are wondering how I plan to get the virus out into the general public. Well, I told a little white lie. There are actually twenty-one vials. The twenty I already mentioned, to kill all of you and an extra one hidden somewhere in the village for the rest of the population. I've made that one slightly different. That one will take about two weeks to kill, just enough time for people to move about and infect others. They are all connected to the same timer. I have exactly ten minutes before I have to go and input the code and I am sure you have many questions. I will be happy to answer anything you ask, but the clock is ticking.

"Why, Andrew? We all loved you." Winnie's voice wobbled as she spoke.

"You know why. I want The Light Elixir."

"Where's Judith?" Rafe shouted.

Anais looked around. She had not noticed before now, but Judith was not at the table. Rafe suddenly looked panicked.

"Ah, I was hoping you'd ask that. Well, I know that I told you she was sleeping, which is the truth. What I failed to mention earlier is that she is sleeping in my bed, a little oversight on my part. She has been drugged and knows nothing about this. I plan for this to remain the case. As I'm sure you would tell her at the first opportunity, I've decided to keep her with me. I'll wake her up when Arcadia comes home with the last pendant and Aldrich brews The Light Elixir. At that point, I'll wake her up and tell her the good news--that she will live forever as my bride."

"You sick..." Rafe jumped over the table and ran towards Andrew, no doubt to finish the job Aethelu had started moments before. Before anyone could stop him, he punched Andrew straight in the face, knocking him to the floor.

"You'll pay for that!" screamed Andrew as Alex ran to grab his brother. "In fact, I think you'll find it very funny indeed." He pulled himself up from the floor, wiping blood from his nose. With that, he pulled out something that looked like a normal TV remote and pointed it towards the back of the room. There was a loud beep and a thick metal door came down in front of the normal door. Andrew ran towards it and ducked under just before it closed.

Anais could see the shocked expressions of everyone around the table apart from Sabine, who looked bleakly at the table. Alex ran to the door to see if there was a way to open it as more metal shutters came down in front of each of the huge windows, plunging them into darkness. Somebody screamed in the darkness, but Anais couldn't tell who it was. Chairs started to move and squeak on the wooden floor as everybody stood up. Finally, the lights came back on, thanks to August, who had been seated next to the light switch. The room was in chaos as everyone tried to process what had just happened.

Winnie and Sabine were the only two still seated and it was obvious Winnie was crying although she held her head in her hands.

"I don't believe it!" she murmured. Aldrich put his hand on his wife's shoulder as a gesture of comfort.

"I'm going to kill him! I'm actually going to murder him." Rafe pounded on the metal door in frustration, but it did not budge. Anais was shocked to see Rafe like this. He could always be counted on to keep his composure. It was actually quite frightening to see him so angry.

"Sit down!" yelled a voice above all the din. Everyone went quiet and followed Aldrich's instructions, even Rafe.

"We need to stick together in this and figure out what we are going to do. If we fall to pieces, he will win. We need to end this. I know it has been a huge shock to us all. Andrew was practically a son to me, but I think we can all agree he needs to be stopped. Now, can anyone tell me what he meant about Arcadia coming home with the final pendant? Has she called anyone to tell them that she has found it?"

It was then that Anais remembered the necklace around her neck. In all the pandemonium, she had totally forgotten it was there.

"I think that's my fault. I told him it was in a safe in Egypt. He's probably already called Arcadia to tell her to retrieve it."

"I take it by your tone of voice that she will be unsuccessful in that endeavour and the pendant is not there. Am I correct?"

"Yes. I made it up. I was playing for time. He was going to kill me."

"I understand why you told him that, but by tomorrow we are going to be in a difficult situation when he realises that he will never get the elixir. We have next to no chance of finding that last pendant."

"Actually..." Anais trailed off. She pulled at the chain around her neck and brought out the last pendant, holding it up for everyone to see. Aethelu gasped.

"Where did you find it?"

"It was up in the attic the whole time, locked in an old jewellery box. I found it earlier this evening before I found out about Andrew."

Aldrich came over to her and took the pendant. He examined it closely.

"This is indeed the last pendant. We finally have everything we need to make the Elixir. The question is, are we going to?"

"Not a chance!" spat Rafe, who was actually looking rather mad. "I spoke to Judith, she knows about us. She never wanted to take any Elixir. She had no desire for eternal life. She just wanted to be happy in this one. I'm not going to let that monster do that to her."

"We have to" countered Sabine. "He'll kill anyone who gets in his way."

"Let him try! Killing all of us won't get him the Elixir."

"Anais is pregnant. I'm not letting that scum-bucket harm either her or my daughter. I say give him what he wants." Aethelu looked determined. Anais held her hand tightly.

"What's that noise?" asked Jennifer in alarm.

At first, Anais didn't know to what Jennifer was referring, but then she heard the hissing sound.

"It's some kind of gas. He's pumping the room full of gas!" exclaimed Alex. He ran back to the door and together with Rafe, they tried to somehow barge through it. August had run to one of the shutters over the windows and was trying to find a way to grip it to pull it up. James was doing the same at the other window.

Anais suddenly found the whole situation ridiculous. She let out a giggle. Aethelu gave her a strange look.

"Why are you laughing?"

Anais wasn't sure. She certainly didn't feel very happy. Suddenly there was a peal of laughter coming from Sabine, who seemed to have gotten over her morose state. Jennifer sat in the corner of the room giggling away to herself with tears of mirth running down her face.

"I think I've figured out what the gas is," said James, who then broke out laughing, as if he had just heard the funniest joke.

"Laughing gas," said Alex between guffaws. Anais looked over and saw that both he and Rafe were so consumed with laughter that they were unable to carry on trying to get through the door. Despite this, Rafe still had a look of extreme anger on his face. It was the funniest thing Anais had ever seen. She laughed so hard that her stomach hurt. On her left, Aethelu was banging her fists on the table in hysterical laughter.

Andrew had rendered all of them useless with laughing gas. They all were now either slumped over double in hysterics or were rolling around on the floor in stitches.

Everything seemed hilarious to Anais, who couldn't stop laughing. Her stomach was now really beginning to hurt because of all the vibrations of laughter running through her. She tried to calm down and regulate her breathing, but the more she tried, the more hysterical she got. She began to worry how all this laughing would affect her baby, but it all seemed so funny that she laughed all the more.

Hours went by and still she couldn't stop. The pain in her stomach was now getting unbearable, but she couldn't tell anyone, as she was laughing too hard to speak. No one would have noticed anyway as they were all consumed by their own laughing. Anais looked around and found that the others were experiencing pain, too. Most of them were clutching their stomachs like she was. Still, the laughing continued. It seemed to go on forever. Some of the family were struggling for breath now. Anais herself was gasping between laughs. Her whole body was exhausted with the effort of laughing. She fell to the floor and curled up into a ball. The pain was intolerable and seemed to radiate out from her middle. Eventually, after what seemed like hours the hissing stopped. Anais didn't move. She couldn't. Her whole body was in agony. The metal door and window shutters came up and air came into the room.

It was such a relief. Although she didn't have the energy to open her eyes and, therefore, couldn't see anyone, she could hear the others gasping for the fresh oxygen. The room became silent. She knew it was because no one else had the energy to move either. They were all totally exhausted from the hours of laughing. She felt cool air on her face coming from the hallway. It was blissful. She took a few lungfuls of air and fell into a deep slumber on the floor where she had fallen.

2

Anais awoke the next morning in considerable pain. Although it had lessened during the night, she was still very stiff from falling asleep on a cold floor, and her stomach had cramped up so badly she felt sick. Her first thought was for her baby, but a little kick from inside reassured her that her daughter was fine. It was as if she knew. Anais brought her hand to her stomach, but even that small movement shot pains up her arm causing her to gasp aloud. When she opened her eyes and eased her painful body into a sitting position, she could see that the others had also slept where they had fallen. Anais herself had fallen asleep under the table, but she could see Aethleu's legs still seated at the table. Winnie and Sabine had both fallen under the table and were both still sleeping. A huge snoring noise from the corner told her that August was also still asleep. She couldn't see anyone else from her position and so she was momentarily shocked when someone grabbed her arm. Turning her head quickly, she saw that it was James.

"Are you ok? I saw you moving. I think we are the only two awake so far."

James pulled her into a standing position, but when he let go of her, her legs couldn't hold her weight and she fell. James lunged and caught her just in time. He placed her on the seat next to Aethelu whose head was on the table in a puddle of drool.

"I have dead legs. I can't feel them," explained Anais to James.

"You will in a few minutes when the blood comes back into them. You are going to get the mother of all pins and needles. Is the baby ok? Do you know?"

"I think so," replied Anais rubbing her legs to get feeling back into them. "She kicked a couple of times this morning. I think that's what woke me up actually."

James smiled. "I'll ask Aldrich to give you a check-up once he's awake."

One by one, the family woke up, each dazed or, like Anais, suffering from varying degrees of pins and needles. The food left over from the night before still sat on the table along with the dirty plates, which had not yet been cleared away. The smell made Anais' stomach churn.

There was a general air of sadness and confusion in the room. Despite the fact that Anais knew that Winnie had slept all night, she still had black circles under her eyes. In fact, all of them looked a little worse for wear after their night on the floor.

"What now?" asked a weary looking August once they were all sat back around the table.

"I'm going to go up there and wring his neck..." said Rafe, standing up. He wobbled for a few seconds before falling back into his chair, "just as soon as I get enough feeling back in my legs."

"Hang on," said Aldrich, taking charge. "You remember what he said last night. Wringing his neck isn't going to help us. We need a better plan."

"Oh, another plan, how droll." All heads turned to see Andrew enter the room. "This family and their plans. It's all we ever do. Does it ever get us anywhere?"

Anais was shocked at his appearance. His once limp hair was styled fashionably, his trademark black t-shirt and jeans had been replaced. He still wore black, but now, instead of the t-shirt, he wore a black shirt and a long black velvet jacket. It was almost as if he had been stealing from Rafe's wardrobe. The fancy style was all Rafe and a far cry from Andrew's usual attire.

He walked around the room to where Aldrich was seated.

"The pendant, if you please."

"What?"

"The pendant, I know you have it." He waited, hand outstretched, whilst Aldrich retrieved it from his pocket and handed it over. "Imagine it being in the attic all this time. Yes, take those shocked looks off your faces. You'd think by the look of you all that I'd not been planning this day for a long time. Don't think that I haven't got every detail planned. That includes hidden microphones in each room. You already know about the cameras. Ha. All this time you thought I'd installed them for security from Jago when, in fact, I installed them to watch the lot of you. I must say, I rather enjoyed watching your evening last night. I even had a chuckle myself. Laughter is contagious, you know." He continued to walk around the table, swinging the pendant as he went. When he passed Rafe, he gave him a hard kick in the shins.

"That's for last night. I don't appreciate being punched in the face."

Rafe looked murderous, but it was clear that his body was just too exhausted to fight back.

"Now, please don't get any more Ideas of beating me up, because you won't. The whole house is booby-trapped and with much worse things than laughing gas. Last night was just a taste of what you can expect. Next time you disobey me, it will be no laughing matter.

Aldrich, now that you have all the ingredients, how long will it take to brew the Elixir?"

"It takes about a month to brew, although we have to wait for the next full moon to begin." He paused. "That is if the ingredients are still usable. They are incredibly old. If they have survived, the chances of them being usable will be negligible."

"Let's hope for all our sakes that they are usable then. Right, I'll go and check on when the next full moon will be. In the meantime, here is what is going to happen. You are all going to continue to live here as if nothing is wrong. I could kill all of you now, which will make my life much easier, but I really don't want the hassle of cleaning up all the mess. I put in a couple of calls last night. Arcadia, Audsley, Ava, and Alfred will be joining us shortly. Of course, they don't know what's going on, but I'm sure you will clue them in once they get here. I need you all in one place so I can keep an eye on you all. I don't want any loose ends. Aldrich and James will make the Elixir and when it's done, Judith and I will disappear."

"Why? Why, Andrew? Why are you doing this?" Winnie asked, repeating her question of the night before, tears falling down her face.

"I've had to live with the lot of you for six centuries. I'm sick of it. All of you have partners, but not me. At first, it wasn't too bad. I didn't mind that Rafe and Alex always had girls falling all over them or that Arcadia was beautiful and popular. It didn't bother me because I still had Alistair and Aethelu. Just like me, they had no one and in that respect, we had each other. Then everything changed. Alistair got a girlfriend. At first, I was happy for him, but then he brought her here. Sarah. He'd leave her here whilst he went out to work. How anyone could leave such a beautiful woman even for a second, I do not know. She got bored, stuck in the house on her own. She used to come and chat with me. She loved chess as much as I did. I made her a chess set. We'd play for hours moving the family pieces around."

Anais remembered the chess set. She'd played with it herself with Aethelu when she was locked upstairs. She'd not known it was made for her mother.

"She was the first woman to ever pay attention to me. I fell in love with her, but all she wanted was him," he spat this last word out with such hate. "Even the chess set wasn't enough for her. I tried to get her to fall in love with me, but all she ever talked about was your father."

This was addressed to Anais.

"Ali this and Ali that. It was sickening. Eventually, they visited less and less. On one of their visits, she told me she was pregnant. Pregnant! Can you believe it? After all, I had done for her. I couldn't believe it. I was so angry that I wanted to kill them both. I did not succeed. He took my love away to America. As you know, I cannot travel by plane due to my phobia of flying. I bided my time. I suppose my love for her lessened over time, but the anger remained. I'd already started talking to Judith over the internet by the time they moved back to England and I had no desire for Sarah anymore. I was shocked at how easy it was to kill them. Things were going great for me then. I'd finally gotten rid of them and had a new love of my own. Judith even talked of coming to live with me in England. The only problem was that she was mortal. Even if she lived to a very old age, we only had another sixty or so years left together. Plus, she'd get old and saggy and wrinkled. I could not let that happen to my beautiful Judith. I needed some of the Light Elixir, but how? I asked Aldrich, but he told me he'd forgotten. I figured he'd remember pretty quickly if I threatened his family and I was right, wasn't I? Here we are less than a year later and we have all the ingredients. All that remains now is to get it brewed, wake Judith and leave forever."

"Aren't you forgetting something?" sneered Rafe, pure anger on his face. "Judith is in love with me. She'd never leave me for you."

"I'll just tell her you died in a horrific accident. It probably won't be far from the truth by the time I wake her up, anyway."

"I should just kill you now." Rafe looked angry enough to, but Anais knew he would feel too exhausted to move and certainly wouldn't have the energy to cause much damage to Andrew.

"We both know that is not going to happen. However, if any of you get any ideas of that nature, I think I should set a few ground rules.

One: None of you is to leave the house under any circumstances. All the doors are locked, anyway. The only exception is Aldrich and James to go to the surgery to brew the Elixir. If anyone tries to escape, the grounds are as booby-trapped as the house and I will think nothing of killing you.

Two: No attempting to contact anyone on the outside. I've jammed all the phone signals anyway, so I don't think this will be much of a problem for anyone.

Three: This is for you, Rafe. Don't attempt to rescue Judith. She is perfectly fine and being looked after. You don't have to worry about her welfare, only your own.

Four: Don't try to defeat me. Last night was only a taste of what I can do to you. I can hear everything you say and see every move that you make. I will pop up where you least expect it and I have enough tricks up my sleeve to ensure that you can never win.

My final rule is that I expect everyone to attend breakfast, lunch and dinner here together every day. I will be here for every meal and if anyone is so much as a minute late for any meal without good cause, I will set off one of my traps. I assure you that they won't all be as much fun as last night's entertainment."

Anais shuddered. Last night had been anything but fun. It had been pure torture. All she wanted to do now was go to bed. She'd had enough listening to Andrew's psychotic ramblings. She knew she should be angrier with him, but all she could think of was her nice, warm bed. She would be quite happy to stay there the whole month or however long it took to brew the Elixir and get rid of Andrew.

"Right, the time is..." Andrew looked at his watch, "nine-fifteen, too late for breakfast. I'll see you all back here at midday for lunch." He turned and stalked out of the room leaving the rest of them, angry, shocked and most of all, shattered. Anais dragged herself up and pulled on Aethelu's hand. The weary pair made their way upstairs and collapsed into bed, not even bothering to undress. At eleven-thirty, she woke up, every muscle aching but feeling slightly more refreshed, thanks to the couple of more hours' sleep she'd had. She left a snoring Aethelu and ran a bath. The warm water soothed her, and she could have lain there for hours, but she dared not be late for lunch, or who knew what might happen. She reluctantly got out after staying in it as long as she could, dried off, and dressed.

After she woke Aethelu, they descended the stairs to the dining room. The dirty dishes from this morning had been cleared away and now platters of sandwiches lined the long table. Anais suddenly felt guilty that she'd not offered to help. Winnie must have done it. She vowed to help clear up this meal and let Winnie have some much-needed rest. Looking around the table, she saw that everyone was already there except Rafe and Andrew. She looked at her watch...three minutes to twelve. Rafe was cutting it close. She hoped that he hadn't done anything stupid or wasn't attempting to defy Andrew by arriving late. The dining room doors opened and Anais prayed it was Rafe, but it was not. Andrew came in, sat down and helped himself to a sandwich. Everyone else sat silently, watching him with fear in their eyes. The grandfather clock out in the hallway started to bong twelve o'clock. Under the table, Anais crossed her fingers. She could barely breathe. Where was Rafe? Then on the eighth bong, Rafe entered the room much to the relief of everyone else and sat down sulkily. Andrew smiled at him, a smile that was not returned. One by one, they helped themselves to the food. No one spoke a word for the whole meal and when he had finished, Andrew simply got up from the table and left the room.

"Thank you for these wonderful sandwiches, Winnie." Anais broke the silence.

Winnie gave a small smile. "You are welcome, love.

August helped, too. How are you feeling anyway? How is the baby? I meant to ask you this morning, but I was just too exhausted to speak."

"I think she's fine. She's kicking like a trooper. I don't think the laughing gas affected her. I hate to think what else he has in store, though. I certainly can't go through last night again."

"I don't think any of us could," said August between mouthfuls of sandwich. "My back's killing me. I'm going to need a bed if he's not going to let me go home. I do need to get Baker, though. I can't leave him at the cottage by himself. Andrew looked after him whilst I was in Egypt, so I think he'll let me go fetch him. I'll go ask him now." He got up, picking up a handful of sandwiches to take with him."

"If Andrew really has told Arcadia, Audsley, Freddie, and Ava to come, we won't have any spare bedrooms. Will you be ok in the dorm room in the cellar?"

"Don't worry about me, Mum, I'll be fine."

"Oh, and can you ask Andrew about food. We have enough for the next few days, but if he doesn't let us leave the house, we are going to run out pretty quickly.

"Will do."

"What are we going to do?" asked Aethelu to the table when August had left.

"What can we do?" asked Anais. "He can hear everything we are saying right now. He's got all bases covered. We all know how clever he is. I hate to say it, but I think our only option is to give him what he wants."

"Give him the Elixir?"

"What else can we do?"

"I'll be damned if I'm going to let him do that to Judith." Rafe slammed down his fist angrily. "She explicitly told me that she had no desire to live forever. She wanted to grow old." He suddenly raised his voice and shouted into the room to no one in particular. "Do you hear me, you evil bastard. She wanted to grow up, grow old, and eventually die. She didn't want to be like us!"

"Calm down, bro," said Alex, putting a hand on his brother's arm.

"Calm down!" Rafe shouted, "Why should I calm down? He has Judith drugged inside his bedroom and we are all sitting here doing nothing about it. Would you calm down if it was Sabine?"

The look on Alex's face answered his question.

"No, I thought not." Rafe stalked out of the room and banged the door loudly on the way out.

Aldrich stood. "I think we all need to keep calm. Alex, Rafe will do something dangerous if he can't keep his emotions in check. Can you stay with him and make sure he is ok? The rest of us need to just hang on and see this out. The next full moon is in about three weeks. From that point, it will take about a month to brew the Elixir. Perhaps then, we can appeal to Andrew's better nature to do the right thing. In the meantime, I say we sit tight and not cause any problems. I know it's not ideal, but I see no way around it at the moment."

Anais put her hand on her stomach. This would all be over by the time Autumn was born--one way or another, Andrew would have what he wanted. She only hoped they all lived long enough to see it.

All the others nodded, all except Aethelu.

"This is ridiculous. How can we just let him get away with this? Appeal to his better nature? I think there is enough evidence to support the fact that he doesn't have one!" she must have known he could hear her, but she made no attempt to lower her voice.

"I don't see that we have much of a choice, Aethelu. My main priority is to keep you all safe. Giving him what he wants looks like the safest course of action at the moment." Aldrich spoke calmly to his youngest daughter.

"At the moment!" repeated Aethelu. "What then? Do you really think he'll just use it on Judith? I can't see her skipping off into the sunset with him anyway. What happens when she wakes up and tells him that she still wants Rafe?"

"I think Rafe is in the biggest danger at the moment, that's why I've asked Alex to keep an eye on him. I want you all to look out for him."

"But what about Judith?" asked Sabine. "Are we going to let him keep her prisoner?"

"Again, I cannot see that there is any other way at the moment. I think we can assume that Andrew will keep her safe for now."

"For now!" repeated Aethelu in a huffy voice.

"I will go and speak to Andrew and see if he will permit me to see Judith. I will check up on her and see how she is doing. Alex, Can you let Rafe know. Perhaps if he knows that she is getting medical care, he will calm down a bit."

Alex nodded and stood up from the table. He took Sabine's hand and led her out of the dining room. One by one, they all trooped out knowing that they would have to be back again in a few hours for the next mealtime.

The next day saw the arrival of Arcadia, Audsley, Ava and Alfred. Anais didn't know what Andrew had told them to make them all come to The Manor, but whatever it was, it wasn't the truth. They all looked pretty happy as they arrived. Andrew had told August to pick them up at the airport and given him very strict instructions not to tell them the truth. At the very first mealtime after they arrived, Andrew himself filled them in. He looked positively gleeful in announcing that he was Jago. Beds were found for everybody, although it was a bit of a squeeze fitting them all in. The only one in the house that seemed happy apart from Andrew was Baker, August's dog. He was positively ecstatic with all the people and, therefore, all the extra attention he was getting.

Every mealtime for the next few weeks followed the same routine. Andrew sat smugly eating every meal whilst the others ate in silence. Rafe always came in last and was the first to leave. Anais only ever saw him at meal times and he looked more and more miserable with each passing day. His usual flamboyant attire had become increasingly dull and boring. Some days, Anais had even seen him wearing jeans, which would have been unthinkable a couple of months ago. His long hair had grown even longer and was now threatening to match the length of Andrew's. The less Rafe seemed to care about his appearance, Andrew, proportionally, became more stylish. Anais' theory that Andrew was taking clothes out of Rafe's wardrobe was confirmed when he appeared one dinnertime with the tiger topped cane that Rafe used to carry around with him everywhere. Not that Rafe seemed to care. He just ate his food and left the table without making mention of it.

Despite the fact that the house was the busiest it had ever been, it was also eerily silent. Everyone was too scared to talk to each other, scared that Andrew might overhear them. Even Ava, who normally couldn't shut up, was finally mute. People moved through the house like ghosts, mostly sticking to their bedrooms and the dining room. Anais found that her only conversations were with Winnie when she offered to help make meals or at bedtime with Aethelu. The thought of being able to have a conversation at the end of the day was the only thing that got her through. Each night, they hid under the covers and whispered to each other. It was the only way they could talk without being overheard by Andrew. Anais wondered how many of the others were having these same whispered conversations with their partners.

They threw around ideas of how to escape, how to stop Andrew, how to save Judith and how to find the vials, but nothing came to fruition. It wasn't long before they gave up on plans for escape and talked about the baby. Anais got lost in the beautiful pictures of the future that Aethelu could conjure up with words. These moments before sleep were the only thing that kept her calm and she came to look on them as a salvation to the horror of each day.

A week before the full moon, Aldrich stood up after dinner to make an announcement. It was the first time in weeks that anyone had said a word at any meal.

"Andrew, if you'll permit me to say a word?"

Andrew looked mildly surprised but nodded his head.

"As you know, we have all the ingredients we need to brew the Elixir. No doubt, you have all checked your calendars and have seen that next Wednesday is the full moon. Thanks to all your hard work, we have found all the pendants with the ingredients in them. August has been growing the Heatherwort, which is coming along nicely. The only thing we are missing is water. Unfortunately, tap water will not work. There is a spring near the village where we used to live. Even as far back as six hundred years ago, it was known as a very magical place. I used its waters for many of my cures when I worked as a healer. I do not think that any other water will have the same effect. Andrew. I need to go to the spring."

"No," said Andrew. "I've already told you that I don't

want anyone leaving the house. You'll have to use tap water."

"Andrew," Aldrich looked him in the eye. "That spring was magical. I do not believe that any other water will work."

"I remember the stories of that spring. It was all superstition and nonsense. They thought it was magical precisely because you used it and cured all those people. It was you that was magical, not the water."

"I've never been magical Andrew, merely a scientist."

"Then you, of all people, should know that there's no such thing as magic water. You will use tap water and it will work. I can't keep my eye on you if I let you gallivant off to the countryside.

"So be it." Aldrich sat down, defeated.

Eventually, the day came when Aldrich and James could start making the elixir. They only had a small amount of each ingredient and so couldn't make a huge amount of The Light. Despite this, Aldrich had asked if Andrew would mind if they split it into two batches. It had been over six hundred years since they had last brewed the potion and they wanted some left over in case it didn't work out right the first time. Andrew eventually agreed when Aldrich assured him that even split in half, there was enough to make a vial of Elixir strong enough for Judith. Anais wondered if the real reason he asked this was nothing to do with getting it right the first time and everything to do with Aldrich not wanting Andrew to have any more than one person's worth of it. He'd said it was only for Judith, but who knew if he was telling the truth or not.

The full moon, rather appropriately, fell on the 31st of October, Halloween. It was a holiday Anais had loved as a child. Dressing up in fancy dress, trick or treating, hand in hand with her father who always dressed up for the occasion. The most frightening part of this Halloween was now living amongst them--a murderer, a psychopathic killer who had shown no remorse over killing her parents. Aldrich told them all over dinner that the first part had gone well. He'd broken into the pendants and found that all the ingredients were still intact enough to make the Elixir.

Anais wondered how potent six-hundred-year-old ingredients really could be as she looked out of the bedroom window over the grounds. Oranges, reds and yellows had turned the grounds into a tapestry of warmth. Anais ached to be outside, just to walk around the grounds and feel the fallen leaves crunch beneath her feet. Fall had always been her favourite season and for some reason she loved it here more than she had in California. As much as she missed the California sunshine, nothing quite beat the beauty of England in Autumn. This was her second fall in the UK. This time last year, she had been working with Winnie in a little antique bookshop in York. How things had changed since then.

A pair of soggy arms wrapped themselves round her making her jump. It was Aethelu, who had just emerged from the little bathroom.

"Urg, you're all wet."

"I've just had a shower. What are you doing?"

"I was just thinking how glad I was that we are naming the baby Autumn. It really is beautiful out there. I just wish I could go out in it."

"Aethelu hugged her tightly. "We will soon enough. Daddy has started making his elixir. If all goes to plan, this will all be over by the time it's your birthday."

Anais was due to turn twenty at the end of November. She would finally come into her inheritance. It reminded her of the thoughts she'd had a few months ago about leaving The Manor.

"Let's get out of here."

"I doubt Andrew will let us. You know his rules."

"I don't mean now, although I'd give anything for a ten-minute walk in the grounds. I meant afterward when this is all over. My parents left me enough money for a house. I'll get it on my birthday."

"You mean, not live here anymore? This has been my home for over a hundred years."

"I know, but I'm sick of it. For me, this place holds nothing but memories of being locked up. I want to be free."

"If that's what you want, let's do it. I suppose it's time I flew the coop, so to speak. Where did you have in mind?"

"Actually, I was thinking of moving near to Arcadia."

"You want to move to the South of France?"

"Yeah, why not? It's sunny, it's beautiful. It's got the coast and the mountains. It's the perfect place for a little girl to grow up. Plus, Autumn will have her Aunty Arcadia there to spoil her rotten and it's not too far to fly from the UK, so the others can visit all the time."

"How will we afford it, though? The south of France is ridiculously expensive. Arcadia's villa is worth millions."

"Obviously we'd not be able to afford a villa, I was thinking we start with a little apartment in town and see where we go from there. Perhaps we could sell some of your paintings and I thought I could open an antique bookshop. I loved working with Winnie at hers in York."

"Winnie didn't make a penny from that bookshop, you know."

"I know, but I was thinking bigger than that, real antique books, not just a few dusty old tomes taken from The

Manor's library. I could source first editions for the rich collectors."

"Sounds like you've got it all worked out. I do like the idea of painting all day in some sunny studio."

Anais took one last look out over the grounds and closed the curtains. She took Aethelu by the hand and led her to bed.

3

Breakfast the next morning started the same as every other. Silence prevailed over the table. When Andrew got up to speak at the end of the meal, it made everyone jump.

"Anais, I'm going for a walk in the grounds. Would you care to join me?"

Anais looked shell-shocked. He'd posed it as a question, but she could tell by his tone, that he expected her to follow him. She knew she had no choice to comply, so she slowly stood up from her chair. Aethelu was by her side in a flash.

"I'm coming, too!"

"I wish to speak to Anais alone," said Andrew, "Your presence is not required."

"I'm not going to let you take Anais without me."

"We are only going for a walk, Aethelu. Please sit down. I assure you, she is in no danger. I'll have her back to you in one piece within the hour."

Anais had no choice but to follow. She kissed a fearful Aethelu and let Andrew lead her to The Manor's main doors and out into the cold air.

The Manor was always kept warm, thanks to underfloor heating and radiators, not to mention the log fires that crackled on really cold nights, so the crisp air of autumn gave her a shock. It looked much warmer than it actually was and she gave a shiver. She could see her breath in the crisp air.

"Are you cold?"

Anais wrapped her arms around herself to try to keep the heat in. She nodded her head.

Andrew disappeared back into the house and reappeared just a few moments later with a coat, scarf and hat for her.

She accepted them gratefully and put them on, instantly feeling much better, now that the chill had gone.

"That was a nice gesture, for a raving lunatic."

Andrew laughed at her. Huge braying guffaws. It was unlike him, but then again she was still getting used to this new Andrew.

"See, I'm not all bad. Walk with me, Anais."

Anais followed him around the house, past the gate to the courtyard and out into the woods.

"Where are we going?" They were following the path that Anais knew would take them to her father's tomb."

"We're not going anywhere. We are just walking."

"Why?"

"Don't you want to? I thought you'd give anything to come outside, and here we are."

Anais thought back to the night before when she'd said those exact words to Aethelu.

"You were listening in to our conversation! Do you eavesdrop on everyone in the house?"

"I have to. I need to make sure you aren't plotting anything against me. It's really rather tedious listening to you all, but is, unfortunately, a necessary evil. I try to listen only to snippets rather than whole conversations. Mostly, it's rather boring. The majority of you are pretty quiet these days.

"Nobody dares to speak. They all think you are listening in on them."

"Well, they are right; I am listening in on them."

Anais didn't know how to respond, so she kept quiet.

They came upon the clearing with her father's tomb in it. Andrew made to walk straight past, but Anais stopped.

"Can I go in and see my father?" She'd not visited the tomb since her first week at The Manor, almost a year before.

"No, you most certainly cannot. We are here to walk and see the trees, not go and look at a musty coffin belonging to Alistair."

As if to emphasise his point, he grabbed hold of Anais' hand and marched her right past the stone tomb.

Anais gave a yelp of shock, which quickly turned into pain as he held her wrist tightly.

"Get off!" yelled Anais and pulled her hand away. To her surprise, he let go.

"Where are we going? Why are you bringing me out here?"

"I told you, I thought you might appreciate the fresh air."

"We are not out here for fresh air, and you know it. Why have you brought me here?"

"You got me. I did have an ulterior motive for bringing you out here. I wanted to talk to you."

Anais was caught off-guard. They had reached the edge of the grounds now, close to where she and Aethelu had climbed over the electric fence to get to the tramway all those months ago. A faint hum told her that the fence was not only operational but turned on.

"What do you want to speak to me about?"

"The baby."

"The baby?" Anais instinctively put her hand down to her stomach. "What about the baby?"

"Don't you ever wonder how you ended up pregnant?"

"Of course, I do. It's impossible and yet here it is. Why are you asking me this?"

She wasn't sure she wanted to know where this was leading, and yet, curiosity kept her from saying anything.

"Judith wants children. She told me once."

"So? What's that got to do with me?"

"I hate children. Messy little things. Really can't stand them. Always underfoot, always in the way. Always covered in stuff, whether it be chocolate or vomit or worse." He shuddered at the thought of it.

"That's why..." he continued "I made sure that nobody's pregnancies went to term. I really couldn't have snotty little rats running around."

Anais wasn't sure what he was saying to her.

"The Light made the Custor Lux women miscarry," she said uneasily.

"Yes. That's what they all thought, but no, it wasn't The Light. It was me. As soon as I found out that any of them was pregnant, I brought them an herbal tea, a little concoction of mine that assured that they would miscarry within a few days."

Anais could barely speak from the shock.

"You killed all those babies? You are sick!"

"It was better than having the little maggots running around and annoying me. Goodness knows how many of us there would be if I had let everyone have babies willy-nilly.

I've done everyone a favour. Of course, I missed a few, you for example. I did actually make your mother the tea, but for whatever reason, she didn't drink it. Sabine and Jennifer were others that were missed. I didn't even know that Amber was pregnant when she left, and, obviously, I never met Sabine's mother."

"Is that why you brought me here? You want to kill my baby. Is that it?"

"Actually, no, as I said earlier, Judith wants a family. I myself could live without it, obviously, but I want her to have everything she wants. As I find your condition repugnant, I really couldn't go through that with Judith, so I have decided to give her a child another way."

"What do you mean?" asked Anais, fearful of what he was about to say. She'd already had a crazy woman try to take her baby away from her. Was Andrew telling her that he, too, wanted her unborn child?

"I just wanted to see if it was possible. I remembered from your failed attempt to get pregnant before that you had an embryo left."

Anais thought back to when Aldrich had tried IVF on her in an attempt to create a baby to save the world from the Jagovirus.

"Did you give me your concoction then? Did you kill my babies?"

"No. I did not. Make no mistake, I would have, but your body rejected them, all by itself."

Anais didn't know why, but she found this thought strangely comforting. Of course, her babies hadn't survived, but at least, it had been natural and not due to Andrew. She'd had one embryo left. She knew what Andrew was about to tell her. Now, she knew how she had mysteriously gotten pregnant. After all her protestations, the baby was

Alex's, after all. He'd been the father of her lost babies and, therefore, was the father of the one embryo they had left. Andrew must have implanted her with the embryo when she was in a coma. The dates fitted.

"Is that why you gave me the Jagovirus? To make me unconscious, so you could use the last embryo to get me pregnant?"

"Yes, clever, huh? I'd already given it to both Rafe and Alex. Rafe, of course, was given it to kill him for taking Judith. I was actually surprised when he pulled through. I tried modifying the virus and tried it on Alex. I picked him because he had started to get close to finding out about me. He, too, survived. I realised that the Jagovirus, as strong as it was, just wasn't a match for the Guardians' immune system. By this time, Alex was beginning to get suspicious, so I gave myself a dose, knowing that I'd survive. Ironically, I nearly died from my own virus. I guess I'm not as strong as Rafe or Alex. I had such beautiful dreams when I was infected, though. Did you?"

Anais couldn't say that she had, but Andrew didn't give her time to reply.

"It was then that I had the idea of giving Judith a baby. I knew that if I gave her a child, she would have to come back to me."

"So you made me pregnant to give a baby to Judith?" Anais asked incredulously. "Are you insane?"

"Quite possibly," Andrew laughed an unnatural laugh.

They were now deeper into the woods than Anais had ever been before. They had been walking uphill for at least twenty minutes. She wondered how long it would be before they hit the top border of the grounds. They couldn't be far from the moorland where Andrew had tried to kill her all those months before.

"Why would Judith want someone else's baby? Your plan is crazy."

Andrew suddenly became angry, his mirth of a few moments ago disappearing to be replaced with something much more scary. His features changed perceptibly. Anais shuddered.

"It's not insane. Have you never heard of surrogacy? Famous women do it all the time. Too rich, or too vain, or just too lazy to give birth themselves. It happens you know."

"Yes, maybe, but it usually happens with consent of everybody involved. Nobody is tricked or forced into it."

"Would you have consented, if I had asked you?"

"Of course not."

"Well, there you go then," said Andrew, as if this answered her question.

"But Judith hasn't consented either. She doesn't even know."

"Ah, but this is where my plan is perfect. I remember you saying that you planned to get a house in the village once you receive your inheritance. I know you said last night that you planned to move to France, but you can do that after. You have the baby in the village. I'll encourage Judith to visit regularly. Once she falls in love and bonds with the little brat, I'll let her bring it here and keep it. Once it's past the disgusting stage, of course. I will not have shitty nappies in my house. After that, I'll hire a team of nannies and then I can send it off to boarding school as soon as it's old enough.
"

Anais could barely wrap her head around his fanatical plan. Insane didn't cover it. The guy was so out of touch with reality. She realised at that point that there was no point trying to show him reasoning or have a rational argument with him. He was not rational. Anais couldn't see any possible scenario where his little plan would work. Still, she knew there was no point trying to tell him that. In his head, he had it all worked out. He would manipulate and if he had to, force everyone to comply. The truly terrifying part of his plan was the fact he planned to be in their lives for a long time. Any hope that he would just give Judith the Elixir and disappear for good, faded. Anais tried to remember when she had told Andrew her plan to move away from the manor once the baby was born. She realised that he must have been listening to her private conversations for a long time now.

The boundary wall appeared in front of them. Anais could just see the top station of the tramway peeping through the trees at the other side of the wall. She'd had dreams of taking Baby Autumn for her first trip on the tramway with Aethelu next summer. It was a dream that would probably never come true, at least, not freely, not without the threat of Andrew over their shoulders. The path curved around to the left following the dry-stone wall with the electric fence on top. Andrew had become silent, probably marvelling at his own cleverness.

Anais was astounded that anyone so clever could be so totally out of touch with reality. For a genius, he sure was stupid. He had no idea how people think. Anais wondered if The Light had robbed him of any shred of humanity he might have originally possessed, or if he had always been like this. He had many of the same traits that Jasmine had possessed. Anais decided to ask Aldrich when she got back if it was possible that The Light could do that to someone. It was too coincidental that the two craziest people she had ever met both had The Light in their system and that it wasn't somehow to blame. The others seemed normal, though. Perhaps she was wrong.

The path curved once more and even though she couldn't see it, she instinctively knew they were heading back to The Manor. She knew that she was safe, at least for now. Andrew would have to keep her and her baby alive if he wanted to put his plan into action. The thought gave her some comfort. Once Autumn was born, that would all change, but that wasn't going to happen until February. After that, who knew? Suddenly, a thought came to her.

"How did you post all those letters?"

"Which letters?" his anger seemed to have dissipated, and he was once again talking to her normally.

"The threatening letters. They came from all over the world." She remembered how, at one point they had thought there were two people as the letters had come from two different countries at the same time.

"Ah, yes, I have to admit it was rather enjoyable watching you all trying to work out time zones and distance travelled. Not once did you consider that I had sent them from here."

"But they had postmarks on them from all over the world."

"Consider this. I have internet friends all over the world. I write letters, put them in an envelope with this address on it but with no stamp. I put that envelope, plus a bit of cash for a stamp, into another envelope and send it to my friend in, say, Australia. He takes it out of the first envelope, buys a stamp, and reposts it as a favour to me. I hadn't counted on two of them posting them at the same time. I thought you'd rumble me, but instead, you just got more scared thinking there were two of me. It was actually rather funny. "

"And the fire?"

"Ah, the fire, well, I have to admit I lost my cool a bit on that one. I threw my computer across the room in a fit of rage and, well, let's just say it caused a bit of a mess. The fire started as it smashed into the other monitors. I passed it off as Jago as I did everything else. Is there anything else you want to know?"

He seemed really quite excited to unburden all his secrets onto her.

Andrew being Jago certainly explained how he got in and out without anyone noticing. It was because he was there all the time. It also explained why they never saw him on the security cameras. No doubt, Andrew had been caught doing things as Jago many times on the cameras but because he was always the one to check the footage, all he had to do was lie about it. It had been so obvious all along. How had they not seen it? It was because Andrew had been such a good actor. They had not suspected him at all because he had played his part well and for such a long time--six hundred years!

"Well?" asked Andrew with a curious look on his face. He was itching to tell her more. She didn't want to hear any more. They were getting close to the house now and she just wanted to be away from him, away from all his revelations of sickness. She wanted to be wrapped up with Aethelu in bed and for all this to go away. She kept silent.

"No? Well, I'm going to tell you anyway." His voice was filled with glee. He reminded Anais of a little child, desperate to tell his mommy what he'd been up to at school. This mommy didn't want to hear it though.

"Didn't you wonder why we didn't come and rescue you earlier when you were in Egypt?"

Anais hadn't actually thought about it before now.

"You didn't know where we were?"

"I did, though, didn't I? I knew you were going to a

theatre. I knew which theatre. I even helped Aethelu get some explosives if you remember."

Anais thought back. He was right. He had helped them. It made sense that he would help them. He needed the last two necklaces for the Elixir. Why then had he left them there?

"So why did you leave us?"

"I waited a few days to hear back from you. At first I thought it must be taking longer than planned, but when I still hadn't heard back from you after two days, I realised something had gone wrong. I had Winnie breathing down my neck 'Have you heard anything, have they emailed?' It's all she ever asked, over and over again. I wanted those pendants so badly and I was so angry with you all for messing it up. I called your hotel and they told me that your things were left in the room, but you hadn't paid your bill. I called The Light of Jasmine hostel, but the line was dead. I assumed that Jasmine had closed it. I didn't know what to do. I was just about to tell everyone what I knew. There are only three theatres anywhere near the hostels. It would have been easy to check them all out and find the right one, but then something wonderful happened. Winnie, pretty much, ordered everyone to go to Egypt to look for you. Winnie herself, Aldrich, August, James and, of course, Rafe were all to go. There wasn't time to sort out the proper visa documentation for Judith. Of course, flying back into Africa would be no problem, but she wasn't sure that she'd be able to fly back out. She decided it was safer to stay in the UK. Of course, I wasn't expected to go with my fear of flying. It meant that I would be here in The Manor with Judith, all alone. It was an opportunity that was just too good to pass up. I hadn't told anyone about the theatre. I led them on a wild goose chase all over Cairo. The longer it took, the more time I had with Judith. Rafe was not happy being apart from Judith but every time he called to say they were giving up, I fed him another phony clue. Those weeks were magical. I had Judith all to myself, and it was almost like old times. She talked about Rafe way too much, but as the time wore on, it became less and less. I was on the verge of convincing her to leave Rafe and be with me when they all gave up and came home. It was maddening, watching Judith running into Rafe's arms when for the last few months she had been happy with me. Then I got that hurried phone call from you. Winnie had overheard and she gathered everyone up straight away. She even called Ava, Alfred, Arcadia and Audsley to fly over there. By that time, Judith had gotten her visa through so, of course, Rafe took her away from me. I figured that if I couldn't have Judith to myself, I might as well go back to my original plan and get the pendants. Of course, it meant that my secret lasted longer, too. I knew that Sabine would recognise me if she came over here. I should have killed her when I had the chance, but that's of no importance now. I quite like everything being out in the open. What do you think?"

Anais felt sick. She'd heard enough. The back door of The Manor was in sight. She opened the little gate of the courtyard and made a dash for the door, hoping it was unlocked. She was lucky. It opened with a slight creak. She rushed in, past a surprised looking Winnie, who happened to be in there doing some baking, and up the stairs to the bedroom. Aethelu appeared a few minutes later.

"Thank god you are back." She ran over to Anais and gave her a hug. "Did he hurt you?"

"Not physically, no, but he told me some awful things. Oh, Aethelu, it was awful." She burst into tears and sat on the bed.

"What did he say?" Aethelu sat beside her, wrapping her arms around her.

Anais jumped up and turned on a little radio on the bedside table. A chart show blasted out. She then got into bed, dragging Aethelu under the covers with her.

"What are you doing?"

"You know that Andrew has got all the rooms bugged," whispered Anais. "He's been listening to everything we say." This is the only place I can think of where it's safe to talk because you can bet your bottom dollar that he's listening to us now. All he will be able to hear is the radio. I'll have to keep my voice down though. She proceeded to tell Aethelu everything that Andrew had told her; about terminating all the pregnancies, about impeding their rescue in Egypt, about his clever way of sending letters to them. She saved the baby news until last. She knew she would have to tell Aethelu that Alex was the father of the baby after all.

"There's something else too," began Anais.

"Something worse than you've already told me?"

"Andrew put me in a coma to get me pregnant. He implanted me with the final embryo from the failed IVF."

"What? Why?"

"He considers me a surrogate for Judith."

"He wants to give Autumn to Judith? Over my dead body!"

"You've not heard the best bit. He wants us to look after the baby until she's out of diapers and then when she is two or three, just pass her over to Judith."

"That's just madness."

"Yes, and I think that's our biggest problem. Andrew isn't just insane; he's so totally out of touch with reality that he thinks it's a great idea and that Judith will just go for it."

"Oh god. The guy is totally loopy. That makes him even more dangerous."

"I agree. We have to stop him. This isn't going to end when he gives Judith the Elixir like we all hoped it might. It's going to carry on. We give him Autumn and then what? It will just be something else. We will never be rid of him."

"We will NOT give him Autumn!" said Aethelu a little too loudly causing Anais to shush her.

"Of course we won't. I didn't mean that. I just meant that he will never stop, no matter what we do. We have to end it."

"What do you suggest? He has us over a barrel. If we kill him, we set off a plague."

"I know. I think we have to find those vials," replied Anais determinedly

"But there are twenty-one of them. Surely he'd notice."

"We have to figure a way to do it without him finding out."

"How? It's impossible."

"I don't know!" Anais rolled over and closed her eyes. The task they had ahead was just too daunting to contemplate. At that moment, Autumn gave a huge kick. Anais pulled Aethelu's hand to her stomach and Autumn kicked again.

"I felt it!" exclaimed Aethelu. "I felt her kick. She just kicked me."

Anais smiled. It was the first time Aethelu had experienced what Anais had been feeling for a couple of months, their daughter just beneath her skin.

Aethelu was silent for a few moments, marvelling at the movement of Anais' stomach.

"Anais."

"Hmm?"

"I don't mind that Alex is Autumn's father. It's actually

kinda nice. It means Autumn will be related to me by blood."

Anais curled up with Aethelu's arms around her. They stayed like that until the alarm went off telling them they had to get up and go to lunch.

4

November came and went in much the same way October had.

The trees were almost completely bare now, and the ground beneath them was carpeted in brown slushy leaves. The riot of colour Anais had seen just weeks before had faded, replaced with a cold misery.

The only respite from the misery was Anais' birthday. Hers was the first birthday since they had found out about Andrew being Jago, so she wasn't expecting anything.

She was pleasantly surprised when on the evening of her birthday, Winnie walked into the dining room with a huge birthday cake in the shape of a heart with HAPPY BIRTHDAY ANAIS iced on it in delicate pink icing. Alex followed her in, carrying a couple of bottles of fizzy pop. No one had drunk any alcohol since Andrew's great revelation, as they all knew they had to keep their wits about them. Anais was quite happy as it meant that she didn't feel left out due to being pregnant.

As none of them had been able to leave, thanks to Andrew's rules, most of them gave her handmade gifts.

Aethelu presented her with a sketchbook full of beautiful drawings, including ones of Anais that she'd not even known Aethelu had drawn. Winnie's gift was the cake. Alex and Sabine had ordered her some fur lined winter boots through the internet. Anais was especially touched by August's gift. He'd made a beautiful changing table out of wood he'd found on the grounds. He'd painted it white and etched the name Autumn into it.

"I'm not exactly sure what it's for, but I found a baby catalogue and it said that all new mothers need one. It has a drawer for nappies, see?" He opened one of the drawers to show her. "I copied it straight from the catalogue. I hope it's ok."

"It's beautiful, August. Thank you." She moved around the table and gave him a kiss on the cheek. It would fit perfectly next to the cot in her bedroom.

Arcadia was the most generous of all. "I've not bought you a gift, as such," she started "but if you ever do decide to come to France, I've bought a little plot of land next to mine. You can build a little house there. I made sure it had a sea view. It's not huge, but it's in a dazzling spot and has enough space for a little girl to run around."

Anais didn't know what to say. She'd not told anyone except Aethelu about Andrew's plans for Autumn, probably because she was determined it would never happen. The thought of living in the South of France in a little house made for three gave her a thrill. She had to get them out of this mess. She hugged Arcadia and thanked her profusely.

When all the other gifts had been given, Andrew came up to her with a flat box in his hand. Anais had been steadfastly ignoring him, as she did every time she had to be in near proximity to him. She'd not spoken a word to him since the walk in the woods, nor had he attempted to engage with her. She was quite shocked when he handed her the box. It was wrapped in yellow wrapping paper with pictures of balloons and cake on it, the type that you might wrap a child's present in. Anais unwrapped it to find a red velvet jewellery box. With some trepidation, she opened the box. She was acutely aware that everyone was watching. Inside was a heavy gold necklace encrusted with a diamond pendant hanging from the front. If it was real, it was expensive. It just looked gaudy to Anais. It was nothing like the kind of thing that she would ever wear.

"Turn it over!" said Andrew, rubbing his hands together in excitement. On the back of the pendant was an engraving. It read 'To the mother of my child.'

It was the sickest thing she had ever seen. She dropped it on the table and then realised she was going to be sick. She knew she wouldn't make it to the bathroom in time and so had to throw up in a nearby waste paper basket.

"How utterly rude!" said Andrew angrily, as Aethelu picked up the necklace.

Aethelu read the inscription and then with such speed that no one was able to stop her, punched Andrew right in the head. He wobbled a bit but didn't fall as he had when Rafe had done the same thing, weeks before.

He snatched the necklace from Aethelu's hand and stalked out of the door. Once again, as before, he activated some remote detector in the room and the door locked. Anais could only watch helplessly as the shutters once again lowered over the windows plunging them into darkness. Audsley turned the lights on and no one spoke. They were all waiting for something else to happen. Anais couldn't bare it if she had to go through another night of laughing gas. She strained her ears for the sound of hissing to tell her that gas was being pumped into the room, but after five minutes of waiting, she realised that they were probably going to be spared.

Anais sat back down at the table and the others followed suit.

"Are you ok, love?" asked Ava, who sat next to her. "What just happened?"

Anais knew this was the time to tell them everything Andrew had told her. She left nothing out, not even the part about Alex being the father of the baby, and how Andrew was going to give Autumn to Judith. How he now considered himself Autumn's father. She worried a little as she told everyone, but Sabine walked around the table and hugged her to show that it wasn't her fault and she didn't blame her. She then went back to her seat and kissed Alex. He squeezed her hand and smiled lovingly at her. If he was upset, or otherwise emotionally affected by this revelation, he didn't show it.

Anais faltered when she told them the reason that they all had lost babies. Almost all the women round the table had lost at least one child, thanks to Jago. Even those who had never been pregnant seemed to understand the misery. Anais bowed her head. She could hear sobbing coming from around the table. Andrew had affected every part of their lives and caused so much pain.

Along with the sobbing, Anais heard something else. At first, she couldn't be sure, but it sounded like singing. She looked up and saw Jennifer singing quietly. It was a lullaby she'd heard as a child. Her father had sung it to her when she was little. When she had scraped her knee or thought monsters were under the bed. It was a song of comfort. Jennifer's small voice sang out so beautifully, hauntingly. Anais joined in followed by Aethelu and Sabine, adding harmony to the vocals. With tears in her eyes, Arcadia held

Jennifer's hand and joined in. Turning to August on her other side, she held on to his hand, too. The crying stopped, as one by one, everyone around the table held on to the hands of the people on either side of them and joined in with the lullaby. Nobody had dry eyes around the table, but everyone was smiling by the end of the song. When it was over, Winnie stood up and walked around to where Jennifer was sitting. She kissed both her cheeks and then mouthed 'thank you' before enveloping her in a huge hug. Anais found herself being drawn into a huge group hug.

Someone had moved the vast dining room table to one side along with the chairs. After a few minutes, someone coughed to get everyone's attention. Anais was surprised to find it was Aldrich.

"Every single one of us here has been affected in some way by Jago. Most of us have lost sons and daughters who should be standing here with us tonight. James and I are very close to finishing the Elixir. Once we give it to Judith, perhaps that will be the end of it. We must pray that he will then leave us alone."

"He won't leave us alone. He plans to take my daughter, just like he took away all of yours," said Anais miserably.

"I don't believe for a second that will happen."

"Shhh." said Sabine. "He'll hear you."

"He can listen to every word I say. I hope he does. I do not think for a second that Judith would want to take Anais and Aethelu's baby."

"But..." began Anais.

"Dad's right. She does want children--lots of them, but she would never take someone else's. Besides, she told me she wants them all to look like me," Rafe added, rather uncomfortably.

"Autumn *will* look like you, bro," said Alex. "I'm her

biological father, and you are my identical twin. She'll look like me and so it goes without saying that she'll look like you, too."

"God help her," said Aethelu, which broke the seriousness of the situation and made them all laugh.

"A toast," said Aethelu, as she lifted a glass. "To all the babies that will never be forgotten and to the future babies in this family." She found a lighter that had been placed next to the cake ready for the candles to be lit. "I hope you don't mind your birthday cake being hijacked, Anais. She lit one of the candles and passed the lighter to her mother. Winnie followed suit, giving all of the women who had lost children a chance to light a candle. Winnie, Ava, Audsley and Arcadia had all lost babies, thanks to Andrew. Finally, Alex and Anais lit one for the triplets they had lost less than a year ago.

They all said a silent prayer before placing the candles back on the cake where they were blown out to much applause.

"Right," said Aethelu, once again taking centre stage, "Enough sadness for one night. We have food, we have drink, we have cake, we have music, and if I remember rightly, it's someone special's birthday still. Andrew doesn't seem to be doing anything particularly horrible at the moment and better yet, he's not here. Let's grieve tomorrow, but let's party tonight."

"Cheers!" yelled August, holding up a huge glass of bright pink pop, which might have been cherryade.

An old record player in the corner was turned on, and old records that had been gathering dust since the eighties, were once again allowed their moment of glory. It was the strangest birthday party Anais had ever had or indeed attended. Despite the underlying sadness, there seemed to be a renewed sense of hope for the future. Although he didn't unlock the doors until the next morning, which meant they all had to sleep on the floor again, Andrew didn't do anything else. Alex had very cleverly brought a load of blankets down after the last time they had been trapped and hidden them in a sideboard, so they were at least warm even though they slept on the floor.

When the doors eventually did open in the morning, they all trooped past Andrew ignoring him as they walked past.

"What about breakfast?" he asked as one by one they walked past.

"Make your own sodding breakfast!" said Winnie to an astonished Andrew, causing Anais to giggle. She had the feeling that he would find some way of punishing her later, but looking at Winnie's determined face, she thought it was worth it.

As they trooped up the stairs, Winnie pulled Anais back and whispered in her ear. Now that we know that it's not The Light killing the babies, do you think we will all be able to have children?"

Anais was shocked by the question. She'd always thought of Winnie as being too old to have more kids. She had five grown children, after all, not to mention, a grand-child on the way. Then she looked at the eagerness in Winnie's face. She didn't want to disappoint her

"I guess anything is possible," she whispered back before following Aethelu into their bedroom.

5

Over the course of the next few days, things mysteriously kept happening to Andrew. Not enough to make him mad, but enough to disrupt the smooth running of his day and generally inconvenience him. It started one lunchtime when his stomach began to gurgle alarmingly. He excused himself and quickly disappeared, only reappearing at dinnertime, when after a particularly delicious chilli, he did the same thing again. The next night Anais noticed a wry smile on Winnie's face as she dished up spaghetti bolognese onto his plate. He looked at her suspiciously before taking a mouthful and deciding it tasted fine. However, before he'd even gotten to pudding, he was once again running off to the bathroom. Winnie caught Anais looking at her, and she winked. Anais smirked as she realised that Winnie had obviously been putting laxatives in his food. It was awfully dangerous. She had to have known that he could see her over CCTV. She must have been surreptitiously dropping them in. As no one else seemed to have been affected, Anais thought she must have been doing it just before she ladled the food up. Unfortunately for Winnie, Andrew had come to the same conclusion. He burst back through the door, his finger pointing at Winnie.

"You are trying to poison me!" he shouted, red in the face.

Winnie's face dropped and she began to look scared.

"Whatever do you mean?" said Winnie nervously. Anais watched as Andrew walked around the table towards her. The fear on her face was evident. Anais could tell that whatever she had put in Andrew's food was now hiding in her pocket. If he asked her to turn her pockets inside out, she'd be caught and then goodness knows what he would do to her.

A moment of inspiration hit Anais.

"Oww," she said loudly. "Sorry, Toilet!" she shouted before dashing out in a rush. She ran up the stairs and into a first-floor bathroom. Seconds later, she heard an urgent knock on the door. It was Alfred. She heard him loudly shouting through the door.

"Is this bathroom free? The one downstairs is taken and I'm afraid it's rather urgent." She could tell, he was shouting more for Andrew's benefit than hers. She flushed the toilet and opened the door. Alfred winked as he passed her and shut the door behind him. As she descended the stairs, she saw various family members dashing off in different directions, presumably in search of available bathrooms.

"You know, I think there must be something going round." She smiled sweetly at Andrew as she sat back at her place at the table. Andrew just grunted and pushed his desert away. His stomach gave another grumble, and once again, he ran through the door, this time to find himself at the back of a very long queue for the toilet. Anais smirked.

It was Winnie getting her own back in her own way, but Anais knew she wouldn't dare try it again. She'd been too close to getting caught. Andrew's mysterious illness disappeared as quickly as it had appeared and everything went back to normal--for a few days, at least.

6

On the last Saturday of November, Anais and Aethelu made their way down to dinner as usual, but immediately, they could tell something was wrong. Andrew had not missed a single meal since he had demanded they all attend every meal. Anais did a quick sweep of the room. Everyone else was there. She checked her watch. It said five o'clock exactly.

She took her seat and waited. Aethelu sat beside her in her usual seat. They both looked towards the door waiting for Andrew.

"Now that everyone is here..." began Aldrich. Anais turned her head to look at him. "I'm afraid I have some bad news. I have already informed Andrew, which explains why he isn't here."

"Can you explain to us?" Alfred asked

"As you know, James and I have been working on The Light Elixir. We finished it yesterday. However, preliminary tests have told us that it has failed."

"What do you mean failed?" asked Rafe.

"Failed, not worked. We tested it out on some rats. They were all dead within hours."

"So that's it then?" asked Ava.

"No, not necessarily, we only used half the ingredients. We are pretty sure where we made our mistake. I told Andrew we needed specific water, but if you recall, he refused to let me go and retrieve some. We have just enough ingredients left to try once more, but next time we will not be able to test it first."

"You mean give it to Judith without testing it first?" asked Rafe angrily. "It could kill her."

"We think we know where we went wrong. The water..."

"Think? Think" Rafe cut him off, his voice raised in volume and pitch with every word he spoke.

"We are pretty sure. I'm sorry Rafe, but there is nothing else we can do. We have to trust that next time it will work."

"If it doesn't kill her first! When will the next lot be ready?"

"We have to wait for another full moon before we can begin. Then we have to stew it."

"So how long, then?"

"It should be ready by mid-January."

"January? Next year?" Rafe slammed his fist down onto the table. "You mean Judith is going to have to stay asleep for another six or seven weeks only to wake up and be injected with something that will more than likely kill her. If it doesn't, she gets to spend the rest of eternity with that madman bringing up my niece as her own child?"

Anais felt uncomfortable having Autumn being drawn into the conversation.

"Not quite," answered Aldrich. "I've convinced Andrew that it is not wise to keep Judith sedated any longer. The longer she is kept under sedation, the less chance he has of being able to wake her up. I've persuaded Andrew to wake her up now. I saw her just before I came down here and she seems to be recovering well."

"She's awake?" asked Rafe and immediately stood up.

"Sit down," ordered Aldrich. "Yes, she is awake. Unfortunately, Andrew would only let me wake her on strict conditions."

"Conditions?" Rafe's face fell and he sat down. "What conditions?"

"He has concocted a story that he wants us all to be a part of. He has told her that Rafe was having an affair with Sabine and in her grief; she turned to Andrew, who comforted her. He's told her that they are married, but she had an accident and lost her memory which is why she's been in a coma."

Sabine's head jerked up at the mention of her name.

"WHAT?" yelled Rafe, Sabine, and Alex, all at the same time.

"You all have to play along. You know what will happen otherwise."

"So I have to pretend to be in love with Rafe when Judith is around?" asked Sabine. "I could probably do that. It's only for six weeks, right? I'll just hold his hand and gaze longingly into his eyes when Judith walks past. Alex, you'll have to act mad and jealous."

"I don't think I'll be acting," replied Alex in shock.

"I'm afraid there's more to it than that. He expects Sabine to sleep in the same room with Rafe and Rafe to ignore Judith completely. If you talk to her at all or try to find a way to contact her or tip her off, he's said he will kill one of us. That goes for everyone. We must all keep up the pretence."

"Arrrgh!" Rafe screamed loudly, causing them all to

jump. He got up from his place and stormed out of the room without touching his food.

"Oh, dear, that didn't go down too well. Alex, can you go and talk to him, please?"

"What am I supposed to say to him?"

"Just calm him down."

"Calm him down? I'm mad as hell myself!"

"Please, Alex."

Alex stood to leave. Sabine held his hand and followed him out of the room.

Anais was just about to get up and leave when Aldrich began again. It seemed he wasn't quite finished.

"Andrew now understands that the Elixir will not work without the correct spring water. He has given me permission to go and retrieve some. Anais, he's asked that you accompany me."

Anais jerked her head up, surprised to hear her name.

"Why me?"

"Andrew doesn't trust me to go alone. It seems you are the only one he trusts. Originally, he just wanted you to go, but I convinced him that I needed to be there to make sure that you went to the right place. I think he'd forgotten that you'd never been there before."

"Why does he trust me?"

"Do you want to try to understand the weird and wonderful world of Andrew's mind or do you want to just be thankful that you are escaping," said Aethelu.

"I'm not escaping. I'll come back."

"I know, I just meant escape for the day. You've been saying that you feel cooped up. You'll get some fresh air. It will be good for the baby.

"Ok. When are we going?" Anais asked Aldrich.

"No time like the present."

Anais felt nervous as she followed Aldrich out of the dining room. This would be the first time she had been in his sole company since she'd been in the surgery. The only time she'd ever spoken to him alone was when she was ill or having check-ups for the baby. With this pregnancy, as she'd had no real problems, Winnie had been keeping an eye on her health for most of the time.

Aldrich had always put her on edge ever since their first proper meeting where he'd asked her to carry Alex's baby in an attempt to save the world from Andrew's Jagovirus.

She'd expected to go out the front door and get into August's Range Rover. So, she was surprised when Aldrich led her down the stairs to the kitchen. He exited through the back door and crossed the courtyard to the huge garage. Anais had only been in there once when Alex had been showing off his Corvette Stingray. She couldn't remember the other cars that were housed there. She knew they wouldn't be taking the Corvette. Andrew had tampered with the breaks, causing Alex to crash into a tree.

When the garage door opened, Anais could see the still crushed Corvette, parked sadly at the end of the other cars. Aldrich ignored it entirely and opted for the little family car that Anais had never been in before. She sat in the front seat and attempted to pull the seatbelt around her huge belly. The car was so old that the seatbelt was stiff. Aldrich leaned across her and clipped it in.

As they set off down the driveway, it occurred to Anais that she would be free of Andrew, if only for a day. She was finally going to be out of the grounds of The Manor. When they got to the gates, she half expected them not to open, and for Andrew to turn up and announce they couldn't go, after all. She was pleasantly surprised when the large wrought iron gates slid back with no problems.

As they passed through them, she looked back to see them closing behind her, trapping the rest of the family in. As glad as she was to be out of the grounds, albeit temporarily, she still felt bad for those she was leaving behind. Aethelu had seemed happy that Anais was going out for the day, but she knew that Aethelu would worry about her. She would worry about Aethelu, too, but it was only for a day. She turned and looked out of the front window and relaxed to enjoy her first taste of freedom in months.

This winter had been much milder than the last, and Anais had yet to see snow. The last few weeks had been drizzly and cloudy, but today, it was if the weather had known she was going out. The sky was blue in every direction, with not a cloud in sight. The air was crisp and even in the car, she could still see her breath. She had forgotten just how cold British winters were and she began to wish she had thought to bring gloves with her. She rubbed her hands together furiously to get some warmth into them.

"Cold?" enquired Aldrich.

"Just a little," she replied.

Aldrich pushed a button on the dashboard and a blast of warm air hit her in the face. She positioned the vent towards her hands and immediately began to feel better. They trundled through the village lazily. Not through choice, she suspected, but rather that the old car could not go any faster. It laboured as it climbed the hill out of the other side of the village.

Apart from the enquiry about the temperature, neither of them had spoken the whole way through the village. Anais still felt uncomfortable around Aldrich and, therefore, struggled for a topic of conversation with him. She would have contented herself with watching the scenery as they ambled by, but the silence was deafening, and she felt that she really should say something.

"How far are we going?" They were now in open countryside. Rolling hills surrounded them and the road was flanked by dry-stone walling with the occasional wooden gate. She'd not seen much of the countryside and in the dusky winter light, it looked almost ethereal. An occasional farm building or old stone house dotted the landscape.

"It's about an hour and a half away from here," replied Aldrich.

"Oh." She couldn't think of anything else to say, her hopes of starting a conversation dashed by his clipped answer. She went back to staring out of the window.

They passed through a number of villages and hamlets before they finally came to a stop in what Anais assumed was the village where Aethelu had been born.

Aldrich found a parking spot, just off the village square and Anais got out. The carpark was cobbled quaintly and surrounded by various shops. A pub called the Black Bull was the main building on the square, although, at this early hour, its doors were closed. Some traders had set up market stalls where early Christmas shoppers found bargains and others bought local produce.

Anais turned to Aldrich expectantly.

"Ok, which way is the spring?"

She could see little houses and buildings all around her, but beyond them lay a patchwork of hilly farmers' fields. She assumed they would be walking up one of them.

Aldrich was quiet for a moment. She thought she saw the glistening of a tear in his eye.

"It's been a long time since I stood here," he said, slowly moving around in a circle to take it all in. "Six hundred years or so. This is the first time I've stood here in six hundred years. Did you know this square was here all those years ago? Can you imagine? It's changed a lot, but it was still here. They used to sell wares here back then, too." He indicated the market. "Aethelu was born here, they all were. We lived just over there, perhaps a few streets away from here." He pointed to the far corner of the square. The tear that had been threatening to drop earlier, now rolled down his cheek. He rubbed it away with his hand.

"Would you like to go see?" Anais asked. "We have all day."

"Would you mind?"

"Of course not." She smiled at him. She thought that she would find it weird to go back to her hometown in California and she had only left a couple of years ago. She could only imagine what it must feel like for Aldrich to come home after six hundred years.

The ground was slippery with frost and the cobbles were difficult to walk on, but that didn't seem to bother Aldrich, who strode off ahead of her at such a speed. She had to keep her eyes on the ground and watch each step, only looking up to see where they were going occasionally, to keep from falling over.

Once they were out of the main square and onto a house-lined street, which, thankfully, was laid with flag-stones instead of cobbles, she was able to catch up. He walked a while and then turned left at the first left-hand corner. They passed a fish and chip shop, which smelt delicious and made her stomach grumble even though it still wasn't lunchtime. Three streets later, Aldrich stopped. He seemed unsure. He looked around in all directions. Anais followed his lead and looked about her.

The houses on the street were hardly new, but they were modern enough for her to appreciate how different it must be from six hundred years ago. All manner of modern day conveniences surrounded her, cars parked on the streets and houses with plumbing and electricity. A young man cycled past, listening to music through earphones. Anais wished she had paid more attention to history lessons at school. What would it have looked like here in the fourteenth century?

"Well, it's changed a bit," said Aldrich, seeming to know what she was thinking.

"Is this it?"

"It's hard to tell exactly. Things have changed so much. It doesn't feel right, though."

Anais wasn't sure what exactly he was supposed to feel, but she followed him as he carried on down the street and then turned yet another corner.

The street that he had turned onto differed from the ones they had just been walking down. The little rows of red brick terraces were now behind them. On this street, the houses had gardens and were spaced out into semi-detached blocks giving it a feel of open space. Between each house, Anais could see the frost covered hills in the distance. The village was so small that they were already coming to the edge of it.

"Ah, this is more like it." Aldrich rubbed his hands and picked up his pace once again.

As they walked down the street, the houses became even more spaced out. The gardens appeared bigger and each house was detached from its neighbour. Unlike the houses on the previous streets, these were cottages made in grey stone with names like Fern Cottage and Dales Cottage.

Finally, Aldrich stopped.

"This is it!" He' stopped outside a pretty house, which had been painted white. Its garden was covered in frost, which sparkled in the weak winter sun. A Mini was parked in the driveway and a swing sat, unmoving in the garden. It was an old house but unlikely to be over six hundred years old.

"How can you tell?" This house looked just like all the others on the street apart from its colour.

"Can you see the hills behind the house?"

Anais looked to where he was pointing. She could see a pathway or a country lane winding up the frosty hillside. Dry-stone walls marked out the boundaries of farmers' fields. Occasional bare trees dotted the landscape.

"Yes."

"I saw that view every day for years. Everything else has changed but that view. It's exactly the same. Come on. I know the way."

Anais thought that he might want to stay at the cottage to reminisce a while, but he was already off, hiking ahead of her further down the street.

She once again had to run to keep up with him. After a few minutes, he turned onto the same lane she'd seen earlier. It was barely wide enough to get a car down, but she could see furrows in the ground where vehicles had made grooves in the mud. Now, though, the ground was hard with the cold.

Grass grew along the edges, along with hardy weeds, which were managing to survive the freezing weather. The path meandered upwards, twisting and turning with dry-stone walls to either side. They passed a man wearing a flat cap coming in the opposite direction, a border collie at his heels.

"Morning." He doffed his cap to them.

"Good morning!" smiled Aldrich cheerily.

"Morning," wheezed Anais, as he walked past her.

The hill got steeper and Aldrich showed no sign of slowing down.

"Aldrich!" she called out and stopped to get her breath back. Carrying a baby uphill was exhausting and it felt like they had already been walking for miles.

He turned to see her wheezing.

"Oh, I'm sorry. I sometimes forget about your condition. Would you like to walk a little slower?"

"Yes, please," she gasped between breaths.

He waited for her to catch her breath, and then once again set off, this time walking at a much more leisurely pace. The little road became narrower and narrower, until it was nothing more than a path. A farm building marked the end of the road, and they had to climb over a stile to get out into the open countryside.

The view from this height was beautiful. The village where they had parked their car now looked tiny, like a toy village. Everything was white as far as Anais could see, thanks to the frost. It was magical. How lucky Aethelu was to have spent her childhood here. She imagined a young Aethelu climbing a tree, no doubt, with Anais' father just behind her.

She couldn't admire the view for long, though, because Aldrich was already walking.

"Is it far?" she asked when she caught up with him.

"Just over the other side of the hill."

She looked up. The top of the hill still seemed like a long way away. It was then that she noticed something.

"Aldrich. I've not seen a stream. Are you sure this is the right way?"

"Don't worry. The stream runs down the other side. I know where I'm going."

After an hour had passed, they had finally crossed to the

other side of the hill and now were heading downwards which was much easier on Anais.

"See those rocks over there?"

Anais looked. Trees surrounded a rocky area on the side of the hill.

"That's where we are going."

It took another ten minutes of walking to get there, but when they arrived, Anais could see why people had thought the spring had magical properties. It looked like a little fairy dell nestled into an indentation of the hill. She could hear the water bubbling up from the earth and a little stream flowed down the hillside.

"This place has energy," said Aldrich. "Can you feel it?"

Anais wasn't sure how to respond. The last thing she could feel was energy. She was exhausted from their long walk up the hill. A sudden thought occurred to her, which made her heart fall. They hadn't brought a bottle to capture the water.

Aldrich must have known what she was thinking, as he pulled a silver hip flask out of his pocket.

He plunged the flask into the clear water and passed it to Anais.

"Drink some. You'll feel better, trust me."

She lifted the flask to her mouth and drank. The water was freezing. She could feel it as it went down her throat.

It revived her, made her feel more alive. Suddenly, she felt her energy return. Her aching muscles from the long walk stopped hurting. Autumn leaped around in her stomach causing her to laugh.

"I told you!" Aldrich said as he took the hip flask from her and filled it once again. This time, he screwed the lid on tightly and returned it to his pocket.

"It was the water from this spring that made me think

about making The Light in the first place. Our village got its water from a stream on the other side of the village, so no one really came up here. This stream runs down and eventually hits a river where its magical properties are diluted. The ground is barren and rocky so there were never any houses between here and the river. No one else noticed this spring's properties. There was talk in the village of a magic spring, but at that time, people either didn't believe it or they were scared of it. Few people came up here."

"But you believed it?"

"No, I don't believe in magic, despite what I told Andrew. I never did. I believe in science. This water is special, though. Whatever is in this water to give it its "magic" (he held up his fingers in quote marks at the word magic) is just the right set of minerals to prolong life. A friend of mine lived up on this hill. Probably in the same place as the last farm building we passed. He was still herding sheep at a hundred and two. His wife lived to be a hundred and five. It's pretty unlikely now, but then, well back then, it was unthinkable. I came up here one day, exhausted, and had a drink of this water. I felt exactly as you do now. I couldn't believe how much better I felt, how much healthier after just a few swigs of water. Of course, my friend swore by it. Told me that was the secret to his old age. I brought a bucket up here and started to use it in my tonics. I was already working as a healer or doctor. Everything I gave to people using the water worked so much better than it had before. I'd already gotten a reputation for being a great healer by then. All the villagers came to me when they were sick. But when I started to use the water, my reputation increased and people from other villages came to me. People would walk for days for me to cure them. The water didn't cure everything. It wasn't a wonder drug, but it sped up the healing process incredibly."

Aldrich sat on a rock so Anais found one of her own to sit on to listen to his story.

"I was so much in demand that I had to enlist Winnie and the older children to help. I'm afraid I got big headed with all the attention. Too big for my boots, if you will. But I saw something in this water. I had an idea. What if I could make a potion that would cure everything. Then I would be able to just hand it out and we all wouldn't be so busy all the time. I started experimenting. When it became too much, I enlisted James to help me. We worked all hours, while poor Winnie was left to heal the village all by herself.

Eventually, we created the Elixir. I didn't truly understand what I had created, but even then, I knew it was something special. I thought that we'd all live to a hundred. I'm as surprised as anyone else that we are all still here over six centuries later. If I'd have known then what I know now, would I have created the Elixir?" his voice grew wistful. "I'm not so sure. It's brought nothing but destruction and most likely the end of the human race."

"It's not the Elixir that's done that. It's Andrew and his Jagovirus."

"Without the Elixir, Andrew would have died centuries ago."

"It's not your fault, Aldrich." She put her arm around his shoulder. He gave a grateful smile and then stood up.

"Maybe there is magic in this water, after all." Anais jumped up, full of energy.

"Aye, lass, perhaps you're right.

7

The walk down the hillside was much more pleasant than the walk up had been. Anais was full of energy. She felt like she could sprint down the hill. Back in the village, it took no time to get back to the car in the village square.

The market was much busier than when they had left, and the pub had opened its doors. Anais walked around to the passenger side of the car and was just about to open the door when Aldrich spoke.

"What time is it?"

Anais looked at her watch.

"Two-thirty."

"Is it really? You must be hungry."

"Just a bit." In reality, she was starving. Her stomach had been gurgling all the way down the hill.

"Let's have a pub lunch. My treat," announced Aldrich.

Anais knew she should protest, that they should get back to the house, but the thought of a hot meal was too good to pass up.

Inside, the pub was very Old English. Black beams held

the ceiling up and brass knickknacks decorated the walls, alongside old black and white photos of the village.

The only clue that this was a modern pub was a flashing one-armed bandit in the corner.

She found a corner seat and sat whilst Aldrich went to fetch her a drink. He returned with an orange juice for her, a pint of ale for himself and two menus.

She ordered a meat and potato pie, which Aldrich decided sounded lovely and ordered the same for himself.

Whilst they waited for their food, Anais sipped on her juice. The effects of the water were beginning to wear off and her legs were beginning to ache again.

Whatever had inspired Aldrich to chat earlier had now gone because he sat nursing his pint and looking out of the window in silence. Anais once again felt awkward and didn't know what to say to him. After a few minutes trying to come up with a topic of conversation, she finally broke the silence.

"What was it like living here?"

"Hmm?" he seemed to have forgotten she was there. "Living here? It was lovely. It was a nice village. We had enough food to go round most of the time. Everybody knew each other. It was a community. Of course, for me, it was perfect. I had a little fame and I must confess to enjoying it. It was idyllic really, until..."

He paused and stared out of the window again.

"Until?" Anais prompted.

"Until the plague came."

Just then their food arrived, cutting him off. Aethelu had already told her about the black death and the fact that it had killed her younger sister, Anna.

Anais wasn't sure whether she should ask him to continue or let it go. The death of his youngest child would obviously be a difficult topic of conversation for him.

She dug into her pie and a waft of steam came out. It smelled delicious. She'd just taken her first bite when Aldrich continued.

"At first, it was nothing more than a rumour. We'd heard of a disease killing people down south. The world was a much smaller place back then and it seemed that it was nothing to be feared. It was a million miles from our little village. As you can see, even now, this is a small, out-of-the-way village. Back then, we barely ever saw strangers, just the occasional few who came to me. That's how we became infected, our village. It was my fault."

"Anais put her fork down." How could it possibly have been your fault? Didn't it kill a third of the population of Europe."

"But our little village was so remote, we should never have got it. Because I'd become rather well known, when the black death arrived up north, people came to me for a miracle cure, bringing the plague with them."

"It was hardly your fault, though. It wasn't as though you had invited them."

"I courted my fame. Once I started working on The Light, I thought I was invincible. I thought I could cure anything. And so, they came. Just a handful at first, but then, they arrived in droves. I did what I could, but I was too busy working on The Light to help them much. Winnie did most of the work. She gave them my tonics and the kids went up the hill daily to bring bucketfuls of the spring water. It improved their condition temporarily and eased their suffering, but most died eventually."

"And then Anna caught it."

"My darling, baby girl, I knew I could save her. I'd just finished The Elixir."

"Aethelu told me that Winnie wouldn't let you give it to her, that she believed that God would save her."

"That's partly true. At that time, we were all religious. The church was the centre of our community. It was unthinkable not to believe in God. I think, though, the more death and suffering we saw, the more our faith dwindled. The real reason that Winnie refused to let me give Anna The Light was that she was scared of what it would do to her. I had spent a year developing it and in that time had experimented on many animals. Some of them, I'm afraid, had suffered the most gruesome of deaths. Even though I was convinced that I had finally gotten it right, I'd never tried it on a human before, and even I could not guarantee what the outcome would be. As some of the plague sufferers had survived, Winnie gambled Anna's life. It turned out to be the wrong choice. Winnie never really forgave herself."

Aldrich became silent once again, but Anais already knew the rest of the story; How they had gathered up friends and relatives and consumed The Light, how James had torn up their house searching for the elixir, and how their appearance had changed. She knew that they had had to leave the village because the other villagers thought that it was the work of the devil, fuelled, no doubt, by the death and destruction that was coursing through the village.

"Is this the first time you have been back?" Anais asked, finishing off her meal.

"It is," replied Aldrich simply.

The drive home was as silent as the drive to the village had been. Aldrich, no doubt, was reminiscing about his past, as Anais watched the scenery. She was looking forward to getting back to Aethelu, but at the same time, dreading going back to The Manor. Who knew when she would be able to leave again? Or if she'd be able to leave. She pushed the thought to the back of her mind as they pulled in through the gates.

Aethelu was waiting for her as she walked in through the kitchen door with Aldrich. Anais noticed Andrew was also waiting for them, seated at the big oak table.

"How did it go?" asked Aethelu.

Anais grabbed Aethelu's hand and led her upstairs. She had no desire to be in the same room as Andrew. Once back in their room, she told Aethelu all about her day. There was no point in keeping her voice down, as nothing that had happened that day was particularly secret. Besides, Andrew was probably too busy with Aldrich to listen to their conversation.

"I wish I could have come with you," said Aethelu when Anais told her everything.

"We can go back and visit when this is all over. To be honest, you didn't miss much, although I can see why your dad needed the spring water as an ingredient. It made me feel amazing. It's a shame it didn't last long, though; we walked miles," she said, whilst rubbing her aching feet.

"Come here, let me do that for you." She sat next to Anais on the bed and took one of her feet to massage. "Andrew was incredibly nervous all the while you were out. He kept thinking you'd just disappear and not come back."

"It's hardly like I'd leave you all here."

"That's what I kept telling him. He doesn't understand love or loyalty at all, though."

"If he did, we probably wouldn't be in this mess in the first place," Anais replied.

That night Anais found herself helping Sabine move all her clothes from Alex's room to Rafe's. Neither man was particularly happy about this turn of events. Sabine, however, was coping very well.

"I plan to go to Rafe's room and then sneak back into Alex's every night," she whispered to Anais. "It's actually quite exciting."

Anais wasn't sure if she'd get away with it, but she kept quiet. Andrew had eyes and ears everywhere. Alex's room was exactly as she imagined it to be. It was a real boy's room with pale grey wallpaper and carpet and bright orange curtains. The bed sheets were in the same shade of orange. The room was slightly smaller than Aethelu's and Arcadia's but had the same sense of grandeur with the chandelier hanging from the ceiling. Guitars hung on the walls surrounded by signed photographs of famous musicians. A grand piano took up most of the space by the window. She was surprised. She'd heard the whole family perform at her wedding, but up until now, she'd not seen any evidence of a musical instrument in the house.

"Is this where they all practice their music?" asked Anais.

"There is a music studio opposite." Sabine pointed at a door across the corridor.

"You are kidding?" She opened the door, and sure enough, there was a huge soundproofed room with yet more guitars, a drum set, a couple of violins and another piano in the corner. "I never knew this was here!" Anais realised that there was a lot of the house she still hadn't seen. This whole wing, for instance, had been left out when Aethelu had given her a tour of the house a year ago. She'd just assumed it was nothing but bedrooms. She closed the door and followed Sabine to another bedroom. Rafe was sat at a desk as they came in. He didn't look up, but he raised his hand to point to an open wardrobe, which had been cleared out for the arrival of Sabine's clothes. Rafe's bedroom was larger than Alex's. It was decorated in muted beiges, dark browns and blacks. Pictures of Venetian scenes dominated the room. Despite its rather neutral colour, it was still the most flamboyant room Anais has ever seen. The bed was huge, elegantly carved out of dark wood. A bright pink duvet with gold embroidery covered it. This in itself was covered with a plethora of gold cushions. The thick curtains that hung at the windows were also gold and the rest of the furniture either matched the curtains or the duvet. Everything was painted gold; the desk, the wardrobe, the side tables--all gold. The chair that Rafe sat on was brilliant fuchsia as was a sofa at the other side of the room. A gold shelving unit held white marble busts and various vases in either pink or gold. The room was immaculate. Not a thing was out of place.

The whole effect made her feel rather nauseous. She gave a silent 'thank you' that Andrew's plan hadn't required that she have an affair with Rafe. If the thought of sleeping with Rafe wasn't enough to make her feel sick, then this room certainly would.

"You can have the bed. I will take the sofa." Rafe turned round and finally spoke to them.

"Don't be silly," replied Sabine. "I'll have the sofa. This is your room. I don't intend to stay here for long anyway. Once it gets dark, I'm planning to go back to Alex's room. I'll sneak back in here before dawn."

"An excellent plan with only one drawback; Andrew can hear everything you say. By now, he already knows of your plans of sneaking away. I'll take the sofa. You can have the bed." He pulled a pink blanket out of a wardrobe and draped it over the sofa.

Sabine covered her mouth and went bright red. "Shit! I forgot," she whispered looking around.

Anais bade them both goodnight and walked back down

the corridor to her own room. She decided to stop off at Alex's room and let him know that his girlfriend would not be joining him in the middle of the night after all.

He would have laughed if he weren't so miserable.

"This whole thing's ridiculous. How does he expect Judith to believe any of it?" he spoke aloud, knowing that Andrew could hear him.

"He knows you will all play your parts well. There is too much at stake to do otherwise."

"Mmm," answered Alex. "I'm glad that the baby is mine. You know I'll always be there for her, don't you? You, too, if you ever need me."

"I'm glad, too. You'll always be part of her life, Alex. She'll know how special you are."

"Will you tell her I'm her father?"

"If Andrew gets his way, she'll not even know I'm her mother."

"She's bound to ask questions when she gets older. I mean Judith is so dark skinned and she will be so pale with The Light in her."

"Perhaps that's what Andrew is planning to tell her. That she is white because of The Light. I don't know. The whole thing doesn't bear thinking about."

She sat next to Alex on the bed and he wrapped his arms around her. She immediately felt comforted by his warmth.

"I'm scared Alex."

"I know. We all are."

"I meant about the birth. I was hoping this would all be over by the time she decides to make her appearance. It's not, though, is it? The Elixir won't be ready until mid-January. I'm due at the beginning of February."

"That gives you two weeks."

"What if she comes early?"

"I read in those baby books that most first babies are late."

"Not all, though. Some come early."

"She'll be on time, our perfect little Autumn. You won't let us down will you?" He put his hand on her stomach.

"Even if she does come on time, what happens then?"

Alex had no answers for her. Instead, he pulled her tightly towards him and held her close.

8

Breakfast the next morning was an awkward affair. There had been quite a bit of seat swapping to accommodate Andrew's wishes. Rafe and Alex were now seated as far away from each other as possible, which meant that Alex now had to sit only one chair away from Andrew, as Rafe steadfastly refused to. Sabine sat between Alex and Andrew, and the seat at his other side had been left empty for Judith. What was already a squashed table became even more so with the extra chair for Judith. It was built to accommodate twelve people comfortably. Five at each side and one at each end, however, there were now fifteen of them all crushed around it. August was so large that he took up more than his fair share of space, so Anais ended up eating her breakfast perched on a corner. Judith looked completely dazed as Andrew pulled out her chair allowing her to take her seat.

No one spoke as Winnie passed around great tureens of hot breakfast food. Anais noticed Judith looking sadly at Rafe, who, in turn, was trying not to return her gaze. She noticed he kept stealing glances at her when he thought Andrew wasn't looking.

It was Andrew who spoke first. "I was just telling Judith how happy we all were when you and Sabine announced your engagement last week Rafe."

Alex opened his mouth in shock "What?" Anais kicked him under the table.

Sabine hid her shock much better than Alex had. She grabbed Rafe's hand and smiled. "We are so very happy and so much in love." She over-egged the pudding a bit, but this was nothing compared to Rafe. He sat there with a smile that was really a grimace.

"Very happy," he hissed. He didn't look very happy to anyone quite the opposite! Sabine wiggled his hand a bit to cajole him.

"And in love, dear," she said and kissed his cheek. Anais could see Alex go red and hoped Judith wouldn't notice. Then she remembered that Alex was supposed to be jealous of his girlfriend running off with Rafe.

"And in love," repeated Rafe in monotone. He added a smile to his lips, but when he looked towards Judith, the pain in his eyes was evident.

Judith herself looked stunned. Tears skirted around her eyes at Rafe's proclamations of love for Sabine. As Anais watched her, she picked up a napkin and delicately wiped her eyes. She was trying to hide her pain, but like Rafe's, it was evident. She clearly didn't know what was going on. The whole thing was a huge shock to her.

"How are you feeling Judith, love?" You must be hungry."

"Thank you," she replied in honeyed African tones to Winnie, who had just walked round the table to heap food onto her plate. "I'm still a little confused. I'm afraid I don't remember very much. My brain feels like it is made out of Swiss cheese. I don't remember the accident or much before it, for that matter. My head is a little fuzzy. I apologise if I have forgotten anything important these last few months."

"Nothing to apologize for honey," said Andrew, grabbing her hand and kissing it. The movement made her flinch, but then she smiled to mask her uncertainty. "Andrew was hazy with the details of my accident. Can you shine any light on what happened?"

Anais looked up from her food... Judith was talking to her. Anais didn't know what to say. She put down her fork and started to um and ah.

"You were with Judith when she had the accident, remember? Just after the wedding." Andrew prompted.

"Oh, yeah..." began Anais. She didn't know what to say. "Yeah, we were in France and you..."

"Our wedding, silly, not yours." Andrew could barely mask his anger at her slip up.

"Oh, yeah, sorry...your wedding. Um, it was beautiful. You looked gorgeous. Had a big white dress. Lots of flowers. Nice, really nice."

"Yes, but how did I come to be unconscious?"

Anais racked her brain to come up with a believable story.

"You, um... You went to get me a drink. You know, because I was pregnant and all."

"You were already pregnant by then?"

Anais felt like she was digging a great big hole. Why hadn't Andrew told her this fictitious wedding had taken place? Or how Judith's 'accident' supposedly happened?

"Um, yeah, I think so. Anyway, you went to get me a drink, tripped over Baker, and fell down the kitchen stairs. Knocked you out cold."

"Oh," said Judith with a look of confusion on her face. "Did we go to Egypt at all? I feel like I remember being there."

"You must have dreamed it, darling," said Andrew. "The bang to your head no doubt caused all kinds of damage to your brain."

"I suppose so," answered Judith, without conviction.

At the end of the meal, Andrew led Judith away. Minutes later, Rafe also left the table.

"Well, that went well," said Arcadia with obvious sarcasm.

"This is going to kill Rafe," said Alex. "How does Andrew expect us to keep this up? It's madness!"

Sabine got up from her place, walked around the table to Alex and hugged him.

"Nice story," grinned Aethelu at Anais.

"I totally forgot that the pair of them are supposed to be married. I'm useless at lying. I'm going to forget what's the truth and what's not."

Suddenly, the sound of raised voices came down the stairs. It was Rafe and Andrew.

Anais, Aethelu, Alex, and Audsley rushed out of the dining room into the main hall to see what was going on. Judith stood at the top of the stairs, clutching onto the balustrade, tears in her eyes. Andrew and Rafe were fist-fighting at the top of the stairs. Rafe was incandescent with rage. The two men were almost a blur thanks to their speed, but it was evident that Rafe was the stronger of the two. He pulled his right arm back and punched Andrew in the jaw, breaking it with a loud crack. Andrew ran towards Rafe, knocking him off balance. Both the men tumbled down the stairs to the sound of Judith screaming. Anais desperately wanted to run up the stairs to comfort her, but she was blocked by Rafe and Andrew.

"Get Rafe. He's going to get us all killed at this rate," shouted Audsley to Alex. Both the fighters had now landed at the bottom of the stairs, but their little fall had done nothing to stop their fighting. Alex jumped in to try to separate them and got an errant elbow in his eye for his trouble. Audsley and Aethelu waded in to help. Between them, they managed to drag Rafe from Andrew's battered body and drag him back into the dining room. Anais followed, just making it before the door shut behind her. Andrew had pressed his remote control once again. Anais didn't think they would get off as lightly as last time, and sure enough, within minutes, there came the sound of gas seeping through some vents.

She looked around her fearfully. Everyone else had the same expression on their faces. What was it this time? No one was laughing, so she knew it wasn't laughing gas again. A few minutes later, she realised what it was. Some kind of itching powder was being blown through the vents. It was so fine that she could barely see it, but she knew it was there. Every part of her skin that had been exposed to the powder had turned red and was beginning to itch.

"Quickly, get under the table."

They all pulled the chairs out and followed her lead by diving under the table. Anais' arms and face were itching so much that scratching was barely easing it. Arcadia, who had been wearing a short dress, had gotten it worse than anyone else had. Her long manicured nails dug into her skin to try to ease the agony of her irritated legs. Blood poured down them where she had scratched too hard. At that moment, Anais would gladly borrow Arcadia's nails, despite the damage to the skin because her own bitten down nails were doing nothing to ease her own itching. Everywhere Anais looked, people were scratching their skin raw. The problem was that the table was not big enough to cover them all. It didn't help that August was so big and was using the table leg to scratch his back, making the whole table wobble and causing more of the powder to drop onto them.

"Stop it, August!" shouted Ava, who had just been showered with powder from the table. Immediately, her neck and arms burned with the powder. Anais jumped up, to the shock of Aethelu. She ran to the sideboard and extracted all the blankets they had used to sleep on last time they had been locked in. Instead of bringing them under the table, she draped them over the top and sides making a tent out of the table. Then she crawled back under and did her best to shake all the powder off her. Unfortunately, her unselfish act of leaving the cover of the table, even for a few moments, meant she was covered in powder. The density of the powder had thickened considerably, and it was now falling like snow. Her hair was now almost as white as Aethelu's.

Her eyes burnt with the pain of the little flakes and her vision became cloudy with the tears running from her eyes. Just scratching her arms and legs was not enough. It felt like a million ants were doing the foxtrot all over her body and no amount of scratching was easing it. Her biggest wish right now was for a giant piece of sandpaper to rub up and down her whole body. She'd gladly have peeled all her skin off if it meant an end to this suffering. By now, she couldn't see anyone else, but she could feel the movement of everyone around her, scratching madly. Her ears could hear the moans and screams of those around her as each of them tried their best to ease their own torture. She couldn't see it, but she could feel something warm and wet dribbling down her leg. She knew it was blood, her own blood. She'd scratched her leg so hard that she'd broken through the skin. Still, that didn't stop her from scratching more. Her short nails broke the surface of the skin all over and rivulets of blood flowed. Her nails became her greatest enemy and her saviour at the same time, but the relief of each scratch lasted less than a second.

"Why am I bleeding so much?" Anais managed to choke out. Her throat itched and hurt in the same way the rest of her body did, and she could barely get the words out. The Light in her blood meant that she rarely bled at all. She'd not had to experience childhood scrapes and bruises like her classmates had. She wasn't used to bleeding like this.

"The powder is not ordinary itching powder," coughed Aldrich. "He's formulated it so it's strong enough for even our bodies to feel. He must have put some anticoagulant in it, something to keep you bleeding for longer if you scratch. The best thing you can do is to not break your skin in the first place. Stop scratching."

This, of course, was easier said than done. Anais couldn't have stopped scratching if her life depended on it. The blankets, forming a tent around the table, offered some protection from the powder, but for Anais, it was too late. Every inch of her was both itching and burning. Her eyes were now so painful that she couldn't open them, and her throat felt like it was on fire. The powder had even found its way into her ears, so even her brain felt itchy. Before long, she descended into a temporary madness. Nothing existed anymore, just her body with its burning, itching, and screaming, along with the writhing of bodies next to her. It went on for an eternity. She became deathly tired, but she could not rest. A second after she stopped scratching, the itching was unbearable and so she continued digging her nails into her skin throughout the night. Unlike the night of the laughing gas, she didn't worry about Aethelu or her baby or any of the others. Her brain just couldn't go anywhere beyond the incessant itching. She couldn't think in any kind of rational way and so when she heard someone talking; it took quite a few minutes to comprehend what was being said.

"It's breakfast time," repeated the voice for what could possibly be the hundredth time. It was Andrew's voice. She finally recognised it although it sounded tinny and distant. At first she thought it was because her ears weren't working properly, but then she realised he was talking to them through some kind of speaker. "Get up and come out. The door is open."

The door was open! They could get out. Anais took a few seconds just to process this information, her brain was so fatigued. Eventually, she realised she should move, but it wasn't easy. Her body felt raw. Any movement stung her skin making her want to cry out. Her throat was now burning so much that she couldn't scream even if she had wanted to. She peeked through the blankets but couldn't see anything through her burning eyes. Everything was a blur. It took a good few minutes to crawl from beneath the table and get to the door of the dining room. Every step was an agony like no other. Her legs and arms felt strange. The skin on them was moist, what was left of it. She felt, rather than saw, her way into the hallway. She could hear the others behind her and in front of her. No one was speaking. It was impossible to.

The small en-suite bathroom next to the bedroom didn't have a shower so she would have to use the shower in the main bathroom on the first floor. First, she would have to climb the stairs to get to it, which seemed like an arduous task. Just lifting her leg to put her foot on the first step was akin to climbing Everest. She couldn't see anything as her eyes were so swollen, but using the banister to guide her was impossible. Every touch against her skin made her nerve endings feel like they were on fire. It was eerily quiet except for the shuffling of feet of those around her. She assumed the reason was that, just like her, no one could scream because of the pain in their lungs, their swollen throats, their sore mouths. She could almost hear the screaming inside the others' heads joining hers in a cacophony of anguish. She knew that she had to wash the powder off or it would continue to burn her skin, but every step up the stairs was an agony beyond any other. She wanted nothing more than to collapse in a heap, but she knew that if she did, any contact with the floor would only hurt more. The going up the stairs was ridiculously slow, but she couldn't have moved faster if she had tried. Judging by the sounds around her, no one was climbing them any faster. After what seemed like an eternity, there were no more steps to climb. A loud banging sound behind her was enough to tell her that someone had fallen down the stairs. A pang of guilt ran through her as she carried on towards the bathroom. In any other circumstance, she would have run down the stairs to help whoever had fallen, but she knew there was nothing she could do in her present state. Even if she had managed to get back down the stairs, there was no way she would be able to help someone up off the floor, much less, up the stairs. No, the best course of action was to wash the powder away first and then see if she could help. Even then, it was unlikely. Her fingers no longer felt like fingers. Instead, they had been replaced by fat, painful, sausages, which shot pain up her arms every time they came in contact with the wall. She had a vague idea of where the door for the bathroom was, but she could have no more opened it with her swollen hands than if it was a bank vault door. Thankfully, someone had got to it in front of her and opened it wide. She bumped into the person in front of her as she got into the shower. Just the contact of her body against someone else's was agony. Only a few seconds later, someone else bumped into the back of her causing her to, once again, silently scream in her own head. The shower cubicle was not made for three people and yet there were at least three of them trying to use it.. The person behind her backed up a little, meaning that she could step away from the one in front and give them the room to turn the shower on. After a few seconds, it became apparent that that was not going to happen. Why did they not turn the shower on? What were they waiting for? Then she realised the person in front would not be able to turn the taps with their own painful, swollen, fingers. She could hear the movement of the person in front of her, trying to turn the taps, but no water flowed over her. Eventually, a small squeak signalled a tap being turned and a cascade of water flowed around her. A millisecond of bliss was quickly followed by the realisation that each drop of water hitting her body felt like a tiny sharp knife on her broken skin. She wanted to run from the pain, but there was still someone behind her trying to get in, and in any case, running was impossible. She had to bear it. Eventually, she got used to it and as the powder washed away, she actually began to feel a little better. She knew she should take her clothes off to wash the powder away completely, but her fingers were in no state to enable her to do this. Instead, she raised her head up and let the water wash her eyes and flow down her throat. She was thankful that the water temperature had been set to lukewarm, as had it been very hot, it would likely have burnt her skin right off. As it was, she felt like her exposed skin was peeling away. The person behind her bumped into her again signalling her time in the shower was up. She got out and slowly walked down the corridor to her bedroom leaving a trail of dripping water behind her. By the time she managed to get to her door, she was so exhausted she didn't have the energy to try to open it. It would have been impossible anyway with her sausage-like fingers. Fatigue and pain finally overwhelmed her and she fell where she stood, just outside the door to her room. Just before she passed out, she felt someone trip over her and land on the floor next to her.

9

It could have been hours or days before Anais awoke. Her body had completely dried, but her clothes and hair were still slightly damp, as was the floor where she had fallen. She tried to open her eyes and found that she could, albeit only a fraction. The corridor in front of her was blurry, but she could just make out the general outline of the person who had tripped over her. She blinked her eyes a few times to try to clear them, but it was no use. She couldn't tell who the person next to her on the floor was, but she assumed it was Aethelu. She patted the body to try to wake them. She was pleasantly surprised to find that, although it hurt her hands, it was nowhere near the agony it had been previously. A slight moan alerted her to the fact that whoever it was, they were still alive and had recovered the use of their vocal chords. She tried to speak herself, to say 'Aethelu' but all that came from her own lips was a strangled guttural sound. She tried to stand, but her arms and legs still hurt. At least she was awake, though, and if she stayed really still, the pain was minimal. She ran her fingers down a patch of bare skin on her arm. It felt like coarse sandpaper. She was almost glad she couldn't see very well. The other person moaned again next to her and she could hear their efforts to get up. After what seemed like an eternity, they must have managed it, because Anais could now feel them pulling on her arm as if to get her to stand. A burning pain shot up her arm reminding her of the early days of herself and Aethelu. This little thought spurred her on and she tried once again to stand with the help of the other person. With much grunting and with an incredible amount of pain, she finally made it upright. Holding on to the other person, she let them guide her to a room and to a bed. Even though she could barely see, the bright red told her that it was Aethelu's room and the bed was hers. The other person fell next to her on the bed. Anais carefully draped her arm over the person who could only have been Aethelu and gratefully fell back asleep.

On next awakening, Anais could finally make out shapes. Everything was still a blur, but at least she could see general outlines of things and not just colours swirling together. She imagined this would be what it was like to need glasses. She tried to move her arm, but it had stuck to the charred skin of Aethelu. She pulled a little harder and ripped her arm away leaving a good quantity of her own skin still sticking to Aethelu. The urge to throw up with the thought of it overcame her, and she stumbled as quickly as she could to the en-suite bathroom. She retched for a few moments, but nothing came up. Her insides were as dry as the skin on her outside. She turned the tap on over the little sink and craned to get a drink from it. The cool water soothed her throat. When she had had her fill, she cupped her hands under the flowing water and threw it over her eyes. Dabbing them dry with a nearby towel, she looked into the mirror in front of her. The water had helped to clear her vision, but now, looking at her reflection in front of her, she wished it hadn't. She was unrecognisable. Not just as Anais, but as a human being. Her skin was blackened, as if burned, with patches of weeping red sores all over her body. Her hair had fallen out in clumps and now she was almost bald with only wisps of hair clinging to her charred scalp. She looked like a burn victim from a house fire--one who hadn't survived. She peeled away her clothes, being careful not to take any more skin with them than necessary. Most of her body had escaped damage, thanks to being covered in clothing. Her torso was certainly red but, at least, had an appearance of living skin, unlike her arms, legs, and head. She gave a gasp. Autumn! Her stomach, still prominent, had a rosy pink glow and looked virtually unharmed, but Anais realised that she hadn't felt her baby kick since being in the dining room and she had no way of knowing how long ago that had been. She brought her hand down to her stomach and willed baby to move, but nothing happened.

A sense of dread filled her, one of guilt, too. In all the time she had been covered in Andrew's itching powder, not once had she thought of her little girl. Prodding her stomach brought no reaction beyond a searing pain down her finger. 'How long should you wait before panicking?' wondered Anais, but it didn't matter, she was already panicking. She couldn't bear it if anything happened to her child. Andrew had already murdered her parents. Had another innocent been added to his list?

She would have cried, but she had no tears to cry. Her tear ducts were probably as burnt as the rest of her. She could only stare in shock at her reflection and try to breathe through her charred lungs. The magnitude of what Andrew had wreaked upon her, upon all of them hit her. Why had they all sat back and let him do this to them? Because the alternative was death? Death would be preferable right now. A noise from the bedroom startled her. Aethelu was moving. Anais turned back to the bedroom and made her way to Aethelu, who was just beginning to stir. Aethelu hadn't fared any better than Anais. Her skin, too, was blackened with rivers of raw bloody flesh peaking through. If Anais didn't know it was her, she would have been hard pressed to recognise her.

"Aethelu," Anais choked and tried to stroke Aethelu's face. The motion made both of them flinch in pain.

"Aregghhh ye k?" Aethelu rasped. Even her voice was not like her own, but that of an habitual smoker.

"I've been better. Can you see at all?"

"Notreallyyou'rejsssablurgghh."

Anais tried to decipher Aethelu's words.

"You need to come to the bathroom. Wash your eyes and clear your throat. I can hardly understand you. The water will help."

Anais desperately wanted to help Aethelu out of bed, but she knew that any skin-to-skin contact would only damage them both. Instead, she waited patiently whilst Aethelu tried pathetically to get out of bed, a little like she had done herself just ten minutes before. Aethelu looked horrendous. There was no other way to put it. She almost didn't want to let her wash her eyes. It would be more humane to let her be blind for a while, at least until they both healed, but Anais knew it was not an option. She knew Aethelu too well. So she guided her to the bathroom as best as she could without actually touching her, and once again turned on the taps. She had been prepared for a complete shock, but she hadn't expected Aethelu to scream. Although, you couldn't really call it a scream. It was barely audible. The horror in Aethelu's eyes as she took in both their reflections was evident. Her mouth was open wide, but her vocal cords hadn't healed enough for her to really scream. Instead, a high-pitched rasping sound came from her.

"Calm down. Please calm down," Anais implored her. She'd have given anything to be able to put her arms around her, but at the moment, it was impossible. Instead, she could only look on helplessly whilst Aethelu went into shock.

"Take your clothes off," Anais said, but she could tell that Aethelu hadn't heard her. The screaming or rasping had stopped and Aethelu now stood with her eyes closed, completely silently. Anais took it as an opportunity to undress her. It was almost impossible as Aethelu wasn't cooperating, and the fabric hurt her hands. It took considerable force to rip the t-shirt off her. Force which made her hands scream in agony, but she knew she should wash them both down. She was glad that Aethelu had been wearing a t-shirt and skirt and not a thick jumper. The skirt was easy to pull down. Anais grabbed the bathroom bin, emptied it out, and filled it with warm water, which she then threw over Aethelu. The bathroom floor flooded, but Anais didn't care. She had more pressing things to worry about than whether the ceiling in the room below them would leak. She filled the bin again and repeated the action. Once she was satisfied that Aethelu was totally clean from the powder, she did the same to herself. Movement was coming a little easier now. Perhaps the restorative powers of The Light were beginning to kick in. She wrapped a towel lightly round Aethelu being careful not to wrap it too tightly, then made her drink some water. Wrapping a towel around herself, she guided them both back to the bed. Any kind of dabbing to dry her body hurt like hell, and when she tried to do it to Aethelu, it elicited a whimper of pain. Giving up, she lay back on the bed and decided it would be easier to air dry the pair of them.

A knock on the door a couple of minutes later made her jump. Who would be knocking at the door? It would have been too painful to bang her knuckles against a hard wooden surface in their present condition. Yet the knocking continued, not a hesitant knocking but persistent, almost forceful. Perhaps the others had healed much more quickly than she had. She wrapped herself in the towel and opened the door. Andrew stood there grinning at her. Actually grinning! The urge to punch him was immense, but she knew the skin on her hands was no match for him at the moment. She's never felt such hatred in her life. How could he smile after all he had done?

"You are late for dinner."

"Dinner?" Was he serious?

"Yes, dinner, I'm giving you all a chance although this will be the only time. I'm afraid it's only pizza. I had to order in as Astrid wasn't up to cooking."

He still called Winnie 'Astrid', the name she had taken for herself when they first became Guardians. She had soon gone back to her given name of Winnie. Had he actually asked her to cook for everyone? He was totally insane.

"I expect you all there within ten minutes. No exceptions." He turned and walked down the corridor. Anais could hear him knocking on another door, probably Alex's.

"I'm going to kill him!" Aethelu spoke behind her. Her voice had improved with the water considerably.

"He'll hear you." Anais closed the door.

"He won't. He's just down the corridor. He can't sift through every second of CCTV footage from the whole house."

Anais turned to look at the thing that used to be

Aethelu. Her beautiful Aethelu was now just a black oozing mess. No white hair remained on her head, and barely a patch of unbroken skin was left on her. Her eyes, though, they sparkled through infinity as they always had. Diamond flecks of light proved that Aethelu was in there somewhere. She was right. He had to die. She could not live through another night living in fear. The only question was how? How would they kill him without killing everyone else? She had no clue, but as she looked at her once beautiful wife, she vowed that she would end this. A small kick from inside her told her that she actually had something worth fighting for. Autumn was ok.

"Come on. Get dressed. We are late for dinner."

10

A horrible sight awaited them at the bottom of the stairs. Aethelu's family were congregated in the hallway. Anais couldn't tell one from another. August was the only truly recognisable one because of his sheer size, but the others could have been anyone. It was even impossible to distinguish between male and female. None of them had much hair left and their faces were unrecognisable. Anais had to figure out who was who by their clothing although most had decided to wear dressing gowns, as it was too difficult to get dressed in anything else. Arcadia, true to form, had not let her melted skin put her off wearing the latest fashion. She had still dressed as if she was going to a royal gala in a short black dress with an auburn wig atop her head. The only difference to her normal attire was the lack of high heels. Instead, she wore some pink fluffy slippers, something she would not usually be seen dead in. There was an argument going on between Rafe and Andrew. Anais would have recognised Rafe even if he hadn't spoken because of his silk robe. It was the same one he had come to meals in previously.

"We are not going in there for bloody pizza!"

"I'm afraid you have no choice. Don't worry. It has been thoroughly cleaned since you were last in there. You have nothing to fear," said Andrew smoothly.

"Nothing to fear?!" Rafe's voice raised an octave. "I don't know what part of my body is what and I resemble a lump of coal. My throat feels drier than Death Valley and you want me to force Pizza down it? I'd rather ram what's left of my fist down your throat."

"I'm sorry you feel that way. Nevertheless, we are going into the dining room and we are going to eat pizza like civilised people."

"Civilised people?" She heard someone whisper under their breath with incredulity.

"Besides," continued Andrew "Your fist would come off a lot worse than my throat at the moment. It's paper thin and ever so painful. I know because I designed the powder to work that way. I suggest you all shuffle in or I'll prove to you just how thin your skin is and how much it can hurt."

"I think we are all aware how much it can hurt, Andrew," said a voice that was unmistakably Winnie's, although Anais wouldn't have guessed who it was to look at her. "Everyone just go in. I'll bring some ice cream up from the kitchen for everyone. If you'll permit me, Andrew?"

"Of course, it sounds like an excellent idea."

Someone (although Anais couldn't tell who) went to help Winnie carry the ice cream from the kitchen. Everyone else traipsed into the dining room and sat down.

Andrew was the only one eating the pizza. Anais' stomach gave a growl. How long had it been since she'd eaten? She knew she should eat for the sake of Autumn, but there was no way that she would manage to get a slice of pizza down her throat. Instead, she occupied herself by trying to figure out who everyone was. In the end, it was easier than she had imagined. They'd all sat in their usual places. Only Judith was missing. It made sense. There was no way Andrew could bring her in here to see what he had done.

"Where's Judith?" she asked. She noticed Rafe look up as she asked.

"I thought the sight of you all would put her off her lunch, so I paid for her to go to a spa. I will be joining her there as soon as we finish dinner."

This new piece of information elicited a few startled looks from the family. At least Anais assumed they were as startled as she was. It was difficult to tell.

"I will, of course, be back in time to input the code. Please don't think about doing anything funny. I will be watching the security footage as soon as I get back. I suggest you spend the evening relaxing and letting your skin rest. If I think you have all behaved when I get back, I might even let you have some cream that will heal your skin quickly. It's quite the miracle cream. I made it at the same time as the powder. I do so want you to be good because, quite frankly, your faces are putting me off my pizza. You really are all so very ugly."

With that, he stood up and left the room. A few seconds later, Anais heard the front door open and then close.

He was gone. He'd actually left the house. She stood up and shuffled to the window. He was jauntily walking down the driveway. Andrew couldn't drive. He must have ordered a taxi.

"He's gone," she said, expecting someone to say something. Nobody did. They were all either too shocked by finally being left alone or just too exhausted to care. Now was the time. They had four hours until Andrew came back.

It gave Anais an Idea. She looked around to find Winnie trying to serve Ice cream. She was struggling with the ice cream scoop with her painful, swollen, hands. Anais walked over and took the scoop out of her hands.

"Sit down, Winnie. Let me do it."

Winnie gratefully let Anais serve the ice cream. Anais started with Aethelu. Just the act of running the scoop through the ice cream was enough to bring tears to her eyes. It was incredibly painful, but she had a plan. As she brought the scoop of vanilla to Aethelu's bowl, she brought her mouth down to Aethelu's ear making sure it was the opposite side to the camera. She whispered as quietly as she could.

"I'm going to look for the vials--*today*. We need to locate them all while Andrew's out. Will you help me?"

She purposely didn't look at Aethelu as she spoke. As she pulled back, she saw Aethelu nod her head almost imperceptibly.

Anais repeated her message around the table until she got to Rafe.

"I don't want any ice cream," he said in a sulk, trying to dismiss her with a wave of his hands."

"It looks really good. Vanilla," said Anais, trying to put the ice cream in his bowl anyway.

"I don't care what bloody flavour it is. I just told you, I don't want it."

"It's really nice. Soothes the throat," said Sabine, trying to help Anais.

"I DON'T WANT IT!" Rafe looked menacingly at Sabine and pushed his bowl away. Anais didn't know what to do. She couldn't force him to eat ice cream, but if she didn't manage to talk to him about her plan, they would be one person short. They needed him.

"Raphael Julian Hyde," said Winnie sharply. "Stop being so rude and eat your ice cream." Anais wasn't sure who was more shocked, herself or Rafe, but he pulled his bowl back and accepted his ice cream.

His mood seemed to improve greatly when he heard what Anais had to whisper in his ear and by the time Anais had returned to her seat, he had brightened up considerably.

In fact, everyone seemed much happier than they had just five minutes before, which Anais took it to mean that they all agreed with her plan. The only problem they faced now was how to coordinate a snoop around the house without Andrew being suspicious. If he were to watch the footage of them all when he got back, he would certainly figure out quickly what they were all up to. Jennifer spoke up and solved the problem.

"Anais, I was thinking of getting a book from the library. Could you show me where it is, please? I've heard so much about this wonderful library, but I've yet to see it. In fact, I've been here quite a while and I still don't know where everything is. Could you give me a tour?"

Anais knew she was trying to figure a way to search the whole house credibly, but Andrew was not stupid. If he saw anyone walking from room to room, he would figure it out soon enough. Alex obviously thought the same thing.

"Actually, I was planning to spend the day in the recording studio today so please could you stay away from there. I don't want any noise disruption once I'm in the zone."

"And I'm planning on attempting to cook something we can all eat. I'm not having pizza for every meal, especially as none of us can swallow it right now. I was thinking of making a huge batch of soup and freezing some. I'd be grateful if you left me to it." Winnie winked at Jennifer.

Anais knew what they were trying to do. They were going to search individual areas. It made sense for Winnie to search the kitchen as she was always there. Making soup was the perfect cover too. She'd have to look in all the drawers and cupboards for a host of ingredients. Alex would search the recording studio.

"Looks like I'll have to give you a grand tour some other time," Anais said to Jennifer "I'm happy to show you the library, though. Did you know there is a secret passageway from there up to the first floor?"

"Fascinating," replied Jennifer, playing along. "I'd love to see that."

"Does anyone else have any plans this afternoon?"

"I feel miserable like this," said Audsley. "I need to do something fun to cheer myself up. Anyone fancy a game of pool?"

"I will," replied Rafe "fancy joining us, Aethelu?"

"Actually, I was thinking of doing some painting. Christmas is coming up and as we can't go out to buy presents, I thought I'd paint a few. Not sure how good they'll be with my hands like this, but I thought I'd give it a go."

One by one, they made plans, each involving different parts of the house. August had decided to use the passageway from the house to his cottage to collect Baker, his Cocker Spaniel.

"Poor thing, I've not been able to feed him for days. Andrew said he'd been looking after him, but I know he's been missing his Daddy August."

Ava, Alfred, and Sabine decided to have tea in the parlour, James and Aldrich were, of course, going to be working on The Light potion. Arcadia had decided to go back to bed.

"I can't stand being out in public looking like this one moment longer. A potato would beat me in a beauty pageant at the moment."

Anais felt sorry for her. She relied on her beauty in her Hollywood world. To look as ugly as she did now must be heart-breaking for her.

"Anais," Jennifer called her "Let's go."

Anais followed her out into the hallway and then directed her to the library. Once they got there, Anais could see that they had a huge task ahead of them. The library held thousands of books. Looking at each one, or more specifically, behind each one, would not be a problem, however, doing it without making Andrew suspicious would be a difficult task. Jennifer came up with the perfect solution.

"My grandmother often talked about this library. She loved to read and found it difficult to get English books in Egypt. Do any of these books belong to her?"

"I don't know. There are some pretty old books here. Some of them could have belonged to her. Winnie would be the best person to ask. She knows this library inside and out."

"My mother used to write her name on the inside cover of her books."

"Ok, then. Let's look."

Between them, they spent quite a few hours searching for one of the vials under the pretence of looking for Amber's books. At one point, Anais thought Jennifer had found one when she shouted out, but she had only found one of the books. She carefully placed it to one side and carried on looking. After three hours of searching, they had found seven books with Amber's name on them but no vial. Anais was fairly certain that if it was hidden anywhere it would be in the electronics section where Andrew usually looked for books, but she couldn't think of a valid reason to check there. Eventually, she came up with cause to check there, but it was pretty lame.

"I need to fix my alarm clock. I wonder if there is a book that will help me?" she mused aloud.

"I think I saw a couple of books on wiring over here," said Jennifer, heading straight to the only unsearched part of the library. Anais followed her over, and between them, they pulled out a good many books. Each time, they checked for some hidden recess behind it. When they could search no more for fear of being too obvious, they sat in the old wingback leather chairs. Anais pretended to peruse a book about clocks to keep up the pretence. Jennifer seemed truly happy to have amassed a collection of her mother's books. She flicked through one of the books, whilst Anais pondered the location of the vial. They had searched the whole library and found no evidence of any vials. The only other place she could think of was the secret passage up to the first floor. She was way too big to fit her pregnant frame down the narrow passageway, but Jennifer would be able to search it.

"Why don't I show you the secret passage? You can take the books up to your room and read them in peace. You will have to take a basket though as there is a ladder to climb at the other end. It will bring you out on the first-floor corridor through a concealed door. Obviously, I won't be able to follow you. I think I'm a bit past climbing ladders in my condition."

"How exciting. A secret passageway." She placed her

mother's books in a basket and followed Anais to the far wall. Anais pressed a button and the wall opened.

"It's pretty dark so you will have to feel your way, but there is only one way to go so you can't get lost."

Anais knew there was a light switch, but she figured that if Andrew had hidden any vials in there, there would be a little light to show whatever mechanism he was using to break them, if needed. If that was the case, Jennifer would see it better in the dark. "Just be careful on the ladder and shout if you need me. I'll wait here until you get to the top of the ladder."

Jennifer hugged her. "Thank you for helping me find some books of my mother's. It means so much to me." With that, she disappeared into the blackness of the tunnel. Anais kept the door open so at least a little light shone through. She heard Jennifer's shoes hit each rung of the ladder and the basket clunking against it as she climbed. Eventually she heard a little click, telling her that the upstairs door had opened and a distant voice.

"I'm up. See you at dinner." Jennifer's voice echoed down the black tunnel.

"See you later," Anais shouted back before closing the secret door.

She sat back down in the chair and looked at her watch. There was just half an hour until she was expected back in the dining room for dinner. The whole afternoon had been a waste of time, well, not a complete waste of time. They had found something that meant a lot to Jennifer, but they hadn't found what they were looking for. She hoped that the others had been more successful. She'd been so sure that Andrew would have hidden a vial in the library. It was a room he used a lot, and he'd want to have those vials in a place he knew well. However, they had searched every inch of it and come up with nothing. Anais doubted that Jennifer had found something in the tunnel. She would have thought of some way of letting her know if she had. Disappointment flooded through her. She didn't know why she thought it would be so easy. Andrew knew this house better than any of them. He'd been the one who had devised all the secret passages and hidden rooms under the guise of improving security. There could be countless hidden places that none of them knew about. It was such a huge house, too. Even without all the secret rooms, searching it without being noticed would be an impossible task. Perhaps they should give up looking. Pretty soon, Aldrich and James would finish The Light Elixir, and Andrew would give it to Judith. Then, whatever happened, it would be better than the hell they were currently living through. She looked at her hands. The skin was flaking off in bits, and thanks to three hours of handling books, they were getting sore. She desperately wanted to rub them, but she knew the fragile skin would just break under the pressure.

She sighed and closed her eyes. She thought back to the first time she had visited this library, a time before she knew about Andrew being Jago. She'd had a conversation with him about the first edition copy of *Alice in Wonderland*, actually, copies. They owned two, and they were worth a fortune. Andrew had been sitting right where she was now, looking at books on wiring or something. He was probably figuring a way to booby trap something. If only she'd paid more attention to what he was looking at. Hindsight was a glorious thing, but it wouldn't help her now. She looked at the shelf where the Alice books had been kept before remembering she'd made Aethelu promise to lock them up somewhere safe. Aethelu had put both copies in the safe. They were out of the light, pretty air tight, and most importantly, locked up, so that no thief would be able to get them. She made her way to the painting over the fireplace, behind which the safe was concealed, and moved it to one side. She dialled the correct numbers and pulled. Nothing happened. Perhaps she had put the numbers in wrong. She tried again, this time more carefully and once again pulled. The safe was still locked tight. Why would someone have changed the code? They all had access to the only thing that was in there, the two books, before. It made no sense to change the code now, unless there was something else in there--something that hadn't been there before--something like a vial. Anais' heart started thumping. She looked down the side of the safe and noticed a hole had been drilled near the back from which wires were now protruding. There was a vial in there! The mechanism to break it was wired up in there, too. Excitement flooded through her, until she realised that she didn't know how to get into the safe. Still, it was a start. They had found a vial. If they could find one, they could find them all. She looked at her watch again...fifteen minutes until dinner. She had an idea. It was pretty outrageous, but if she was careful, it might just work. She ran out of the library as fast as she could, which wasn't actually very fast, thanks to her swollen sore legs. Upstairs in her room, she casually went to her alarm clock and shook it. She hoped that Andrew wouldn't be able to tell that it actually did work and show the correct time, but she needed an excuse to go back to the library. She unplugged it and made a big show of wrapping the wire around it just in case Andrew were to look at this footage of her from the security camera. On the final wrap around, she casually knocked a few of the items from her bedside cabinet onto the floor as if by accident. Cursing loudly, she placed the clock on the bed and bent down to pick up the fallen items, her bedside lamp, a hairbrush, a novel, and her camera. The same one she'd bought in the airport that had led them to Sabine. She carefully switched it to the film function and pressed record before imperceptibly putting it up her sleeve. She picked up the clock and took it downstairs to the library. The book on clocks she had picked out earlier was still sitting on the side table. She sat down with the alarm clock and picked up the book. Pretending to read it, she flicked through the book while at the same time examining her clock.

The front door opened, alerting her to the fact that Andrew was back, and she was running out of time. Placing a fake satisfied grin on her face as she pressed a button on the alarm clock, she stood up and took the book back to the electronics section from whence it had come. She placed the book back on the shelf at the same time as pulling out the camera. She angled it as best she could towards the fireplace, hiding it behind a particularly large book. She thought she'd done a good job of hiding her true intentions, but the whole plan would only work as long as the battery on the camera lasted. She couldn't remember the last time she'd charged it. Still, she could only pray that it would work, and that Andrew wouldn't notice the camera. She only just made it to dinner on time. She would have preferred to wait until after dinner to mention the book, but she didn't want to chance the battery on her camera running out.

"Anais, just in time, I was about to come looking for you and that would have displeased me immensely." Andrew smiled despite his unkind words. "It is a good thing that I'm feeling very relaxed and refreshed after my spa afternoon. It does wonders for the skin. I will be checking the security footage this evening, and if you've all been good in my absence, I will distribute the cream that will help your skin. What have you all been up to?" he asked jovially.

"I've been cooking this for you," replied Winnie ladling soup into his bowl. He looked momentarily suspicious, until she ladled some into Aethelu's, then Anais' bowl. Aethelu picked up a spoon and guzzled hers down.

"I wasn't very successful, though," she started looking straight at Anais. "I couldn't find any coriander."

Anais knew she was talking about the vials. There wasn't one in the kitchen, or if there was one, Winnie hadn't found it.

"I can't say I had a successful afternoon either," said Alex. "I couldn't hold the drumsticks very well with these stupid hands and I couldn't get anything to sound right."

No vial in the recording studio either.

"You've been recording?" Andrew asked, dipping his spoon into his soup.

"I tried to. I can't do anything with these hands, though."

Anais suddenly burst into tears, startling Aethelu, who stopped eating and put her arms around her.

"What's the matter? What's happened?" There was genuine concern in Aethelu's voice. Anais wished she could tell Aethelu that she was putting on, but there was no way she could without alerting Andrew.

"The baby..." she sobbed.

"What's happened to the baby? Is everything alright?"

Everyone was looking at her with concern now. Even Andrew seemed mildly surprised by the outburst.

"I wanted to read my *Alice in Wonderland* book to her, but because of my fingers being so sore I couldn't get into the safe," she sobbed. She had no intention of announcing that the safe code had been changed.

"Is that all?" remarked Aethelu with obvious annoyance.

"I thought you were ill. Why on earth do you want to read to the baby?"

Anais kicked her under the table and then wailed more loudly. Aethelu gave her a quizzical look. She had no idea what was up, but the kick under the table was enough to alert her to the fact something was happening. She quickly hugged Anais.

"Pregnancy hormones!" she announced to the rest of the table. "Don't worry; I'll get the book for you if you really want it."

"Surely, any book will do," said Andrew hurriedly. "It's not as if it would be able to understand anything you say to it anyway. It probably wouldn't even be able to hear you."

Anais hammed it up a little further, wondering how far she could push it. She'd managed to conjure up real tears, but they burnt her raw skin as they travelled down her face.

"It's no big deal. Anais honey, don't cry. I'll get the book for you, if you don't mind, Andrew?"

"Actually, I do mind. We are having dinner."

"Ok, no problem. I'll just go get it after dinner."

"For goodness sake," snapped Andrew. "I'll get the bloody book for you. Perhaps we can all eat in peace then!"

He jumped up out of his seat in a huff and left the dining room.

"What was all that about?" asked Alex. His wasn't the only confused face around the table.

"I just wanted to read Alice, that's all," replied Anais, wiping her eyes with a handkerchief that Rafe had passed to her. "I've heard that reading to a baby in utero will make me a successful mother."

She'd chosen her words carefully. Emulating both Winnie and Alex by using the word 'success', she hoped she'd get her message across.

Alex's mouth formed a perfect 'oh' shape as comprehension dawned.

"Well, I think reading to babies is to be commended. Well done!"

Andrew stalked back into the room and threw the book on the table in front of Anais. Usually, she would have been horrified at the mistreatment of such a priceless book, but she was too happy to care.

"Thank you, Andrew." She gave him a sweet smile, which Andrew did not return.

"Just eat. You've all put me in a bad mood now!"

The rest of the meal was spent in silence, but Anais could see the smiles on everyone's faces. They'd found one vial! The only one not smiling was Andrew. He sat sullenly throughout the meal, but at the end, he surprised everyone by passing out tubes of cream to them all.

"I don't feel as if any of you deserve this, but as you all look hideous at the moment, I want you to use it. I don't want Judith coming back home to think she's moved into the reptile house at the local zoo.

That evening Anais hugged Aethelu and whispered to her what she had done. She knew she couldn't get away with going to the library again, so instead, she sat with Aethelu and read out loud passages of Alice to Autumn. After an hour, she asked Aethelu to take it back to the library for her. Aethelu knew what she must do. Anais had told her where the camera was hiding. She only hoped she'd find it without much fuss. It was so difficult to do anything knowing that everything they did could be watched. She trusted Aethelu though. As Aethelu left, she called after her.

"Don't put it back in the safe; It will hurt your hands too much. Just put it back on the shelf. The security is so high at this house that no one will be able to steal it anyway."

Aethelu came back into the room, kissed her and then left once again leaving Anais with a smile on her face. She would have crossed her fingers for luck, but her fingers were so sore that she didn't want to rub them together. The thought of it reminded her of the cream that Andrew had given them all at dinner. She opened one of the tubes and sniffed. Was this another of Andrew's tricks? Would this cream cause even more discomfort and burning? It smelled vaguely of vanilla. She cautiously dabbed a little onto the back of her right hand. For a second, nothing happened but then it started to burn. She was just about to run to the bathroom to wash it off when the burning turned into tingling. It still felt warm, but now, it was a pleasant kind of heat. As she watched, her red and black charred skin turned a rosy pink. The outer layers were dead and flaked off, but the skin underneath appeared healthy. She quickly applied more to the whole of her right arm. The intense burning as she applied it was incredibly painful and she let out a murmur. However, just like before, it quickly gave way to the tingling sensation, which reminded her of how she used to feel when Aethelu touched her. After a couple of seconds, she ran to the bathroom and held her arm under the tap. She was amazed to see the old skin slide off and wash away leaving only the pink skin underneath. She held her right arm up to the left one. The difference was staggering. The cream really was a miracle. She quickly threw her clothes off and doused herself in the full tube. She covered her hair--the little she had left--and worked her way down, making sure the cream touched every inch of her body. She tingled so much that she was barely able to turn the bath taps on. What she wouldn't give for a shower right now, but the nearest shower was down the hallway. Instead, she had to make do with fitting as much of herself under the bath tap as possible and washing herself bit by bit. The little bit of hair she did have left, fell out when she tried to towel dry her head, but at least she didn't hurt anymore. Her image in the mirror looked like her again, albeit a much redder balder scarred version. At least, she looked like a human being again.

"Oh my god!" screamed Aethelu from behind her, making her jump. She'd not heard Aethelu come in.

"You look like you again. You are beautiful!"

Anais looked back at her reflection. She actually resembled a giant tomato, but she was thankful for the kind words.

"It's the cream. It works. I've left a tube for you on the bed. Use it all. Be careful, though. It stings like hell when you first put it on, but it's actually quite pleasant after that. Do me a favour, though. Do it in the shower down the hall. Look at the state of the bath with all my dead skin in it."

"Ugh!" Aethelu exclaimed and then grinned. Brill, I'll go do it now. I managed to put the book back successfully."

That word again! Aethelu had managed to retrieve the camera. She just hoped it would show Andrew dialling in the correct combination to the safe.

"Great. Whilst you are showering, I think I'll go and speak to Arcadia about borrowing a couple of wigs for us. She has plenty."

Even though Arcadia's bedroom connected to theirs through the bathroom, she thought it would be rude just to walk in. Instead, she cleaned out the bath and then walked the short distance along the corridor and knocked on the main door.

"I'm not taking visitors!"

"Arcadia. It's me, Anais."

"I'm only coming out when I absolutely have to at meal times."

Anais smiled. Oh, vanity.

"I take it you've not tried Andrew's miracle cream yet?" Anais shouted through the door.

"Of course not, I'm not putting anything that vile man made on my skin. Who knows what it will do?"

"Do me a favour. Put the cream on and then have a bath. The bathroom's free. Aethelu is using the shower down the hall. I'll come back in half an hour. You'll feel better, I promise."

"Have you used the cream?"

"I have, and if you would only open the door, I can show you how amazing it is."

A few seconds later, the door opened with a crack.

"Wow! It works. Was it just the cream that did that?" Arcadia grabbed her hand and dragged her into the room. She ran her own peeling hands up and down Anais' arm.

"It feels so soft and even smells nice, too. I don't believe it."

"Believe it. It works. It won't save your hair, though. That's why I came to you. I was hoping to borrow a couple of wigs."

"Go right ahead. Take whatever you want." Arcadia gestured to her collection of wigs, which sat atop numerous wig stands. With no embarrassment at all, she threw her dress over her head and stood totally naked covering herself with the cream.

"Ow! It hurts!"

"It soon passes," said Anais, averting her gaze. It was hard to imagine that Arcadia had appeared on the cover of many fashion magazines looking at her as she looked now.

"Do you think you could do that in the bathroom? I've cleaned the bath for you."

"Oh, yeah, sorry." She opened her door and ran into the tiny bathroom, not bothering to close the door behind her.

Anais rolled her eyes and walked over to the wigs. She tried an auburn one on that had looked stunning on Arcadia. On her, however, it clashed terribly with her rosy red skin. She tried a long blonde one on which looked ok, but wasn't her. She put it to one side for Aethelu. It was much closer to her colouring. Eventually, she picked a dark and curly one, much closer to her own hair colour, and placed it on her head. She looked like the old Anais again.

As Anais was about to leave, she heard a shout from the bathroom.

"I know you must think awfully of me. I know I'm vain."

Anais sat on the bed, took the wig from her head and put it next to her, and waited for Arcadia to emerge from the bathroom. She sensed that Arcadia might need someone to talk to. With all the secrecy, Arcadia had no one to talk to. She must feel so lonely cooped up here, away from her swanky lifestyle and Hollywood friends.

When she finally did come out of the bathroom, she was wrapped in a white towel with a matching one wrapped around her head.

"I don't even know why I've got this round my head. It's not as though I've got any hair left to dry." She gave a wistful smile. "Still, it will save me a fortune in waxing."

She was making light of the situation, but Anais could see that she was struggling. She'd always been beautiful. She frequently made the world's top 100 most beautiful women lists in the glossy magazines.

Even now, with her skin a cherry red and numerous scars on it, she still had a certain beauty to her.

"You'll heal. You'll be beautiful again." Anais tried her best.

"Will I? Who knows what Andrew's powder has done? Perhaps this is how I'll always look."

"Even if you do always look like this, you are still more beautiful than most people. Make-up will cover the red skin and you wear wigs so often that no one knows what your natural hair colour is anyway."

"How do you do it?" Arcadia looked into the mirror and winced at her reflection.

"Do what?"

"You are so confident. You seem totally relaxed sitting there with no hair. Isn't it freaking you out?"

"Of course, it is. Why do you think I came in here to borrow a wig? You will be fine, Arcadia. You'll be back on the front cover of Vogue before you know it."

Arcadia made a non-committal grunt. Tears coursed down her cheeks.

Anais continued, "If you don't, so what? You have a great life. You are beautiful on the inside."

"Isn't that just code for 'ugly'?"

"Not in this case. You are beautiful inside and out. You are successful and have the world at your feet. I doubt you'd let having no hair keep you back. I know that if Andrew hadn't blocked all the phones, it would be ringing non-stop with calls from various A-list actors. It's actually about time you gave someone else a chance with all these hunks anyway."

Arcadia smirked through her tears.

"You are so great...and so silly!" she hit Anais with a pillow. She was pleasantly surprised that it didn't hurt.

"Honestly, you'll be fine."

"Thank you, Anais. I'm so glad you came into our family." She paused. "I actually have something to tell you. The land I gave you for your birthday. I have to admit it was purely for selfish reasons. I wanted you all near me. I want to see little Autumn there growing up."

"You will."

A door opening and closing alerted them to the fact that Aethelu had come back from the shower.

"I'd better go back. Thank you for the loan of the wigs."

"Not a problem. Keep them. Oh, and, Anais?"

"Yes"

"Thank you."

Back in her room, Aethelu was already back and in bed. Anais threw her a wig. It was slightly longer than Aethelu's natural hair, but the colour was a good match.

"Did the cream work? Can I see?"

"Cheeky! Come into bed and you can see all you want."

Anais skipped over to the bed and dove under the covers.

"I can't see your skin if you put the covers over both our heads!" teased Anais.

"You can see it later, but I have something to tell you first," Aethelu whispered.

"What could be more important than seeing your body?"

"I found one."

"One what? A vial? I know. It's in the safe. Let's look at the camera. Hopefully, Andrew wasn't in the way when he opened the safe." Anais made sure she kept her voice down as she spoke.

Aethelu passed her the camera. Both girls watched the little screen, in anticipation, as it played back the recording from the Library earlier. They waited a few minutes until Andrew could be seen at the edge of the frame. He yanked back the painting that covered the safe and mumbled as he turned the dial. Anais held her breath. She could see the dial perfectly. He turned it to three, then seventeen, followed by twenty-two and eight. The door to the safe opened and he carefully brought out one of the two copies of Alice. His care was not because the book was priceless, but because he did not want to accidentally break the vial that sat behind it. Anais could hear him grumbling away to himself as he closed the safe door and replaced the picture.

"Stupid book, why do they need to keep it in the safe anyway? Trust them to want something where I've hidden the virus."

He'd moved away from the camera by now, but they could still hear his voice. It got quieter and quieter as he headed away from the camera and towards the library door, but his last words were unmistakable.

"They'd better not ask to go for a drive for the stupid sprog."

Anais and Aethelu looked at each other.

"Drive? Do you think he's hidden one in the garage?"

Aethelu looked at her with excitement on her face.

"I bet he has. Why else would he mention it?"

"So we've found two vials already."

"Actually, that's what I was trying to tell you earlier before you turned the camera on."

"You've found another one?"

"Yes. It was in the painting studio. I noticed one of my paintings had been moved slightly. When I looked closer, I could see a wire just peeking out from behind it."

"Excellent. That's three vials."

"Four. Rafe found one wired to the Jukebox in the games room."

"Oh, my goodness. Brilliant! Do you think Andrew will suspect anything?"

"I didn't move any of the paintings. It was just as if I was really in there to paint. I started on your Christmas present, by the way. It won't be as good as last year because I could barely hold the brush, but hopefully, now my fingers are ok and I'll be able to finish it."

"Christmas? Is it nearly Christmas?"

"Next week, silly."

"Wow. The days have just passed me by. I didn't even realise the date."

"I don't think you are the only one. We've all been a bit preoccupied, what with having all our skin dropping off and the threat of being killed and all."

"This is brilliant, though. We could put up Christmas decorations all around the house. If I remember, last year, the whole house was covered in them. There was tinsel on every surface."

"Winnie is usually very festive. I guess she forgot this year. Do you really feel in the mood for Christmas decorations?"

"What better way to search the whole house without Andrew being suspicious?"

"Oh brilliant!" she turned to kiss Anais. "Just let me be in charge of the mistletoe."

If Andrew had been listening in to their room that night, all he would have heard would have been the sound of giggles.

11

The next morning, Anais and Aethelu came down to breakfast to the sound of shouting coming from the dining room. Both of them had worn Arcadia's wigs and their skin had turned a much healthier pink colour overnight. In fact, Aethelu, who usually was as pale as snow, looked more human than Anais had ever seen her. This must have been what Aethelu looked like before she consumed The Light all those hundreds of years ago.

"Who's shouting?" asked Anais on the stairs.

"It sounds like August. That's strange. It's not like August to shout.

It was a strange sight that greeted them as they entered the dining room and took their seats. It looked like everyone had used Andrew's miracle cream, but only some of them had borrowed wigs from Arcadia. Arcadia, herself, looked almost back to her usual stunning self, wearing the auburn wig that Anais had discounted the day before. Ava, Audsley, and Winnie had all borrowed wigs, although none of them had found ones that were like their normal hair. Audsley had attempted to make hers match by dying it hot pink.

Winnie had found a light brown bob wig and it suited her. It actually knocked years off her. Anais would have complimented her on it, was it not for the tension that surrounded the table. Sabine had tied a silk scarf prettily around her head and Jennifer had decided to remain bald. Either that or she didn't know about Arcadia's immense collection of wigs. She looked strangely majestic, though, and she was one of those few women who could carry off baldness. None of the men had gone to any effort to conceal their baldness. August was barely recognisable without his mop of hair and shaggy beard. He had Baker curled up on his lap. He was as red as Anais had been the day before, but it was due to anger.

"I don't care what you saw. It was bloody dangerous. It was your fault that Baker was all alone in the house for days in the first place. He'd nearly starved to death." He picked up a slice of bacon and offered it to Baker who greedily swallowed it.

"Of course it was dangerous. It was supposed to be dangerous." Andrew was almost apoplectic with rage.

"Can someone enlighten us to what is going on, please?" asked Aethelu.

"It seems that August found Baker playing with one of Andrew's vials back at the cottage and he buried it in the woods somewhere," Rafe said, barely hiding the amusement in his voice.

"Oh!" replied Aethelu, at a loss for anything else to say. This was both good and bad. It was good because they had found another vial. Found and as good as destroyed by the sound of it. The bad news was that Andrew looked like his head was going to explode. There was no telling what pain Andrew still had in store, ready to inflict on them at a moment's notice.

Anais held her breath, waiting to see Andrew's response.

"Just tell me where you buried it, August, and nobody has to get hurt." He sucked air through his teeth.

"I don't remember. I do remember burying it deep where Baker wouldn't be able to dig it up. It's out in the woods somewhere."

"You'd better remember soon, August, because if you don't, you'll all feel my wrath."

"Oh? What can you do that you haven't already done? I've got less body hair than a snooker ball, most of my skin has washed down the plughole, and worse still, I've not had a proper meal in ages."

Anais could barely breathe. This was the first time that someone had stood up to Andrew so brazenly. She had thought that it would be Rafe having this argument with Andrew, not August. It was electrifying and terrifying all at once. August had pushed Andrew too far. She could see his face was almost purple. August, on the other hand, looked perfectly calm serving himself some scrambled eggs from a tureen in front of him.

"I... You..." Andrew spluttered before standing up and storming out of the door, slamming it behind him.

Anais waited with baited breath for the grills to come down over the windows. After a minute of silence, Jennifer stood up and checked the door.

"It's open," she said, and to prove it, she opened it and closed it a few times before returning to her seat.

"August, what did you just do?" Arcadia looked at him wide eyed.

"Oh, he's just full of himself. I'm sick of all this. I just called his bluff, that's all."

"Well done, August!" Rafe clapped his hands.

"Pssh!" replied August before returning to his breakfast.

"Well done?" squealed Audsley. "He's probably got us all killed."

"The door's open, nothing horrible has happened and August has managed to get rid of one of the vials. I'd say he's done us all a favour."

"Just because the door is open and nothing bad has happened yet, doesn't mean that it won't," argued Audsley. "You saw his face when he left. He was steaming mad."

"Let him be angry, who cares. The thing is, we are one vial down." Rafe countered.

Anais realised that this conversation was getting dangerous. She was sure that Andrew would be watching them and listening to what they were saying. If they carried on, they would let slip that they were looking for vials.

Just then, she noticed that Judith was still not among them. "Is Judith still at the spa?" she enquired.

"No," replied Rafe sullenly. "He doesn't trust that Alex, Sabine, and I can keep up the pretence. That's what we were fighting about before he locked us all in here and pumped itching powder in. He'd told me that he felt it was in his best interest to put her back to sleep. Induce another coma."

"And you told him that it wasn't in her best interests."

"Those weren't the exact words used but essentially, yes. Sorry guys."

Everyone was silent. They couldn't blame Rafe for standing up for Judith but because of it, they were now all bald and scarred.

"You know it's Christmas Day in a few days and the house is looking very sad. Aethelu and I thought we'd put up the decorations today if anyone wants to help?" It was a way to break the tension.

There were a few mumbles from around the table. It was

obvious that nobody was in much of a mood to celebrate Christmas.

"I'll help," offered Ava.

"Thanks, Ava. We were thinking of going a bit mad this year. Cover the house, the *whole* house, top to bottom." She'd emphasised the word 'whole' in the hope that people would realise that they planned to use it as an excuse to search the house. It seemed to have worked as suddenly she was inundated with responses.

"Yeah, it needs cheering up..."

"I'll get the decorations out of the attic..."

"We could really deck the halls..."

In the end, everyone agreed to help with the exception of Aldrich and James, who were going to carry on their experiments in the little surgery.

After breakfast, Rafe, Alex, Audsley and Sabine ventured into the attic to bring down the Christmas decorations. Boxes and boxes of tinsel and baubles were passed to the rest of the family who waited patiently. Anais was handed an old cardboard box labelled "Xmas Decs" It had seen better days, yellowed at the top and practically falling apart at the bottom. She set it on the floor and opened it. Inside she found old newspaper wrapped around lots of small objects. She opened the first and was delighted to find an exact replica of Arcadia dressed in a winter blue dress. A bit of ribbon at the top indicated it was to hang on a tree. Anais recognised the work at once. It was just like the chess set. Beautiful. Perfect. Andrew had lovingly carved, then painted this. She knew she would find the rest of the family in miniature if she unwrapped the rest of the objects. How could someone who had created something so wonderful, turn out to be so despicable, so cruel? He had obviously loved this family once upon a time. She wondered what had happened that had changed him. But she knew the answer. Her mother. He'd loved her, and when she told him that she'd never love him, because she was in love with Anais' father Alistair, he'd killed them both. When it happened again with Rafe and Judith, he'd just snapped. He'd probably spent centuries watching the beautiful Rafe, Alex, and Arcadia effortlessly attracting partners. Even Aethelu had been best friends with Alistair before Sarah had come along. Andrew had never really had a best friend and when he finally found one in Judith, Rafe took that away from him. No wonder he snapped. Anais suddenly realised she was beginning to feel sorry for Andrew. She placed the miniature Arcadia back into the box carefully and took it downstairs to where the tree would be erected. Aethelu joined her a few moments later with a box of her own. Anais showed her the Arcadia bauble.

"Oh, wow, I'd forgotten about these." She took it from Anais and twirled it around in her fingers. "I've not seen these for years. These must be over a hundred years old. If I remember correctly, there are ones of Abel and Amber in there, too, which will date them. They were made before they left."

Anais unwrapped the next one and found an exact replica of her father in miniature.

"Dad!" He was depicted next to a snowman.

"Heh, yeah, I think we had actually tried building the biggest snowman, ever, that year. That's probably why Andrew made him like this. I think mine is holding a carrot for its nose."

"Did you manage it? The biggest snowman, ever?"

"I think we got it about eight-foot tall, thanks to August, who was the only one tall enough to lift the head on."

Suddenly, the sound of Christmas music drifted down the stairs.

"I thought we could do with some Christmas cheer," came a voice followed by its owner, Alex. "I rigged up a sound system to play festive music throughout the house. I thought it would liven up the place.

"Did someone mention Christmas cheer?" asked Winnie, who had just appeared from the kitchen carrying a tray with eggnog and still-warm cinnamon cookies. "I've had the cookie batter in the fridge since yesterday. It's so nice to have an occasion to use it. Anais, darling, I've made hot chocolate for you."

"Thanks, Winnie." Anais took the hot chocolate and sipped it. The cinnamon cookies melted in her mouth.

"Thanks, Mama," said Alex, grabbing a handful of cookies.

August, having obviously seen Andrew's lack of response to his blatant defiance was now breaking the rules once more. He'd taken Baker out for a walk in the woods. His excuse was that he was going to find the best tree in the forest and cut it down to use as a Christmas tree.

Anais and Aethelu unpacked boxes of Christmas ornaments and stacked them neatly in anticipation of the arrival of the tree, whilst the others brought more boxes from the attic.

August may have felt that he had gotten one over on Andrew, but Anais knew that his flagrant disregard of Andrew's rules would cost him. There was no way that Andrew would let him get away with hiding one of the vials. She had to push the thought to the back of her head or she would have been overcome by fear. The Christmas music and the joy in everyone's faces managed to put her in a good mood, but the thought that something bad was about to happen stayed with her all morning. Eventually, August returned with a magnificent tree, which he potted up and placed in the same place the tree had been the previous year. Anais had such a wonderful morning decorating the tree with Aethelu, that she almost forgot the real purpose of the exercise. She could see the rest of the family running around with various sparkly decorations, and she knew they were on task. At one point, Alex returned and held some mistletoe above her head. She blushed, but as Alex kissed her cheek, she heard him whisper. "We found two vials in the attic."

It was the best news she could have hoped for. She grinned, which made Aethelu give her a perplexed look. Alex kissed his sister on the cheek and judging by the way her face lit up, he'd whispered the news to her, too.

They had now found seven vials. One in the safe to which, thanks to the camera, they had the new code, one that August had buried in the grounds, one in Aethelu's painting studio, one in the games room, a possible one in the garage and two in the attic. They had located seven out of twenty, no, twenty-one. There was still a single vial in the village. Still, it was a start. The day just got better and better. Andrew didn't turn up for lunch, which made the food tastier, at least in Anais' eyes. It was probably because the stress levels were much lower without him there. Winnie had made a huge Sunday dinner even though it wasn't Sunday. She'd cooked a huge turkey and done all the trimmings.

"I'd been saving the turkey for Christmas day but for some reason I felt like cooking it today. Andrew had all this food delivered. I figure we may as well celebrate whilst we can. I've even managed to bring up a couple of bottles of champagne. Let's just forget our current situation and enjoy being together."

"Here, here!" replied Aldrich, who uncorked the first bottle with a resounding pop.

Everybody's spirits were up with the morning of music and decorating the house. Even better news was to follow. Sabine told the table how she'd had a very successful morning followed by Alfred saying the same.

Two more vials found! That brought them up to nine vials found in total. There were only eleven more left in the house and that one vial in the village.

"It seems that putting the decorations up was a good idea," Anais said as she poured herself a glass of juice.

"It certainly was," replied Winnie. "The house looks beautiful. Anais and Aethelu, you've done a wonderful job with the tree. It looks magnificent, and August. Thank you for getting it for us."

"Three cheers for August" yelled Rafe and raised his glass. Anais knew he was being toasted for standing up to Andrew and not because he found the tree. She raised her glass and smiled. She felt better than she had in months.

After the huge lunch, they all went back to decorating the house. Anais and Aethelu had finished the tree in the morning and so, were at a bit of a loose end. Anais couldn't help grinning as she thought of the progress they were making, looking for all the vials. Nine vials in only a couple of days. Andrew wasn't as smart as he thought he was. Anais then gave herself a mental kick for thinking it. She should know better than to underestimate him. Just because they had found nine, didn't mean that they would find the others so easily. She remembered then that, technically, they had only found eight of the vials. The one in the garage was only a guess, based on what they had heard Andrew muttering to himself in the library. She had to know for sure, but how? Andrew would surely see if she went out to the garage, and she couldn't think of a plausible reason to be in there. She hadn't seen Andrew since his argument with August at breakfast, but that meant nothing. She knew he could be watching them all from his room.

"I don't think we have enough decorations up in here," she said, looking round the main hall.

"It looks like a Christmas factory exploded in here," exclaimed Aethelu. She did have a point. Every surface glinted light off sparkly tinsel. "We usually rotate the decorations and have a colour theme. Last year was red and gold, if you remember. I think this year we've used them all."

"May as well. Who knows if there will be a next year to decorate," replied Audsley solemnly, as she passed them on her way upstairs.

They were all quiet for a few seconds, the impact of Audsleys words sinking in. Would they all still be here to celebrate next Christmas? Autumn's first Christmas.

"Yeah, well," started Aethelu to break them out of their reverie. "It looks amazing this year."

"I think there is something missing?"

Aethelu looked at her incredulously, and Anais began to feel stupid. She wished she'd thought of something better to say to have a reason to go to the garage.

"Are you kidding?" There is no space for any more decorations. All we have left to do is pin the hats on the portraits like we do every year.

"I'll get them," shouted Audsley from the top of the stairs.

"No, that's not it."

"What then?"

"Do we have any more decorations?"

"I think they are being used around the house. Alex has already emptied the attic of everything vaguely Christmassy."

"Oh, that's a shame. Don't we have any more anywhere else? Any storage cupboards we've not searched? The garage, maybe?"

Comprehension dawned on Aethelu's face followed by a look that Anais couldn't quite fathom. Exasperation?

Aethelu didn't even bother to cover up the fact that she was going to whisper something in Anais' ear.

"That's so lame! Andrew knows that there are no decorations in the garage and he knows that I know, too. We can't just waltz down there with that excuse. He'll see through it straight away. We are skating on thin ice as it is."

Anais knew Aethelu was right. How else would they get into the garage to check? Andrew would be on them like a shot if any of them left the house. The only ones allowed to leave were Aldrich and James, and that was only to go to the surgery--Aldrich and James! That was it! Andrew would think nothing of them leaving the house. They did it every day. The door to the garage was right next to the surgery door. They could easily slip into the garage for a few minutes without Andrew noticing. They'd probably have to keep the lights off and search in the dark as it was inevitable that there would be a camera in there if there was a vial. She quickly whispered her plan to Aethelu, who nodded. It was much safer than using silly excuses. Anais decided to ask James, the next time she saw him.

Just then, Audsley appeared at the top of the stairs with a pile of Santa hats in her hands.

She quickly divided them into three piles between the girls.

"Actually," began Anais. "I think you are right. These hats will be a great finishing touch to the entrance hall.

Anais started at one side near the steps. There were only two she could reach, Arcadia's, and the one of Alex and Rafe. Audsley put up some stepladders and started at the end with Alistair's portrait, whilst Aethelu did the same in the middle. Anais watched her take a hat and pin it right over Andrew's face on his portrait. She'd not even attempted to set it straight. Anais held back a giggle at Aethelu's little act of defiance. She picked up three of the red and white hats and some pins and walked up a few of the stairs to Arcadia's portrait. She could see, up close, little holes where pins had been pushed through in years past for the very same reason. She carefully pinned the hat to the picture atop Arcadia's curly white painted wig. Moving on to the portrait of the boys, she lifted up one of the hats to Alex's head. She had to stand on tiptoes to reach him. Rafe's portrait on the same canvas would be too far to reach without a stepladder or someone taller to help her. As it was, she could barely reach to pin Alex's on. As she reached up, she noticed that the portrait was stuck out away from the wall, only slightly, a couple of millimetres, at most. She pushed the frame back, but it wouldn't stay flush to the wall. Looking to the side of the frame, she spotted what it was that was stopping it from going back. A vial was taped to the back of the painting. She pulled back quickly, bumping the frame and causing Alex's hat to fall off.

"Aethelu, Can you help me with this one. I thought I could reach, but I can't, sorry." Excitement bubbled through her. Another vial had been found. Instead of finding a way to whisper her discovery to Aethelu when she pushed the stepladder over, she elaborately moved her eyes to the side in the hope that Aethelu understood her. Judging by the grin that erupted on her face, she had gotten the message. Once the hallway had been decorated, they decided to go and find the others to see if they could help somewhere else in the house. Every hallway and room looked amazing, as they made their way through the house. Holly, tinsel and festive statues covered every wall and surface. It was far more extravagant than it had been last year.

Just then Alex and Sabine appeared. "Hey, you lot, there's a party in the parlour. I think we are done for the day with decorating, and Mama has spread out a cold buffet."

"But we only just finished lunch a few hours ago!"

"Yeah, but you know Mama. I think she knows us, too. August has already eaten half of it!"

Anais followed everyone down to the parlour, where a party was in full swing. Party lights twinkled around the room and music was playing from speakers in the corner. Like last Christmas, the furniture had been pushed back so there was a dance floor in the middle. Anais thought back to last Christmas when Arcadia had given her a makeover, dressing her in the most amazing dress she'd ever worn. This year, she was nearly eight months pregnant, huge, and wearing maternity jeans and a wig. Not quite as glamorous, but she was determined to make the most of it. Aethelu grabbed her and spun her round the dance floor, whilst the others danced around them. It was as if the horror of the last year had been forgotten and the terror that they were now facing had been put on hold for one night. There was much to celebrate. Autumn was kicking away, almost to the music much to the delight of Aethelu, who could now feel her through Anais' stomach. Despite not feeling hungry earlier, she was soon grateful for the spread Winnie had set out. Even Rafe managed to find cheer in the impromptu party although that could have been the copious amounts of alcohol being served. Anais, not being allowed to drink, was the only sober one.

Soon, Aldrich and James appeared, arriving from a day's work in the surgery. She ran over and accosted James before he had time to sit down. She quickly told him that she thought there was a vial hidden in the garage and asked him to go find it.

"You'll need to do it in the dark," she spoke quietly even though the loud music would more than likely drown out any conversation.

"I don't know. What if Andrew sees me going back to the surgery? Won't he wonder why?"

"Just make up an excuse. I'll cause a diversion." She didn't know what, but she'd think of something. It only had to be for a minute, whilst James slipped into the garage door. Once he was in there, as long as he kept the light off, he'd be fine."

"Aldrich," James shouted over the music. "I think I forgot to turn that Bunsen burner off. I'll be right back" He winked at Anais, who grinned.

Aldrich nodded and went to join Winnie by the food.

Anais ran quickly across the room to where Aethelu was talking to Jennifer about Egyptian Christmas customs.

"Spill some water on me!" she whispered.

"What?" asked a confused Aethelu.

"Just do it!" Anais hissed, "Lots of it, down the back of my trousers."

Aethelu might not have known what was happening, but she was getting used to Anais talking in code. She looked around for some water, but there was nothing nearby. The only thing she could see was a huge pitcher of mulled wine complete with various chopped up fruits floating in it, which Winnie had made.

Anais had turned her back to her and had engaged August in a conversation about dogs.

Aethelu picked up the pitcher and whilst pretending to pour herself a glass, accidentally on purpose slipped and threw the whole lot down the back of Anais' trousers.

"My water has broken," shouted Anais loudly, in a rather dramatic fashion. Everyone turned round to look.

"Oh my god she's bleeding!" shouted Winnie, in alarm. The whole family crowded round to see if she was ok.

Bleeding? Anais looked down at the huge puddle on the floor below her. It was red. She could see bits of spiced orange in it.

"Actually, I think it's mulled wine," said Jennifer. "See, there are chunks of fruit in it."

"Oh," said Anais, turning as red as the floor beneath her.

"Are you ok, love? I think you just spilled something."

"Actually, that was my fault. Sorry, everyone," Aethelu said sheepishly.

"Yeah, false alarm. I'm fine."

"You'd better go change out of those jeans, whilst I go and get something to clean the floor," said Winnie, before turning to Aethelu. "Honestly, Aethelu. You can be so clumsy. Now, there's red wine on my beautiful, pale, carpet. Come and help me get something to clean it before it stains."

As the three trooped out of the room, Anais to go to her room to get changed, and Winnie and Aethelu to go to the kitchen to get clothes, Anais whispered to Aethelu.

"Why did you chuck wine on me? I said drop water."

"I improvised, sorry. It's all I could see and in my defence, I didn't know what you were doing."

"Stop jabbering, Aethelu. Come on quickly. I don't want my carpet to stain!"

"Yes, Mama." Aethelu dutifully followed her mother to the kitchen, whilst Anais climbed the stairs to her room.

She pulled the soggy jeans off and threw them on the bathroom floor. The red wine had stained her legs so she looked like she had a huge strawberry birthmark covering most of the back of them. She decided to have a quick shower before she headed back to the party. Her idea of a distraction had gone horribly wrong, but she hoped it would be enough to get James into the garage unnoticed. She only hoped that Andrew didn't see through her horrific, hammed-up, acting and suspect it was a ruse.

Still, there was nothing she could do about it now. She wrapped a big towel around herself and went to the wardrobe to pick out another outfit. She found a maternity dress that Arcadia had bought for her months before. It was the only maternity dress she had, and she'd never worn it, preferring to wear large t-shirts and comfortable jeans. It was the only non-red item in the wardrobe, surrounded as it was by Aethelu's blazing attire. This was a lovely cream wraparound dress with some gems and pearls around the top, presumably to take the focus away from the giant bump below it. She slipped it on and was pleasantly surprised at how she looked in it. She actually looked pretty. Well, if you discounted the scarred skin, although even the scars were fading well now. There was nothing she could do with her hair, as she was wearing Arcadia's wig. She found a lipstick that didn't clash too much with her reddish skin tone and applied it using the mirror in the bedroom.

Not bad, she thought to herself. Nothing compared to last year's Christmas party but the best she could do under the circumstances.

Back at the party, Winnie and Aethelu were scrubbing the floor furiously. Furious was also a good word to describe

Winnie's expression, as the stain wasn't coming out. It had paled to a light pink, but was still very noticeable on the pale, grey, carpet.

"Maybe we could just move some furniture over it?" said Aethelu weakly, which only elicited further angry looks from her mother. Anais felt a bit guilty, but then again, she had said water, not bright red liquid.

"You look lovely," said Sabine, who had appeared by her side with a big glass of wine.

"Thank you. I thought Aethelu had spilled all the wine?"

"August brought some more up from the kitchen."

"Ah, I can't believe Winnie let him after the last lot ended up on the floor."

"I don't think she's noticed yet. I think we are all planning to drink it before she does notice and bans it." Sabine gave a cheeky and slightly drunken smile.

Anais looked around and could see that Sabine was right. Everyone had a glass in their hand, and despite their situation, all but Winnie were enjoying themselves. At that moment, James slipped into the room. He searched for Anais and when he found her, he gave an almost imperceptible nod of the head. He'd found the vial in the garage. Anais grinned and almost wished she could drink the wine herself. Instead, she poured a large glass and took it to James.

Then, to put Winnie or, at least, Aethelu out of their misery, she went over and whispered the reason why Aethelu had dropped the wine in the first place. She followed it up by handing Winnie a large glass and practically forcing her to drink it. It seemed to work, cheering Winnie up. Finding a vial was worth a bit of spoilt carpet any day.

It was after 8 pm when Anais heard the front door opening. She slipped away from the party to find Andrew in the main entrance with Judith. He was helping her remove her coat. So spilling the mulled wine had been pointless after all that. Andrew hadn't even been in the house.

"Judith!" Anais smiled and moved forward to hug her. If Andrew had been out all day with Judith, it would explain why he hadn't shown up at lunch or at dinnertime. It was the first time Anais had seen her since the itching powder incident a few days before. If Rafe was correct, she would be put back into a drug-induced coma very soon, probably tonight.

"Anais, it is so good to see you again," she spoke in lilting African tones, but there was a slight slur to her words.

Anais was confused. Judith was not herself. When Anais looked closer, she could see that Judith's eyes were struggling to keep their focus. She was still drugged on whatever Andrew was giving her, just not enough to put her to sleep yet. Had he changed his mind about putting her back to sleep and just given her a mild dose to keep her from fully functioning or was this merely to get her home from the spa hotel without wondering what had happened to them all?

Surely, Judith would wonder why most of them were bald and why their skin was so strange and scarred. If she did notice, she didn't say anything about it.

"The house is perfect, so sparkly. I love the tree."

"We decorated it for Christmas. We are having a party in the parlour. Would you like to join us?"

She knew Andrew would object. He wouldn't want Judith around them whilst they all looked so strange. He was probably planning to sneak Judith upstairs so he could knock her out. Anais, bolstered by August's blatant rule-breaking and the festive cheer, didn't care. Judith deserved one last party.

"A party? But it's not Christmas for a few days," replied Andrew looking annoyed.

"We decided to start the celebrations early."

"Ooh, I'd love to, thank you." Judith swayed but grinned.

"I don't think so Judith. I'm not sure you are up to it." Andrew tried to steer her away from Anais by grabbing her arm. She pulled it away from him forcefully.

"Up to it? I'm not an invalid. I've been in a five-star spa hotel, not a hospital."

"But you said you felt tired in the car," he moaned.

"Well, I suddenly feel more awake." She put her arm in Anais' arm and walked away from Andrew to the parlour. Anais expected Andrew to follow them and force her back, but he didn't. He didn't enter the parlour at all.

Everyone jumped up to hug Judith when they saw her, all except Rafe. Anais could see him, sitting in the corner. She knew he would have given anything to cross the floor and take her in his arms, but he couldn't. Andrew would be watching remotely, and they all knew it. Winnie handed her a glass of champagne, which Anais took straight off her, instead passing her a glass of juice.

"Why did you do that?" whispered Winnie.

"She's on drugs. You can tell by her eyes. Andrew is keeping her drugged so she doesn't suspect anything. I don't think mixing whatever she's got rattling around her system with alcohol would be a good idea."

"Oh, poor girl."

She seemed fine, though. Jennifer, who had never spoken to her before, had grabbed her hands and was now twirling her around the floor. Everyone seemed to be dancing with each other except for Anais, who was finding it too difficult to manoeuvre her huge bump between the other dancers. Every so often, someone would come and rest and chat with her for a bit before getting up to dance again. Anais enjoyed herself from the sidelines by tapping her toes and clapping her hands. At one point, Judith came to sit with her.

"How are you feeling, Judith?"

"I'm fine...At least I think I'm fine. My whole life feels so very foggy. I have big expanses of time I do not recall. I remember my childhood perfectly. I remember the party here last Christmas. I remember dancing with Rafe. I remember it like it was yesterday."

"But?"

"But I don't remember marrying Andrew. Isn't that terrible?"

"You've not been well, though," Anais said kindly. She couldn't remember it because it had never happened. She knew she could not enlighten Judith of this, though.

"I know. Andrew said that spending time in a spa hotel would make me better, but it hasn't worked. I still don't remember anything. I still feel like my brain has been numbed."

Anais kept quiet. What could she say?

"I don't love him, Anais. I mean, I did at the beginning, don't get me wrong. I wouldn't have left my family if I hadn't, but when I got here, I realised he's not the man I thought he was. I'm in love with Rafe." She burst into tears. Between sobs, Anais just barely heard her say that she was a terrible person. Anais' heart broke for her. Rafe loved her, too. She could see him watching the pair of them from across the room. The concern on his face was apparent. Anais prayed that Andrew couldn't hear this conversation above the loud music. He would not be happy to hear Judith talking about her love for Rafe.

As if on cue, Rafe stood up and walked towards them.

"Is everything ok? I saw you crying, Judith."

"I'm fine, thank you." She looked up and smiled. Mascara had run down her face, but it did nothing to diminish her beauty.

"Dance with me."

He held out his hand. Anais expected her to say no, but she didn't. She took his hand and embraced him. He slowly twirled her around, arms round her waist whilst she rested her head on his shoulder. Her eyes were closed, but she had a look of completeness. As if she was finally home. Anais knew it could only mean trouble. Everyone else was too drunk and was oblivious, but she knew that Andrew would be watching, and that he'd be mad. She sneaked a peek at the red pinprick of light in the far corner of the room, the camera. Whatever was about to happen, she didn't want to be there when it did. She grabbed Aethelu, who was dancing with James and pulled her into the hall.

"What's up? I was having fun."

"I'm tired that's all. Come to bed with me."

"Ok. Sure. Come on party pooper." She grinned, as she walked up the stairs.

"I wouldn't be so tired if I wasn't carrying this around," she pointed towards her bump. "And when she's born, the term party pooper will be a whole lot more literal."

"Yuk!" Aethelu made a face.

Both girls collapsed into bed. Aethelu tired from excessive amounts of alcohol was asleep in seconds. Anais took much longer to fall into oblivion. Something was going to happen; she just didn't know what.

12

The next morning, Anais was apprehensive about going down to breakfast. Something was different, but she couldn't put her finger on what. As she rounded the corner to the top of the main stairs, something caught her eye. It wasn't the same as it had been yesterday. It took her a good few seconds to realise what it was. The big star that Aethelu had placed on top of the tree was missing and something else was in its place.

"What's that?" asked Aethelu, who had also seen it. A few steps down and Anais realised what it was. It was Baker. He was dead. Blood dripped from his neck. Someone had cut his throat. Andrew!

"It's Baker." Anais suddenly felt sick.

"Oh, god! August is going to die when he sees this."

"It's Andrew's idea of a warning, telling August not to mess with him again. He did this because August got one over on him yesterday. Watching Rafe dancing with Judith can't have helped his mood either."

"Oh god!" repeated Aethelu.

They moved into the dining room to find the rest of the

family seated around. Judging by the number of wet eyes, everyone else had seen Baker on top of the tree.

"Ah! Anais, Aethelu. I'm glad you are here. I prepared breakfast this morning. Thought I'd give Winnie a morning off. I hope you all like it."

There was nothing set on the table except one silver serving tray with a lid. It was set in the middle of the table just in front of Anais.

It looked ominous, just sat there in the middle of the table. What was in it? It had to be something horrible. All the places had been set with china plates and cutlery. Andrew put his hand on the handle. Anais knew she didn't want to see what was under that lid. He lifted it in slow motion. Anais wanted to close her eyes, but she couldn't. She watched as the lid was raised. Underneath was a lump of meat. She could barely process what it was. Without the normal bushy hair, Augusts head was barely recognisable. Andrew had removed August's head from his body and actually cooked it. The unnatural smell of cooked human flesh hit her nostrils and she could hold it in no more. She threw up all over the floor by her feet. She could hear the others scream and gasp as they realised what Andrew was serving them.

She looked at Andrew with hatred in her eyes.

"What Anais? Not hungry? Come on, let me cut you a nice bit, He picked up a large knife and sliced a bit of flesh from behind Augusts ear. He placed it carefully on Anais' plate. She just looked up at him.

Everyone else around the table sat still with shock. Even Winnie was quiet, even though she must have seen what had been laid out in front of her.

"Come on eat up. It's protein. Good for the baby."

Did he actually expect her to eat it? She looked around

the table for help. No one was looking at her. All eyes were on what used to be August's head. Sabine started to heave and Ava was breathing very fast as though she was having a panic attack. Arcadia fell off her chair, having fainted at the sight of her oldest brother's roasted head.

"Andrew. What are you doing? Leave the girl be. She's done nothing to you." Alfred leapt to her defence. Ava held his hand on the table.

"Nothing?" spat Andrew. "I heard her talking to Judith last night."

"I didn't say anything! It was all her. You can't blame me that she doesn't love you." Anais knew she had taken it too far, but she didn't expect the slap she got from Andrew.

"Look here people," he shouted at them all. "I've had it up to here with you all. I've tried being nice, I've tried to hurt you, I've even killed some of you, and yet you continue to undermine me at every turn. I'm sick of it. Judith will have to remain in my room. I've put her back in a coma. Rafe is also out of the way. He dared to dance with my Judith!

"You've killed Rafe?" asked Alex in a fearful voice.

"Silence! Did I say you could talk? Did I give you permission? Aldrich, I hope you and James are nearly ready with the Elixir. I can't wait to be gone from all of you. Once the Elixir is made, I'm taking Judith and leaving. You'd like that, wouldn't you? Well, good news for you all, I'll be gone."

"It's going to be another six weeks, Andrew. I already told you that."

"Fine, you've got six weeks. It had better work. In the meantime, I don't want to see any of your faces. You can stay out of my way."

"What about meal times?" asked Aethelu.

"I don't want to see you, any of you. You can all get your

own food, or starve, for all I care."

He turned to leave the room.

"Where are August and Rafe's bodies, Andrew?" whimpered Winnie quietly, as he retreated.

He replied by slamming the door behind him.

Winnie broke down and wailed. Both Aldrich and James ran to her side and held her as her body wracked with grief. Alex sat blankly looking ahead, stunned, whilst Sabine put her arms around him. Jennifer and Alfred helped to pick Arcadia up, whilst Ava fanned her with a napkin. Audsley picked up the silver platter lid and covered up August's head. She then returned to her seat and bowed her head.

Anais retreated to her room along with Aethelu. She would have liked to stay to comfort Winnie, but she felt too nauseous. After spending the next hour throwing up in the little bathroom, she fell into bed with Aethelu. They both cried and fell asleep in each other's arms. It was too much to take in--August and Rafe dead. She couldn't cope with the overwhelming grief. Her whole body just seemed to shut down due to the pain of it. Neither girl moved for twenty-four hours. It was actually Autumn who woke Anais up. She sat up with a feeling of guilt. She'd not eaten for a whole day. The sun shone beautifully through the lace curtains, casting soft illumination through the room. She had to eat. She also had to pee. She got up, leaving Aethelu snoring softly.

After using the bathroom, she cautiously made her way down the corridor. She walked all the way downstairs without seeing another person. She expected the kitchen to be empty as well, so her heart jumped when she descended the winding staircase to find Alex sitting with an empty bowl in front of him. His eyes were dry, but they were red, as if tears had fallen.

Anais knew there was nothing she could say. She placed a hand on his shoulder. He turned and hugged her tightly. She could feel, rather than hear or see, him sobbing silently. His whole body shook, taking hers along for the ride. There was nothing to do but stroke his head until he calmed down.

"He killed them, first Ali, then August and Baker."

She noticed he had left out Rafe. Andrew had killed Rafe, too. Perhaps he was still in too much shock to absorb it all. He was Rafe's twin, after all.

"I know, honey, I know." She did her best to soothe him.

"He's got Rafe somewhere. We have to find him."

"He killed Rafe, too. I'm sorry Alex."

"Rafe's not dead."

"He is. Andrew told us."

"He's alive. I know it. I can feel it."

"Why would Andrew lie about it? If anything, Rafe had upset him more than August had. Did you see him slow dancing with Judith? Andrew would have seen it, too."

"I don't care what Andrew says. Rafe is alive. There's no proof that he's dead. We saw Ali's body, we saw August. No one has seen Rafe's body. Don't you think that if Andrew had killed him, he'd be rubbing our noses in it? Putting his body somewhere where we can all see it? You saw what he did with Baker and August. Why not Rafe? Because he's still alive somewhere."

Anais didn't know how to respond. She knew that twins shared a link like no other, but was it really possible to know when your twin had died? She doubted it. It was Alex's mind in denial. There really was no reason to keep Rafe alive.

"What happened to Baker and August?" She didn't want to say bodies.

"Dad, James, and Alfred took Baker and August's head

down to the cottage garden. Apparently, Andrew gave them permission, although he refused to tell them where August's body was. Just another way to hurt us all, I suppose."

Anais got up and fetched herself a bowl, which she placed on the table next to his. She brought some cereal and milk and a couple of spoons. She then made them each a coffee before sitting down on the seat next to Alex.

"How long have you been sitting down here looking at that bowl?"

"I dunno, an hour, two."

"Come on, eat up. It will do us no good to starve ourselves. Eat quickly, though I don't want to be here when Andrew comes down for breakfast."

"He's already been and gone. He went out ages ago."

"He's gone out again? He's been going out a lot recently."

"Judith's not in his room. He's changed the code to the cellar and put her down there on one of Dad's hospital beds. No one is allowed in or out except Dad."

"Why Aldrich?"

"Because he is keeping an eye on Judith's condition. He doesn't know the entry code, though. He can only go down once a day to check up on her when Andrew lets him."

"Poor Judith, she's just as much a victim in all this as the rest of us, probably more. At least we know what's going on. Goodness knows what all the drugs Andrew is giving her is doing to her brain. The last time I spoke to her, she barely knew which way was up.

"He's going to have to drug her forever if he does give her The Light. I doubt that she'd stay with him, otherwise."

"She won't, will she?" It was a rhetorical question, but it made Anais think. How could Andrew ever expect Judith to stay with him? He'd killed his biggest rival for Judith's affections, but she would mourn Rafe. She'd probably do it secretly, but when Andrew killed Rafe, he killed off a part of Judith with him. What kind of hell it would be to live for all eternity with someone you didn't love?. Surely, she would find out what Andrew had done. The whole family couldn't keep it a secret forever. She realised then that Andrew wouldn't give them the chance to tell her. He was going to kill them all. Anais could see it clearly now. Andrew couldn't let them live, any of them. Once Judith had taken The Light Elixir, they were all as good as dead. He was probably only keeping them all alive now to make sure Aldrich and James carried on with their work.

"He's going to kill us all, isn't he?" she asked Alex.

"Probably!" He brought his empty cup down hard on the kitchen table and left Anais without saying another word.

His cereal was left untouched.

She washed up the bowls, spoons, and cups before grabbing a couple of pastries and a bottle of water for Aethelu.

It was with a heavy heart that Anais walked back up the stairs to the bedroom. If Aldrich and James finished the Elixir on time and she was correct in her assumption, then Autumn wouldn't even see the light of day. She'd never be born. How could anyone kill a child before it even breathed its first breath? She decided not to share her thoughts with Aethelu. What was the point? There was nothing that Aethelu could do any more than there was anything Anais could do. It was true that they had found a lot of the vials, but who was to say they would find any more?

Aethelu had just woken up when Anais got back to the room. She sat up and rubbed her eyes.

"Where were you?"

"I just went down to get some breakfast. I brought you some." She threw the pastries towards Aethelu, who caught them and took a bite out of the first one.

"I don't like you going out by yourself. Did you see Andrew?"

"No, just Alex, he told me that Andrew had gone out."

"Out? Again? Where is he going?"

"I don't know."

Anais joined Aethelu on the bed and took back one of the pastries. She was still hungry, even though she'd already eaten breakfast. Autumn was growing so fast. It didn't seem to matter how much Anais ate; she always seemed hungry. Her ever-expanding stomach reflected this. She placed her left hand on her rounded belly, thinking of her little girl, growing bigger every day, getting ready to be born. But would she? Even if she did survive, what was her future going to be? Aethelu's hand joined hers. It comforted her slightly but wasn't enough to really cheer her up. She smiled a sad smile and kissed Aethelu lightly on the cheek, leaving a few pastry crumbs there.

"If Andrew is out, how is he programming the code into the computer to stop the virus escaping?"

"I don't know, perhaps he did it before he left and plans to be back within a four-hour period...although..." she trailed off, deep in thought. Aethelu had a point. Andrew had left the house before. The time he went to the spa to see Judith, he'd been out a long time...longer that four hours, surely?

"I think you're right. He has been out for longer than four hours sometimes. So how does he stop the virus going off?"

"Hmm," Aethelu appeared deep in thought. "I can only think of four options."

She paused.

"Which are?" Anais prompted.

"One: someone else is inputting the code for him."

"There is no way that anyone in this house would be doing that."

"Yeah, but we never suspected Andrew until he told us he was Jago."

Anais thought for a few seconds. It was true. She'd have bet her life that Andrew wouldn't hurt a fly before his true colours emerged. How easy it was to lose trust in everybody once someone you trusted broke it so badly.

"Do you honestly think that anyone could do that? Remember, all of us have been hurt by Andrew. Do you believe that anyone in this house would let August and Rafe be killed the way they were?"

"No. I don't. I trust everyone in this house. I just had to eliminate it as an option."

"Ok, eliminated, what's option two?"

"Andrew has made the whole thing up. Either the vials we have found are full of harmless solution or they are not set up to break."

"Why hide any at all then? It seems a bit pointless to hide a load of vials when he could have just told us he had hidden them and not hidden anything at all. They weren't easy to find either, the one in the safe for example. It's a lot of effort for no reason."

"Ok, strike that. Option three, he turns the mechanism off when he goes out and turns it back on when he gets home."

"That's a reasonable assumption. He could do it, I suppose. He's trusting that we won't think of that and go hunting for the vials whilst he's out, though."

"Yeah, but why would he think we would find the vials? He doesn't know that we've already found a lot of them."

"Ok, that could be it. What was option four?"

"Eh?"

"Option four? You said there were four options."

"Oh, yeah, perhaps he inputs the code by remote control or maybe by telephone. I imagine it would be easy to set something like that up for Andrew."

"Remote control! I bet that's it. He's operating it by phone. He's probably got a phone linked up to the device somehow."

"Oh, my god!" Aethelu sat up so suddenly that she knocked the rest of the pastries on the floor and made Anais jump.

"What?"

"If he is doing it by remote control, what's to stop us stealing his phone, checking the last number dialled and ..."

"And?"

"Well, I dunno, tying him up? Imprisoning him? Somehow incapacitate him?"

"Incapacitate him?"

"Chop the bastard's head off, for all I care, just like he did to August, anything, just to stop him causing any more atrocities. Get rid of him, once and for all. If we know the number to stop these viruses escaping, it will buy us as much time as we need to figure a way to disable the mechanism permanently, either that, or find the rest of the vials so we can destroy them."

The thought terrified her. Andrew had instilled such a sense of fear in her that the thought of killing him was almost as scary as the alternative, letting him live. However, what if Aethelu was right? Could it really be that easy? After all that they had been through, could they just kill him and take his phone? A thrill of anticipation ran through her. What if? What if Autumn had a future, after all? What if they all did?

They couldn't do it alone. They spent the rest of the day

going through scenarios and hatching plots, thinking of different ways to finally kill Andrew. They agreed that they had to tell the others the plan, the more people that knew, the better. Then, if Andrew somehow escaped, they could gang together to catch him.

For the first time in a long time, Anais felt that she might, just, with a whole lot of luck, have a future. It was almost exciting coming up with all these plans. They decided that they would have to wait for a day when Andrew went out again to tell everyone the plan. At dinnertime, Aethelu went to the kitchen to get them some food. She came back with a basket of sandwiches, the same basket that Anais had used when they had been living in the studio. It seemed like such a long time ago now. Along with the sandwiches, Aethelu had also brought fruit, cakes, and a couple of bottles of water.

"I'll give the slimy toad some credit. He's made sure that the kitchen is fully stocked. These cakes look delicious."

"Did you see anyone?"

"No, the kitchen was empty. I think everyone must be in their rooms."

"What about Andrew? Do you know if he's back?"

"I didn't see him either. He could have come back. I think that when we decide to kill him, we should take it in turns to keep watch at the window. We have an excellent view of the driveway so we'll see him leave. As soon as he does, we can run around the house to tell everyone our plan and figure out a way to kill him, hopefully a painful one."

It all seemed so easy, but Andrew was clever. Would he really leave himself open to attack like that? Anais suspected that Andrew wouldn't let himself be beaten so easily. What was the alternative though? Wait like sitting ducks to be murdered by him. Would they even be able to come up with a plan before he found out what they were doing? Only when Anais went to bed that night, did she realise that he already knew their plan. They'd been discussing it all day and forgotten the most important thing--the fact that the room was bugged.

"Aethelu," Anais nudged her awake.

"Hmm?" she answered sleepily.

"We've been talking about killing Andrew all day!"

"I know."

"He has cameras and microphones in every room."

"Crap!" even in the dark room, Anais could imagine the look of shock on Aethelu's face. "I'd totally forgotten. It's so easy to forget you are being watched and listened to. Do you think he'll have heard us?" Aethelu's voice had dropped to a whisper.

"I don't know. There are a lot of microphones and a lot of people to listen in on. There is a chance that he hasn't heard us."

"But we were talking about it all day. If he tuned in to us at any point during the day, he'd have heard us making plans to murder him."

"Either he has or he hasn't. Either way, there is nothing we can do about it now."

Aethelu slipped out of bed. Anais could hear a loud scraping noise cutting through the dark.

"What are you doing?" whispered Anais.

"I'm moving the chest of drawers to behind the door. If he's going to kill us then at least, I'm not going to make it easy for him."

Anais sighed. If Andrew wanted to kill them, a chest of drawers wouldn't stop him.

13

Anais woke early the next morning. A noise had startled her. At first she thought it might be Andrew at the door ready to murder her, but then she realised it was just a bird on the window ledge outside. Her breath caught in her throat. Every little noise was making her nervous. Her dreams had been plagued by nightmares and she'd woken numerous times.

"Are you awake?" whispered Aethelu.

"I am now. The bird woke me up."

"Yeah, I heard it, too."

She was quiet for a few minutes.

"Hold me!"

Anais put her arms around Aethelu and held her tightly. It felt warm and comforting. She didn't feel the tingles anymore. It had been a long time since she had felt the power of the light sending shivers of electricity through her. She didn't know whether it was just because she had gotten so used to them that she didn't feel them anymore or that it was just that there was nothing to trigger them in Aethelu. The Light's effects were especially powerful in moments of high emotion such as excitement or anger. Stress, fear, and bereavement dulled its effects. Anais knew that Aethelu was feeling all three, so it was no surprise that The Light had dimmed in her. She missed it, though. She missed the days when just the slightest touch from Aethelu would set her on fire. Anais stroked the nearest bit of naked flesh she could find, Aethelu's side, just above the waist in her pyjamas. She kissed Aethelu lightly on the lips. Then, briefly, she felt the tiniest of sparks. It wasn't much, but it was there. They were both still alive. She didn't know for how long, but for that second in time, they were both still alive.

It was only when Anais' stomach started to growl so loudly that neither of them could ignore it, that they realised that they'd have to leave the room if only for food. Aethelu moved the chest of drawers away from the door. She made Anais promise to move it back when she had gone and only move it away again when she knew it was Aethelu at the other side.

Aethelu took the basket and left. Anais wasn't sure how advisable it was for an eight-month- pregnant woman to be moving a heavy chest of drawers, but she managed it without hurting herself by using her back and legs to push.

She paced the room the whole time Aethelu was gone, but it was only ten minutes later that she heard a knocking and Aethelu shouting, "It's me." through the door.

Once again, she stood with her bottom to the chest of drawers and put her full weight against it. It pulled the carpet as it went, but she managed to push it enough to leave a gap wide enough for both Aethelu and the basket.

"You were quick. I thought you'd be gone for ages. Did you see Andrew?"

"No. I didn't see anyone. I grabbed enough food and drink for a few days. It's nothing too exciting, but it will keep us going for a while. I don't want any reason to leave this room.

She placed the basket on the floor along with a carrier bag that was also full. Aethelu had obviously just thrown in everything higgledy-piggledy. Anais got everything out and put it neatly on a nearby table. There were a couple of loaves of bread, a block of butter, a block of cheese, some packets of meat, some tomatoes, cucumbers, olives, oranges, apples, some yoghurts, a couple of pints of milk, a box of cereal and a handful of chocolate bars. She'd also managed to fit in a couple of plates, bowls, two cups and a knife, fork and spoon each.

"This is a lot of food."

"I don't want to leave this room unless I absolutely have to. Not until we can be sure that Andrew didn't hear us the other day. I think this could last about three days.

"What about the milk, cheese, meat, and yoghurt? We don't have a fridge up here."

I thought we could open the window and put them on the sill outside. It's cold enough out there. I got the milk for you. You need all the calcium you can get. I'll drink water from the bathroom tap."

Anais made them both ham and tomato sandwiches, which they finished off with a yoghurt each. Then, when Aethelu was washing the plates in the bathroom sink, she put the food that needed refrigerating on the sill outside the window, making sure that it was covered in case the bird came back and fancied an easy meal.

The next two days passed so slowly, they felt like a month to Anais. Every time either of them heard a noise, they stopped what they were doing and waited for it to pass, fearful that it was Andrew coming to get them. More often than not, it was just Arcadia using the shared bathroom. Anais would have liked to talk to her, but Aethelu had barricaded that door too and only moved the bookshelf when either of them wanted to use the bathroom. Arcadia never answered the door on her side of the bathroom when Anais knocked, anyway, so pretty soon she gave up trying.

At the end of the third day, the milk, yoghurts and fruit were finished, the bread was beginning to get stale, and they had not heard a peep from Andrew. Anais was also sick to death of sandwiches.

"I'm going to the kitchen."

"What about Andrew?" Aethelu adopted a look of fear.

"What about him?"

"What if he heard us? What if he tries to kill you?"

"If I have to eat another sandwich, I'm going to kill myself."

"Oh, ha ha," Aethelu stuck out her tongue. "I'm serious."

"I know. If he'd have listened into that conversation, we'd already be dead. It's been three days. I think we are safe. Besides, the bread is going stale. I think it's turning green. If anything is going to kill me, it's that."

"Ok, ok, you win. I'm coming with you, though." She leapt up from the seat, knocking the book she was reading to the floor."

Anais would have liked to protest, but the truth was, she was relieved not to be going out alone. She gathered up the leftover bits of food from the room and put the rubbish into the carrier bag to dispose of in the kitchen, along with what was left of the bread. Once again, they saw no one on their way to the kitchen. The kitchen itself was also empty although the fridge was fully stocked and fresh bread was laid out on the counter. Aethelu made to pick up the bread, but Anais stopped her. "Let's eat here. I can't face another picnic on the bedroom floor. I'm going to make us a hot meal."

"But what if Andrew comes down?"

"If he does, he does. I'm hungry. She opened the fridge and pulled out some beef and tomatoes. She instructed Aethelu to find some chilli powder and rice whilst she chopped an onion she had found and fried it along with the beef. Soon, they were able to serve up a delicious chilli.

"Not quite as good as Mama's but not far off. I think she puts chocolate in her chilli."

"I wonder how she is. I think the worst thing about all this is the fact that we are all so isolated from each other. Andrew has us just where he wants us. Full of fear scared to talk to each other."

"I'm going to take in the view from the window first thing tomorrow," replied Aethelu.

It took a few moments for Anais to realise that Aethelu meant 'keep a look out for Andrew leaving.' She'd almost forgotten about the plan they had spent the whole day coming up with just three days previously.

"It's certainly a great view," she replied, her acceptance of the plan implicit.

There was still a good amount of chilli and rice left in the pans so before washing up, she emptied them into dishes, covered them and left them in the fridge ready for someone else to microwave if they wanted. She turned the taps on to fill the sink, but Aethelu gently pushed her aside.

"I'm washing up. You cooked."

Anais wasn't about to argue. It wasn't one of her favourite jobs. She grabbed a chocolate bar from the counter (Aethelu talking about chocolate earlier had given her a craving for dark chocolate) and stretched her legs by wandering around the kitchen. She was so huge now that she couldn't see her feet at all. Her back ached from sitting, but the walking around didn't seem to help either. It wasn't just her belly that was huge; it seemed her whole body had grown. Her ankles felt like tree trunks, and her breasts were bigger that they had ever been. They felt like lead balloons. At least, they weren't sore anymore like they had been at the start of her pregnancy. She just felt tired now. She'd been pregnant for over eight months and was ready for it to be over. The thought of giving birth in the state they were all in was more terrifying than keeping this baby inside her, so she pushed thoughts of it to the back of her mind. On her third lap of the kitchen, she suddenly heard a noise. The larder door opened so suddenly that she almost walked right into it. It must have shocked Aethelu, too, as she gave a small scream and dropped the plate she was washing, smashing it into a thousand pieces on the tiled floor.

"Sorry, sorry, I didn't mean to startle you." It was Aldrich, evidently emerging from the cellar lift.

Aethelu jumped over the broken bits of plate and ran into his arms, much to his surprise.

"Daddy!" tears sprang to her eyes.

Aldrich awkwardly patted her back as he hugged her. He was not used to seeing so much emotion.

Anais ran over and pulled a piece from the kitchen roll for Aldrich to pass to Aethelu to mop up her tears. She couldn't blame Aethelu for crying. Her father was the first member of her family she had seen since two of her brothers had been murdered. Instead of getting involved, she found a dustpan and brush and cleared up the shards of plate from the floor.

Eventually, Aethelu stopped crying and then looked embarrassed at her show of emotion.

"Sorry," she sniffed.

"Don't be silly. You've nothing to be sorry for." Anais took over from Aldrich and hugged Aethelu.

"How is she, Aldrich?" She assumed he'd been in the cellar checking up on Judith.

"She's fine for now. He has her so heavily sedated that she doesn't even know where she is, the poor girl. There's nothing I can do for her. She needs to come off all the drugs, but Andrew keeps pumping them into her. If he keeps it up, he'll eventually kill her. The human body is not made to put up with that amount of drugs. I don't think it will be too much longer before her organs begin to overload and then shut down."

"He's going to let her die?"

"Maybe, maybe not, the Light elixir is nearly ready. Perhaps it will be done before she dies."

"So she'll either die or live for eternity with Andrew?" asked Aethelu. "I know which one I'd choose if I had the option." She blew her nose loudly.

"Well, she doesn't have the option. Either her body will hold out until she gets the elixir or it won't."

Suddenly the lift in the larder started to descend. She was about to ask if Judith was conscious enough to get into it by herself when she remembered what Alex had told her. He'd told her that Aldrich could only get into the cellar with Andrew punching in the code.

"Is that Andrew?"

"Probably, he always comes down with me when I visit Judith."

Aethelu grabbed Anais' wrist and pulled her towards the stairs. Anais gladly went with her. She had no desire to bump into Andrew. They had just reached the top of the kitchen stairs when the larder door opened. Without a backward glance, Aethelu opened the kitchen door and flew through it dragging Anais behind her. Both girls ran all the way back to the bedroom and Anais was grateful when Aethelu pushed the chest of drawers back in front of the door. She knew it would not stop Andrew, but it offered her comfort, nonetheless.

Anais collapsed on the bed. Her huge frame was not made for running and she was out of breath. After a couple of minutes, it became apparent that Andrew had not followed them. Although that was a good thing, she really didn't want to have to run again. Autumn kicked her hard, just to add to her pain.

The next morning saw Aethelu up bright and early. She was already seated at the window gazing out to the driveway when Anais awoke.

"Morning, I brought some breakfast for you."

Anais looked to where Aethelu was pointing. It was difficult to make anything out in the dark, but she could just about see the outline of a packet of cereal on the nightstand along with a bowl and a bottle of milk.

Why was it so dark? She looked over at the readout on the clock. 5:47 am. No wonder it was dark.

"It's so early. Why are you awake?"

"I told you I was going to watch out for Andrew leaving today. I'm sick of feeling scared all the time. I've had enough. Today is the day. As soon as I see him go, I'm going to get all the family together and carry out our plan."

Anais was very well aware that Aethelu was talking out loud, but she supposed it didn't matter. If Andrew was about to go out, he'd not have time to listen to what they had said. Of course, if he had gone back to his room, there was a chance that he'd be listening now. When he hadn't shown up at their door ten minutes later wielding an axe, she conceded that he probably hadn't heard Aethelu.

Anais picked up a novel she'd been meaning to read and flipped to the first page. She became so engrossed in it that it was only when Aethelu patted her on the shoulder, three hours later, that she realised Aethelu was talking to her.

"Did you see him leave?" she asked.

"No, nothing, it's your turn to take watch now. "

Anais took the place at the window that Aethelu had occupied all morning. She hadn't expected being a lookout to be a fun job, but she'd also not anticipated just how boring it was. After only ten minutes, the boredom was beginning to set in. It was a beautiful view, but nothing moved. The trees were all bare, which gave her a slightly better view of the nearby village, but apart from an occasional car passing in the distance, she couldn't see much else. It wasn't the best time of year to be doing this, she mused. In a couple of months, the trees along the driveway would be lined with a dazzling display of cherry blossom. In the summer, the garden was alive with wildlife, birds, squirrels, and an occasional fox frolicking amongst the trees. Autumn was the best season of all for the grounds of The Manor. Reds, oranges and browns painted a picture of fire amongst the tops of the trees. Now, though, the trees were as sad as she was, and the dull weather echoed her emotions. It was drizzling slightly, which made her miss the California sunshine she was brought up with. It had been a long time since she'd thought of her home in California, but now, for the first time since she'd arrived in England, she was homesick. She'd give anything for one last trip to the beach. For a second, she had visions of herself teaching little Autumn to surf, just as her father had done for her so many years ago. A lone blackbird hopped across the garden taking her out of her thoughts. She watched as it flew up onto the bird table. It was empty. It was a job she had enjoyed doing in the past, putting birdseed out, but, of course, there was no one to do that now. The bird, on finding no food, took flight in search of another food source. How she envied him. If only she could just open the window and fly away. Autumn gave a kick and then did a kind of flip-flop around in her stomach. Her belly was so much lower than it had been and she knew from reading the one book she could find on pregnancy that it just meant that the baby was getting into a good position for birth. The fear of giving birth once again crept into her consciousness, so she concentrated on watching the rain run down the window. The hours passed so slowly that she was very grateful when Aethelu appeared by her side with lunch. Instead of moving away from the window to eat, Aethelu joined her and they ate, sitting opposite each other on the windowsill. Aethelu took over the watch in the afternoon, much to Anais' relief and it was with great pleasure, she went back to her book.

Three books and five days later, Andrew still hadn't left the house. The girls had only left their room to go to the kitchen to get food. On one of the lunchtimes, whilst it was Anais' turn to get food, she ran into Sabine in the kitchen. It was nice to talk to her, but Sabine was in the same position as everybody else. Bored, cooped up in her bedroom, scared to come out and talk to anybody. Anais asked how Alex was, just to be told that he was depressed, understandably, about the loss of his twin and his older brother. There was very little left to say, so after saying goodbye, Anais, once again, walked through the quiet house back to her room. Despite the monotony and boredom that had set in, she was relieved that she still had Aethelu to talk to. She was devastated by the loss of her brothers, but at least she still talked, made plans. She still had a spark in her, no matter how small. It seemed that Alex had lost his. She only hoped that this plan of theirs would work. They all needed it to.

After they had eaten, Anais took her, now familiar, position by the window. She'd taken to playing silly games with herself to pass the time. This particular afternoon, for example, she was counting birds. It was boring, but it was better than nothing. When she had counted her seventeenth bird, there came a knock on the door. It made her jump up. Aethelu looked at her, unsure of what to do. It was the first time someone had knocked on the door in a long time.

Anais shrugged her shoulders. "Who is it?" she asked.

"Anais? Aethelu?"

"It's Sabine. Quick, open the door!"

Sabine must have decided to speak to them both after seeing Anais in the kitchen

Aethelu pushed back the heavy chest of drawers out of the way once again and dragged Sabine in, giving a quick peek down the corridor just in case she had been followed.

"Sabine!" Aethelu hugged her. "How are you doing? How's Alex?"

"He thinks Rafe is still alive." Sabine sat at the dressing table and absentmindedly picked up a book, which she flipped through without looking at it.

"I know," replied Anais. "He told me."

"When did he tell you?" asked Aethelu. "You never told me that."

"I saw him a few days ago in the kitchen. He said he could still feel Rafe was alive."

"Do you think he is?" asked Aethelu, a look of hope in her eyes. "They always did seem to know what the other was up to."

"I don't see how it's possible. Why would Andrew lie about it?"

"When we were kids, Alex and Rafe were separated for a few days. Alex had stayed at home, whilst Rafe had gone to get supplies with August. They had gone to another village a few days away. Anyway, Alex started to complain of really bad pains in his leg. Mama did everything she could to ease his pain, but nothing worked. When Rafe got back, August told us that Rafe had fallen and badly damaged his leg at just the time that Alex had started complaining of pain."

"That could be just coincidence, Aethelu. I think you are stretching a bit there."

"No, stuff like that used to happen all the time. It was like they instinctively knew when the other was hurt or in danger."

"Do you really think Rafe could be alive?" asked Sabine.

"If Alex says he is, then I think he's right. I trust Alex when it comes to Rafe."

Anais wished Sabine had not come to visit. Now, she'd gotten Aethelu's hopes up, as well as Alex's. There was no proof that Rafe was alive, besides a feeling that Alex had.

"Did you come to see us about Alex?" asked Anais, keen to get off the topic of Rafe. She didn't want Aethelu to have false hope.

"Actually, yes I did. I'm sorry Aethelu, but as much as I'd like it to be true, I don't think Rafe is alive. I came because Alex has got it into his head, and I'm afraid he is doing something stupid that will get him killed."

Anais didn't like where this was going, but she was sure that wherever it was, they didn't want Andrew to hear it. She turned on the radio and set it to maximum volume. Andrew might see that they were having a private discussion, but he wouldn't know the content of it.

Sabine moved over to the bed where the other two girls

sat. She spoke as quietly as she could, just enough to be heard over the sound of the radio.

"He's been going out at night."

"Going out? Where?"

"I don't know. He won't tell me. I woke up a couple of nights ago, and he wasn't in our room. I called out for him, but he wasn't there. I was too scared to go looking for him."

"Did he tell you where he has been going?"

"He said he was just going to the bathroom."

"Perhaps that's it then. Maybe he was telling the truth."

"For three hours? It's happened every night since Rafe died. I don't know what to do."

"Do you think he's just grieving? Maybe he just needs some time to himself. If he was up to anything dodgy, Andrew would have caught up with him and put a stop to it already," said Anais as kindly as she could.

"If he just needed space, he could have asked for it. I know he's hurting right now. That's not it."

"So where do you think he's going?"

"I think he's searching for Rafe. He dresses up in dark clothes so as not to be seen by Andrew."

"He really thinks Rafe is alive?"

"He's positive. I'm sorry Aethelu. However much I'd like to believe Alex and you. I don't see how he could still be alive. I hate to say this, but half of me hopes Alex will find Rafe's body so he can grieve properly and not put himself in danger."

She started to cry. Anais felt sorry for her. She didn't know what she would do in the same position.

"Have you tried to follow him?" asked Aethelu.

"No. He's strictly forbidden it. I'm too scared to wander the corridors as it is, let alone in the middle of the night. It took all the courage I could muster to come here to speak to you two."

"What do you want us to do?" Anais didn't see how she could help in any way.

"Can you talk to him for me? You might be able to talk some sense into him."

Anais sighed. If Alex got something into his head, it was unlikely that she'd be able to change it.

"Would you like me to go now?"

"Would you? Oh Anais, thank you." She grabbed Anais and hugged her tightly, a fresh outpouring of tears accompanying the hug.

"You can't go out there alone," said Aethelu.

"It's only down the hall. I'll be back before you know it." She stood up to leave.

"Andrew might be there!" said Aethelu, suddenly sounding scared.

"Aethelu, as much as we'd both like to believe that chest of Drawers is keeping us safe from Andrew, you know, as well as I do, that if Andrew wanted to get in, he could in a heartbeat. He's probably playing mad scientist up in his room or down in the cellar with Judith. Even if I did see him, I doubt he'd do anything to me."

"Well, I don't want you taking that chance."

"I'll be back in ten minutes. Just a quick talk with Alex and I promise to come straight back. Now would you please move the chest for me?"

Aethelu looked to be of two minds, whether to move the drawers or stand in Anais' way. Sabine stood up and flung herself around Aethelu.

"Thanks, both of you. I really appreciate it."

Aethelu rolled her eyes and extracted herself from the sobbing Sabine.

"Come on then. You can help me." The two girls moved the drawers back as Anais slipped through.

"I'm leaving this door open so you can run back through if you need to. If you get into any trouble at all, just yell."

Anais smiled. She felt so safe with Aethelu having her back.

Despite knowing that Aethelu was watching her as she made her way down the corridor, she still ran and was out of breath by the time she knocked on Alex's door.

He opened it an inch and then pulled it wide to let her in.

"I wondered where Sabine had gone. Has she told you to come and find out where I've been going at night?"

Anais walked over to the bedside table and turned the radio on. A talk show was on. She turned it up to the maximum.

"She's worried about you. I'm worried about you."

"I've just been going to the toilet. I already told her that."

"She's not stupid, Alex. She thinks you are going out looking for Rafe."

Alex looked surprised at this. "She does, does she?"

"Are you?"

"Does it matter? You all think he's dead anyway."

"Of course it matters. If Andrew catches you..."

"If Andrew catches me, what?" Alex cut her off. "He'll kill me. So what" He raised his voice.

"He won't stop there. He'll kill Sabine, too, torture her, and then do you think he'll stop there?"

"He's not going to catch me. He's been going out at night. I've been watching him leave."

"You can't have. We've been keeping watch on the driveway for days."

"He leaves by the tunnel to August's house. I've seen him go. I've been following him."

Anais gazed at him, wide-eyed with shock.

"So you've not been looking for Rafe at all?"

"Actually Sabine is right, I did set out to look for Rafe. I thought he might have escaped. It would make sense that Andrew wouldn't want to tell us, for fear that we would all try to get away. Then he'd have no one to make The Light for him. It is easier to say he'd killed Rafe. That way it still looks like he's in charge."

"But if we all leave, he'll just set the Jagovirus out into the world."

"He could, yes, but it's not what he wants, is it? He's only using it as a threat. He wants The Light Elixir."

Alex's words made a strange kind of sense. She began to feel a glimmer of hope that Rafe might just be alive, after all.

"Anyway," continued Alex, "I've still not found Rafe, but I have seen what Andrew is up to."

"What?"

"He's going up to the top of the tramway."

Anais tried to remember the one time she had travelled on the old-fashioned tram. She pictured the little station at the top. It had a tiny room where the controller set the tram going and a little shop that sold postcards and sweets. She could think of no reason that it would hold any interest to Andrew.

"Why? There's nothing up there."

"There is a huge building opposite. It used to be a shop selling souvenirs, but it closed in the eighties. The top floor used to be the shopkeeper's accommodations. It's been for sale for years. I guess Andrew either bought it, or is squatting there, because he's been going into it for the last week, every night like clockwork. He's either not noticed me following him, or he doesn't care that I am. I suspect the former, though. He seems very preoccupied when he's going out."

"What is he doing?"

"That bit, I don't know. The bottom half of the building still has shutters over the windows from the days when it was a shop. He doesn't open them. He goes in at around midnight and leaves at around 4 am. I think he might have Rafe in there."

Anais had been very sceptical about Alex's theory that Rafe was alive, but now, she wasn't so sure. Perhaps Rafe was alive, after all.

"Why haven't you told Sabine this?"

"Honestly? I'm worried that she'll want to come with me when I plan to rescue Rafe, and I don't want her to be hurt."

"You should have told her, Alex."

"I know." He paused "I suppose you are going to tell her now?"

Anais thought about it. She had an idea.

"Actually, I think you should. Maybe she should come with you, maybe some of the others should come, too.

"No!"

"Why not?"

"What if he sees us? It's dangerous. Does it matter what he's up to anyway?"

"You, obviously, seem to think so. You are the one following him."

"But ...but..."

Anais waited until he came up with his next argument.

"You aren't coming, you are just about to give birth!" was all he could come up with.

"I didn't mean me, but whatever Andrew is up to, I think we need to know. If he's not seen you, there is a good chance he'll not see the others either. Besides, there is no chance that Aethelu will leave it alone, once I tell her. She'll go, whether you like it or not; you know her."

She proceeded to tell him of the plan she and Aethelu had developed.

"You want to kill him? How will you stop the mechanism from breaking the vials?"

"Well, he told us that he had to input the code every four hours. You know yourself that he leaves for more than that every night. He must do it remotely, probably by phone. We take the phone from him and see what he's imputed, then do it ourselves until we can find the rest of the vials."

"But what if he's locked his phone?"

Anais hadn't thought of that. It was such a silly thing to overlook. "You are good with stuff like that. Can't you break the login code?"

"I doubt it. If I were Andrew, I'd have it rigged so that if the wrong number was entered, it would automatically set the vials to break."

Anais felt stupid. Of course, that's what Andrew would do. They'd been so set on the part where they killed Andrew that they hadn't thought it through at all.

"I still want to know what he's up to. Come on. Let's tell Sabine and Aethelu."

As Anais and Alex walked down the corridor, she could see Aethelu peeking out of the bedroom.

"Thank goodness, you are back. You've been gone ages."

She pushed the chest of drawers back from the door when they had both come through it.

"Alex wanted to talk to you both," Anais said as she once again turned on the radio to drown their voices out.

He proceeded to tell them everything he'd told Anais.

As Anais had anticipated, Aethelu jumped on it.

"I'm coming with you tonight," she said to Alex.

Anais looked over at her. She was positively brimming over with excitement. She gave Alex a look as if to say 'I told you so'.

Alex only sighed.

"Fine, but just you."

"What do you mean just her?" asked an indignant Sabine.

"I don't want loads of people following him. He'll spot us."

"I'm coming!" Sabine said, and stomped out of the room.

Alex sighed again. "I guess I'd better go," he said indicating the now open door.

"I'll come to your room at 11.30," Aethelu called after him.

She pushed the chest of drawers back in front of the door and joined Anais back on the bed.

"So what do you make of that?" Aethelu asked.

"I don't know. What could Andrew possibly want with a huge building?"

"Who knows? It's away from all of us though, isn't it? Whatever he is doing, he wants to keep it secret. Any secrets he has are bad news for us. We need to know everything if we hope to beat him."

"I knew you'd say that. I agree. Just be safe tonight, though. Follow him, see what he's up to, and get back in one piece."

Aethelu cuddled her. "I promise not to do anything stupid. I know better than to just jump in and act when it comes to Andrew. Intel gathering only tonight! I can't believe we've sat up here like idiots watching the driveway, and he's been sneaking out through the tunnel this whole time."

"He's really got us where he wants us, doesn't he? We are all too scared to leave our rooms and talk to each other. He's using fear to imprison us. That's why Alex has been able to follow him without being caught. Andrew is so arrogant that he thinks we are all too scared to take action. It's just not occurred to him that anyone would leave their rooms long enough to see that he's disappearing every night. I bet he's not even bothering to listen to our conversations anymore."

The hours passed slowly. Anais insisted that Aethelu go to bed early, to get at least a couple of hours sleep before she had to go out. Anais herself didn't sleep for worry, and she suspected neither did Aethelu. Eventually, the alarm beeped signalling the time for Aethelu to leave. She quickly dressed in all black and kissed Anais before slipping out.

Anais knew that she wouldn't sleep whilst Aethelu was gone, so she didn't even try. She decided to go down to the library and get a book to pass the time. She waited ten minutes or so to give the others time to leave and crept out into the corridor. She didn't turn the lights on, instead, moving through the house by the light of the moon and stars coming through the windows. Even though she knew Andrew wasn't in the house anymore, she had been conditioned to feel fear whilst out of her room. The house was silent, though, as she opened the door to the library. She was surprised when she saw that the lamp was burning. Then her heart nearly jumped out of her chest when she saw Andrew seated in one of the chairs reading a book.

He seemed as surprised to see her, as she was, him.

"What are you doing here?" she asked, before realising she was dangerously close to putting her foot in it. He had every right to be here.

"I could ask you the same question," he replied briskly.

"I wanted to read a book," she stammered, panic rising through her.

"I'm not getting the Alice book out of the safe again, so don't even bother asking."

"Err, I, actually, I was just going to pick something off the shelf." She grabbed a book and left as quickly as she could. She passed a confused looking Alex, Sabine, and Aethelu on the first-floor landing.

"He's in the library," she whispered as she ran past them and back to her room.

She hoped she hadn't messed anything up. She glanced at the clock. It was three minutes to midnight. According to Alex, Andrew was usually gone by eleven thirty. She wondered if Andrew had just changed his mind about going out tonight. If that was the case, Aethelu would be back shortly.

Anais paced the room for ten minutes waiting for Aethelu. When it became apparent that Aethelu was not returning, she sat in a chair and opened her book. Andrew must have gone out, after all. It didn't take long until she drifted off to sleep.

When Anais awoke, her whole body ached with cramps from the unnatural position she'd slept in. She brought her hand to her neck to massage it and opened her eyes. Light shone in through the window. It was morning. Anais quickly stood up, ignoring the pain in her body. She looked over at the empty bed and quickly scanned the room. Aethelu wasn't there. Fear began to rise through her. She checked the time. Six thirty-five. Aethelu should have been back hours ago. The chest of drawers had been purposely left away from the door to let Aethelu get back in during the middle of the night. Anais peeked out of the door and down the empty corridor. In a state of panic, she ran through the en-suite bathroom and straight into Arcadia's room.

Aethelu wasn't there either, but the noise of the door opening woke Arcadia. She sat up in bed and removed a baby blue satin sleep mask.

"Anais? What's going on?" Her nightdress matched the sleep mask in the same baby blue; and even in bed, she wore a wig, although goodness knows who she thought was going to come into her room.

"Have you seen Aethelu?" asked Anais in a panicked voice.

"No. I thought she'd be in with you."

Anais was just about to explain where Aethelu had gone when she heard a door bang in the next room. She ran back to find Aethelu, Alex and Sabine just getting in. Aethelu quickly pushed the chest of drawers back in front of the door.

"What's happening?" asked Arcadia, who had followed Anais into her room.

"You guys should sit down," said Aethelu to Anais and Arcadia. Anais took the chair next to the one Alex sat in. Aethelu and Sabine sat on the edge of the bed. Their muddy shoes had left a trail along the red carpet.

Alex jumped up, offered Arcadia his seat, and then went to bring another one for himself from Arcadia's bedroom.

"What is going on?" repeated a bewildered Arcadia, her eye mask now perched atop her head.

"Just a minute," Anais turned the radio on. A local station belted out a disco classic. Taking her seat, she turned to Arcadia. "Andrew has been sneaking out at night. Alex thinks Rafe is still alive. These guys followed Andrew last night." She turned to Alex. "Did you find him?"

"No, he's not there," replied Aethelu.

"Just because we didn't see him doesn't mean he's dead, though," retorted Alex.

"So, what happened? Why are you so late getting back? I expected you back hours ago."

"Oh, man, where to begin?" Aethelu started. "He left later than usual. You saw him in the library. He almost caught us all on the stairs and we thought we'd lost our chance. Thankfully, he took his book and left not long after you saw him. We waited a few minutes for him to go down into the tunnel to August's house and then left through the front door."

"Why didn't you just follow him down the tunnel?" asked Arcadia.

"I did the first time I followed him, but I had to keep so far back for fear of him hearing or seeing me that by the time he'd got to August's cottage and out into the grounds, I was too far back to catch up with him. He has a remote to disable the electric fence. The second night, I was just in time to see him hop over the fence and re-enable it. It only goes off for a couple of minutes, so you've got to be right behind him, but without him seeing you. Since then, I've just walked down to the cottage and waited there for him. That's what we did last night."

"But if you are so close to him, doesn't he see you?"

"Actually, he's been pretty preoccupied these days. You've not seen him so you've not noticed, but whatever he is up to, it's taking all his concentration. I think he's relying on our fear to keep us in check these days. I don't even think he's been watching the CCTV or listening to our conversations for a while now."

"We just jumped over the fence a bit further down from where he was," interjected Aethelu. "He wouldn't have seen us in the dark. You can hear it humming. When the humming stops, that's the cue to jump over. Thanks to Alex, we already knew where he was going so once we were over the fence; we didn't have to keep him in our sight."

"So what happened?" asked Anais impatiently.

Alex continued. "We followed him up to the old shop at the top of the hill near the top tram station. He has rented it out, I think." He said this for Arcadia's benefit. Anais had already heard where he was going. "He's been going there every night for days. At least since I've been following him, but judging by what we saw last night, he's had the place for a long time."

Anais was really getting impatient now.

"Just what did you see?"

"I'm getting to that," replied Alex. "Anyway, he went into the old shop and closed the door behind him. Usually, at that point I just give up and wait for him. He locks the door behind him, so it's impossible to follow him in. I wouldn't like to try anyway. He'd probably spot us."

"The shop backs onto woodland," cut in Aethelu. "We had to walk through a ton of nettles and brambles, but around the back, there was a window. It was the only one without shutters. We had to climb up to the roof using a tree, but it was an easy job to lower ourselves down to the window from there. The window frame was pretty much rotted through, so we were able to jimmy the window open without making too much noise. The upstairs of the house was empty. Andrew hadn't bothered to do anything with it. The shop's living quarters were up there. The room we got into was the master bedroom. It hadn't been decorated since the eighties, at least, and there were mould and dust everywhere. The whole upstairs was the same. He'd not touched it. Downstairs, though, that was a different matter."

Anais, by this time, was on the edge of her seat. "What

was down there?" she could see that Aethelu was enjoying keeping her in suspense.

"Put it this way, what we found explains a few things."

"Like what?" asked Arcadia, who was also gripped by the story.

"He had a laboratory down there. The whole downstairs was an open plan so it was difficult to even get down there without being seen."

"So how did you?"

"Andrew fell asleep. I don't think he planned to, but he fell asleep on a couch. That's why we were so late back. We couldn't get back over the electric fence until he did.

"You just walked around his laboratory whilst he was there?" asked Anais.

"He was asleep!"

"But he could have woken up at any second!" replied Anais incredulously.

"He almost did, at one point, when Alex dropped a picture on the floor." She shot a look at Alex, who shrugged his shoulder apologetically. "What else could we do? We had no choice if we wanted to find out what was going on."

Anais shook her head. They were either brave or stupid; she wasn't too sure which. She remained silent to let Aethelu continue.

"The laboratory was obviously where he'd made the Jagovirus and all that other stuff. It looked like he had been experimenting for years, which would explain a lot. Scientific equipment took up most of the room. Things were bubbling away in test tubes and machines were buzzing and whirring all over the place."

"What was he making?"

"I don't know, knowing Andrew, something horrible. It made me realise, though, that he really has got a virus in those vials. It's not just some big con. He knows what he's doing. It wasn't the laboratory that shocked us; it was his diary."

"You found his diary?"

"It wasn't a diary, as such," Sabine spoke for the first time. "He had a wall with all sorts of stuff pinned to it: photos, blueprints, letters, and such. We managed to piece together a lot by what we found. It seems that Andrew started experimenting a lot earlier than we thought. We found dated recipe lists from over a hundred years ago."

"Recipes?"

"I don't know the English word for it, a list of ingredients. Judging by what was on the lists, we think he was trying to emulate Aldrich and make The Light."

"A hundred years ago? I thought he only wanted to make The Light when he fell in love with my mother. He wanted her to live forever, just like he does with Judith now."

"That's what we thought, but it seems this has been going on for much longer. He had hundreds of scraps of paper; all with scribbles and bits added or crossed out. There were dates of each experiment. He's been chronicling everything he's been doing."

"Don't we already know everything he's been doing?"

"Not quite."

"He's been performing these experiments for years, at least a hundred. Unlike Dad, he's not been using animals to experiment on."

"He's been experimenting on humans?" Anais looked at Aethelu in horror.

"It seems that way. Dad used animals for his experiments. He hated to do it, but he knew he would save lives with his cures. He's always felt bad about it and donates tens of thousands of pounds to local animal charities to this day.

Andrew, on the other hand, decided to bypass the animals and use humans to test out his concoctions."

"But how? Surely, we'd know about it if he'd hurt anyone."

"We did know about it."

"What do you mean?" Anais had no clue about any human experimentation.

"There were photos and news clippings all over his wall, missing girls. Some of them we'd seen in the news. About fifty years ago, a few girls went missing from the village on the way home from school. We even helped search for them. It was all over the news for months. They were never found. That's what I mean about us knowing about it. Of course, we didn't know Andrew had taken them."

Anais held her hand up to her mouth.

"Oh, my god! What was he doing with them?"

"It's hard to be sure exactly, but it looks like he used them as lab rats. He wrote about testing the Jagovirus out on a girl as little as two years ago. She was taken from a village a couple of hundred miles from here. It looks like he cast his net wide for girls to kidnap."

Anais felt sick. All those innocent girls, she could hardly bear to think about it.

"He performed other experiments, too, ones involving his DNA. He tried to add his own DNA to some of these girls. He doesn't want to go down the route of getting married and having children, you know, like normal people do to spread their DNA. He's actually trying to turn girls into a sort of female version of him."

"What on earth for?"

"He's the only person who has ever liked him, I suppose. It's his way of making sure his mate doesn't run away from him. It would be like running away from yourself."

Anais thought about it for a second. She thought that if she were mated with herself, running away would probably be the first thing she would do. Who on earth would want to be with someone their exact duplicate? It would be hell. You'd see all of your own bad points there in front of you. The guy was seriously twisted.

"I suppose his only alternative would be to lock these girls up and keep them as slaves."

"Judging by one of the rooms upstairs, he'd already gone down that route. I guess it hadn't worked out too well for him."

"What do you mean?

"We found shackles and blood in one of the upstairs rooms. He's held at least one person there already, although there were probably more.

He's written down his plan to do the same to Judith once he's given her The Light."

"But if these experiments end up killing people and never work, what's the point? He'll only end up killing her."

"He's managed it one time before. Of all the girls he's tried to merge his DNA with, there's been only one it has worked on."

"You mean there is someone out there with part of Andrews DNA?"

"Yep and if you think about it, it probably won't take long for you to figure out who?"

Anais thought hard, but she could not imagine. Had it been one of the family?

"Who?" she asked.

"Put it this way, who is the only person we know who could have rivalled Andrew in the crazy department?"

"Jasmine?" Anais was in shock. "He did this to Jasmine? That's why she did the things she did?"

"It kinda makes sense don't you think? It was a very strange coincidence that we knew two crazy serial killers with a penchant for killing for youth and everlasting life. I think we can assume that Jasmine was pretty normal up until she met Andrew."

"But she never met Andrew, did she?"

"That's what we all thought until tonight. We found some of Andrew's notes made at about the time Jasmine was a young child. It seems that Amber once brought Jasmine back here. She was finally going to come clean about running away and having a child and I guess she thought bringing her granddaughter would help her case. She brought her here to the house. As it happens, the family had all gone abroad for a holiday at the time. Andrew, with his fear of flying, had elected to housesit whilst they were all gone. Jasmine must have seemed like an ideal opportunity for him to test out some of his experiments. Perhaps she was the first he tested. Anyway, according to his notes, Amber and Jasmine stayed at The Manor for two weeks. I don't know what story he told Amber to be able to get Jasmine alone long enough, but I think we can assume that it was him that caused Jasmine to be the way she was."

Anais' head was spinning with it all. Poor Jasmine, yet another life ruined by Andrew. It would add Amber and Abel to the tally of deaths for which he was responsible. Who knew how high that number was now?

"So why didn't Amber stay until everyone got home?" asked Anais.

"I don't know. Andrew's notes didn't say. It could have been because she began to get suspicious of Andrew or perhaps he told her that Mama hated her. Either way, I don't remember Amber and Jasmine ever being at the house, so he did a good job of scaring them off, however he did it."

"There's one more thing I should tell you." Aethelu looked her square in the eye. This wasn't going to be good.

"What?"

"I think he may plan to do it to Autumn, too. I found scribbled notes on how he plans somehow to splice his DNA into hers. He seems to think she will be the ideal candidate as she will be just a baby when he does it."

"Over my dead body!" Anais put her hand on her stomach protectively.

"Don't worry. Of course, we won't let him. But we need to get those vials before we kill him. As Alex pointed out, my idea of getting his phone is stupid. If we kill him, we'll have a maximum of four hours before the mechanism sets to break the vials."

"So what do we do now? We know more about modern day Frankenstein, but we are no closer to beating him." Anais wasn't sure how the information would help them at all.

"Actually, knowing what we know now does help us a little, or it makes more work for us. I'm not sure which" said Alex.

"What do you mean?"

"Well, I'm guessing that whatever Andrew is brewing up in there, it's not good. I suspect he has more of the Jagovirus brewing as a backup. Lots of it, judging by the sheer amount of liquid bubbling away."

"So actually, we've got twelve vials left to find, and then twenty to destroy, plus the stuff in Andrew's building. I'd say that's more work to do, not less."

"Yep, that about sums it up."

"So, to repeat my last question. What do we do now?" She looked around at the others. Everyone was silent. It looked like no one knew how to deal with the situation any better than she did. Eventually, Sabine yawned.

"I don't know what to do about Andrew, but I do know that I've been awake all night and can't think straight."

Alex agreed. "We need to sleep. We'll come back this evening once we've slept a little and look at it again.

Aethelu agreed. She flopped on the bed as the others made their way out.

Anais joined her. She'd not slept too well herself, and she was exhausted. She only hoped a brainstorm would come to one of them in the next few hours.

It wasn't long before she had drifted off to sleep.

"Anais, Aethelu?"

A knocking on the door awoke both of them a few hours later.

"Audsley?"

"Yeah, it's me. Can I come in?"

Aethelu jumped up and pushed the chest of drawers out of the way to enable her to open the door.

"Wowee, who were you expecting? The bogeyman?" asked Audsley, pointing at the chest of drawers.

"Exactly!" grinned Aethelu, who ran to her cousin and hugged her. It was the first time Anais had seen her smile in a week. Anais rushed over to hug her once Aethelu had let go.

"It's so good to see you. It's so isolating, being stuck in the room all the time."

"Tell me about it. At least you two have each other. I've taken to talking to the TV just to pretend I have company."

"You have a TV?" asked Aethelu in amazement.

"Yeah, of course, I ordered one online."

"Why didn't we think of that?"

Anais was quite glad they hadn't. She might have been

bored, but she wasn't one for watching a lot of TV. She preferred to be outside. She thought back to the last time she watched a lot of TV. It was at August's cottage when Aethelu wasn't speaking to her. She smiled a sad smile at the thought of August. She missed him.

"Anyway, I'm afraid I'm here for a reason. His highness has asked all of us to go into the dining room."

"Why?" asked Aethelu, suddenly afraid. Had he somehow found out about the plan? Had he heard them, after all? Did he see them following him? It was no use not going down with Audsley. He'd only come up and get them himself, or find some other horrible way of getting them down there--something like emptying a nest of bees into the air conditioning system.

"I don't want to go!" exclaimed Aethelu.

"Neither do I, but I don't think he's giving us an option."

"Do you know what he wants?"

"Nope, Auntie Winnie came and asked me to tell you to come down. I think he came to her directly and asked her to pass the message on."

Aethelu ran around the room, searching until she found the thing she was looking for. When Anais saw what it was, she raised her eyebrows. It was a coat hanger.

"What's that for?"

"I thought I could use it as a weapon if I needed."

"Do you plan on hanging him up in your closet to death?"

"It's wire. I could strangle the bloody bastard until he chokes to death with it."

"Aethelu, you know that's not going to happen. Put it down."

Aethelu begrudgingly put the wire coat hanger on the bed and followed her wife and cousin out of the door. Just as they reached the dining room, Anais heard her whisper in her ear.

"If he tries anything funny, we kill him!"

Anais wasn't sure if she wanted him to try anything or not. The thought was too scary.

In the dining room, there were a few empty seats. Of course, the ones usually occupied by Rafe and August were empty, but there were a few others they were waiting for. Winnie was there, looking apprehensive, as were Alex and Sabine, Ava and Alfred and Arcadia. Just as Anais, Aethelu and Audsley sat down, Jennifer came in and took her place. Andrew stood at the end of the table looking extremely pleased with himself, a sick smile plastered on his face. It didn't bode well and Anais fought a shiver.

"Ladies and gentlemen, as you know, we have all been waiting for a very important day--The most important day of my whole life."

Anais tried to think what this day could be. She didn't have to think for long.

"Aldrich kindly informed me this morning that The Light Elixir is finally ready. Today, I shall finally have Judith as my bride and we shall live together as husband and wife for all eternity."

I have asked a local priest to come and perform the ceremony to make it all legal. Welcome to my wedding!

Anais didn't know what to say. She didn't want to point out how ludicrous his plan was. For a start, Judith was barely conscious, not to mention the fact that he'd told her they were already married. She'd be very confused if they got married again. How, on earth, had he managed to persuade a priest to come and marry them? Surely, no one would stay and marry a woman who barely knew her own name because of all the drugs?

A doorbell sounded.

"Ah, that will be him now."

Andrew left the room to answer the main door. Anais looked around the table at the shocked faces surrounding her. It seemed that no one expected this to happen. Still, it beat the alternative of him inviting them down to kill them all, which was what Anais had been expecting.

The priest, a small man in his early fifties with grey hair was ushered into the dining room.

He seemed very surprised by the wedding guests. More so than the wedding guests themselves. Anais looked around the table once more and tried to imagine what was going through his mind. Andrew was the only one not in his pyjamas except for Arcadia, of course, who was wearing a beautiful pink silk dress with matching high heels. She was one of the few who had bothered to put a wig on, too. In fact, she was the only one who actually looked like she should be at a wedding. Sabine had put a wig on, as had Anais, Aethelu, Audsley, and Ava. Jennifer and Winnie had not bothered. Short stubble had begun to grow on their heads, white for Winnie and jet black for Jennifer. Fading scars still marked their bodies and faces from the itching powder. They had lessened, but they were still visible. The family made a very strange looking party, indeed.

The priest, obviously, thought so. He looked rather uncomfortable.

"Is this...erm...the wedding party?"

"Of course, it is," snapped Andrew, but then he smiled at the priest.

"Hmm, well, this beautiful young lady must be the bride." He walked towards Arcadia only to be pulled back by an agitated Andrew.

"No, you imbecile, that is not the bride. The bride will be

here shortly. I've paid you a year's salary to do this, so just stand there and shut up until she gets here."

The priest looked like he was about to argue back but thought better of it. He moved to where he was told and kept his mouth shut. A year's salary, that would explain it.

A couple of minutes later, James and Aldrich appeared at the door. They were carrying Judith, who obviously was too drugged to stand up by herself. They placed her on the chair nearest, Andrew. As they set her down, her head lolled forward and she jerked it back quickly. Her eyes rolled around in their sockets for a few seconds before she managed to gain control of them and focus.

"Ah, here she is, my beloved, Judith." He plucked a pink lily from a nearby bunch and placed it in her hair.

The gesture was not the act of a loving man. It was sick. The whole charade made Anais want to vomit. The priest looked like he felt the same way.

"I don't think she is very well. I don't think I can do this."

"You'll do it. I'll pay another ten thousand pounds. Besides, she'll be fine in a few minutes."

The priest smiled, but it was not a happy smile. Anais could see him struggling between thoughts of riches and performing a wedding with a barely conscious bride.

Andrew picked Judith up and placed her on the table. She was too drugged up to resist. She closed her eyes. Andrew kissed her lightly and then snatched something out of Aldrich's hand. It was The Light, The Elixir of Life. He inserted a needle into the vial and extracted the amber coloured liquid. As he held it up to the light of the window, Anais could see the telltale flecks of light glinting in the weak sun. He brought the needle up and then plunged it directly into her heart.

The priest looked like he was about to faint.

All was silent for a few seconds, then a piercing scream filled the air. Judith jerked up to a sitting position on the table, still screaming. Then she stopped. Something else was happening. Something that Anais had heard about but had never witnessed. Anais had only half The Light, which she had inherited from her father. Sabine, Jennifer, the priest, and Judith herself had no clue what was happening, but Anais knew this was The Light changing Judith's very DNA. All the others round this table had experienced this very same thing over 600 years ago. It was brutal and shocking, and beautiful all at the same time.

Judith's eyes already a deep brown turned black. Light danced in them making them shine. Her once black hair turned silver-white which seemed to look more shocking on her than the others, because it contrasted with her dark skin. Even that was beginning to lighten. She didn't turn as pale as Aethelu or the others. She was still dark skinned, but now it looked paper thin, almost translucent. Anais could just about see the light travelling through her veins. If anything, it made her look golden. Judith's posture straightened and her skin took on a slight sheen. However beautiful she was before was only enhanced by the light. She looked like a goddess.

The looks of shock around the table were nothing compared to the shock coming from Judith.

"What's happening?" she whimpered.

"You are now my queen on your wedding day." Andrew looked positively delighted as he helped her stand down from the table. The Light had beaten the drugs in her system so she was now completely steady and coherent, but she was scared and confused.

"Rafe?" She looked around the table, desperately searching for her love, for someone to cling to in her fear.

"What about him?" shouted Andrew. "He's dead. I killed him. It's just you and me now."

The priest, who already had lost all colour from his face, now turned green.

"I don't think I can do this." He was terrified. He turned to leave.

Andrew drew a gun out of his pocket and pointed it at the head of the priest.

"You will do it!" Andrew was mad with rage.

"Rafe!" screamed Judith desperately searching the table, hoping that Andrew was lying.

"HE IS DEAD!" shouted Andrew a look of pure evil on his face.

"I want Rafe!" Judith collapsed to the floor in floods of tears, which was when all hell broke loose. Andrew turned bright red with rage. He shot Judith right in the head before turning the gun on the priest, who had run to the door in an effort to escape.

Someone else screamed. Anais didn't know who. It could have even been her. Shots were being fired in all directions and people scattered everywhere. She saw Alex pick up Judith's body and run out along with Sabine. Someone grabbed her hand and she felt herself being dragged out through the door. All she could hear were screams and gunshots and above all that, the bellowing voice of Andrew screaming his rage above all the other noise. She was being pulled up the stairs at such a speed that it was making her feel ill. She could just about make out Alex and Sabine in front of her. Eventually, they ended up in the large attic. Only when she stopped to breathe, did she realize it was Aethelu who had grabbed her. Jennifer had also somehow ended up in the attic with them. She sat down and a pain like no other ripped through her. To one side was the bleeding body of Judith. The others were throwing every piece of furniture they could find down the attic stairs in an effort to block the door and stop Andrew getting in. Anais didn't want to point out that they had effectively trapped themselves in and made themselves sitting ducks.

Another pain tore through her body. She gasped. It was Autumn. The baby was coming. The pregnancy book she had read said that labour would start gently, like a tightening around her middle and gradually become more painful in time. This was nothing like that. It felt more like having a thousand knives plunged into her belly. She sucked in her breath and held back a scream. The others didn't need to know just how dire the situation was. It was bad enough that they were trapped in a room with a homicidal maniac on one side and a dead woman and a pregnant woman on the other. They didn't need to know that the said pregnant woman was also in the middle of giving birth.

She concentrated on watching the others piling up furniture behind the door in an effort to ignore the immense pain she was feeling. Then, as quickly as it came, the pain receded. She blew out a breath and relaxed. If this was, indeed, labour, she knew that another pain was on its way. She started the stopwatch function on her watch, just in case, and watched the seconds fly by. A minute passed, nothing. Two minutes...Three. Then...

"Ouch"

The pain came again. Daggers were searing through her middle. It had been three minutes and a bit. Were contractions supposed to come so quickly? She tried a breathing technique she had learned from the book, but it didn't help. She wondered if she had read the book wrong because it wasn't helping her manage the pain at all. Eventually, the pain once again passed. No one had noticed her gasping in pain. They were all too busy piling everything they could find behind the door. The sound of breaking and falling furniture filled the air. It was chaos. She reset the stopwatch and waited. One minute...Tw... A noise came from beside her. She looked around in shock. It was Judith. She wasn't dead. She was breathing. There had been a bullet hole shot right through her head, but the dried blood had masked the fact that she had healed quickly. The Light had saved her. Anais was just going to turn her over to see if the bullet had exited her brain when she had another contraction. Judith started to moan just as she did. She let the pain ride over her and tried to concentrate on Judith. The others were making so much noise that they hadn't heard either of them. Once the contraction was over, she moved a little closer to Judith. She gently tilted Judith's head forward and saw blood on the back of her head. The exit wound. The bullet had gone right through her head. Anais was just wondering how having your brain ripped in two with a bullet would affect someone with The Light when Judith opened her eyes.

"Anais?" she asked, quietly and rather uncertainly.

"It's me." Anais cradled Judith's head on her lap and stroked her silver white hair. A tear fell onto Judith's face and Anais realised it was hers.

"What happened?"

Anais was just about to answer when another contraction came on.

"Just a minute," she gasped, before becoming unable to speak with the sheer force of the pain.

"Judith!" Aethelu shouted. She must have turned and noticed Judith speaking "Guys, She's alive!"

Alex, Sabine, and Jennifer crowded round Judith, just as Anais' contraction subsided.

"She's alive. She can talk," Anais told them. Just then, Judith attempted to sit up.

Alex caught her and helped her become upright.

"How are you? Can you hear us?" asked Sabine.

"I feel strange, really strange. My head hurts, but I feel amazing. I feel better than I ever have. It's like I've woken up from a really weird dream. I have no memory of getting here, though. Everything feels like a blur. The last thing I remember is being in Egypt in a theatre. There was a fire. I can't remember it really."

"You've got a lot to catch up on."

"Oh my god! OH MY GOD!" Judith had caught sight of her hair. It was draped over her shoulder so she could see the ends of it.

"I'm one of you! I've been made one of you. What did you do?" She began to panic and tried to stand up.

Alex laughed mirthlessly, just as another contraction descended on Anais. She held her breath. No one had noticed her pain yet. They were all fixated on Judith.

"Please sit down." He gently put his hand on her shoulder, effectively stopping her from standing. "You are now immortal, yes."

"But Rafe promised me. We made a deal."

Anais could barely make out the rest of the conversation as the pain filled all her senses. Then the pain softened as it had before, and she could hear Alex's reply.

"Rafe didn't do this to you. Andrew did."

"Andrew? Why?"

"It's a long story. It's a good thing he did, because right after that, he pulled a trigger that shot a bullet right through your brain. There is no way you would have survived it if you hadn't just been given The Light. It must have been really strong for you to survive a bullet through the brain, probably because it had just changed you. I doubt that any of us would survive that after all this time."

"Andrew shot me?" Judith once again looked confused.

"Right through the brain, I'm amazed you can still speak, even after taking The Light. Do you have any gaps in your memory except for the last few months?"

"I remember my childhood. I remember coming to England and falling in love with Rafe. Where is he, by the way?"

Anais didn't hear her reply. Another contraction had come on suddenly. She gritted her teeth, but this time it was too much. She let out a long moan of pain. As soon as she heard it, Aethelu was over by her side.

"What's up? Is something wrong with the baby?"

"Anais caught her breath and answered, "She's coming. I'm having contractions. I think they are about three minutes apart."

"You're kidding. Are you sure?"

I feel like I'm being stabbed in the stomach every three minutes. It's the most intense pain I've ever had, and I can barely breathe through it. I'm pretty sure that means I'm in labour.

"Oh, dear lord!" Aethelu started to panic. "This is the worst possible time for this to happen."

"I'm sorry, I'm sorry," cried Anais. She felt like she was putting them all in danger.

"Don't be silly. This isn't your fault." Aethelu hugged her tightly and kissed her forehead. "Oh, god, what are we going to do?"

Aethelu looked terrified as she looked at the others for help.

"I have delivered babies. I helped my sister deliver her two sons. I can help Anais through this," offered Judith.

"But you've just been shot in the head" replied Aethelu, rather stupidly.

"Just let her help," cried Anais as another pain came on. Now wasn't the time to argue.

"Ok, what do you need?" asked Alex.

"We need to make her comfortable. We need water and blankets."

Jennifer ran over to the side of the attic and came back with some old pillows and some thick blankets.

"No water," she announced.

"There is no water supply up here. It's just an attic." Alex passed the information to Judith.

"Then we will have to make do without."

"What else?" asked Aethelu.

"Nothing, now we wait."

"That's it? Wait?"

"Just wait. The baby will come in its own time."

Aethelu looked like she was just about to faint. She stood up and started to pace the floor and mumble to herself in a panic.

"Aethelu, can you help me push this furniture closer to the door? We need to keep Andrew out of here as long as possible." Sabine put her arm around Aethelu and led her to the furniture pile. It didn't need anything done to it, but if it kept Aethelu occupied, then, Anais was grateful for it. Alex excused himself to help, too, leaving Judith and Jennifer.

"Ok, I want you to listen to me. This is not going to be easy, but I know you can do it. I need to take a look and see how far you are from giving birth. Is that ok?"

Anais could hardly say no. She was just grateful there

was someone there who knew what they were doing. Jennifer stayed up by her head and stroked it, whilst Judith did goodness knows what at her other end. Jennifer began to sing a sweet, soft, melody, which calmed Anais.

"Egyptian lullaby," she smiled.

"Right, I'm afraid we are going to be in for a long night. You are going to have to listen to everything I say. It might not feel right, but it will help you deliver this baby safely. I want you to pant through each contraction and let me know when each starts so I can count them.

"Now!" gasped Anais and closed her eyes.

"Ok, breathe like me...Anais, I need you to look at me." Anais opened her eyes and looked straight at Judith. Her eyes were pools of glittering ink. She could see her own reflection in them, contorted in pain.

"Now breathe like me." She gave little pants, which Anais copied.

"Good, good, you are doing a good job. We are going to do that for each contraction. It helps to stop you panicking and regulates your breathing. It will give you something to focus on instead of the pain."

"Ok," replied Anais. She could feel beads of sweat starting to form on her forehead. Jennifer pulled an old-fashioned handkerchief out and dabbed it on her forehead.

An hour later, which seemed like much longer to Anais, nothing had changed. Her contractions were coming hard and fast, barely giving her a chance to catch her breath between them. Judith was still offering her encouragement and Jennifer was still singing her lullaby. Anais had no idea what the others were doing, but they were making enough noise, so they must have been doing something.

'What a stupid situation to end up in,' Anais mused between contractions, 'In full on labour whilst being chased by an immortal maniac trying to kill both me and my baby.' She'd have laughed at the absurdity of it if she weren't in so much pain.

"I don't think we can secure the place any more than we have," said Aethelu, returning. "How is she?"

"She is doing well. Things are progressing well. I think we should see this baby before morning."

Anais looked at the grandfather clock by the wall. It read 7 o'clock. It was only 7 pm. This baby would be here by morning? Was Judith insane? She felt like she was being ripped inside out and she'd only been doing this for an hour.

Aethelu took her hand. "Hear that honey? Autumn will be here before morning."

Anais wanted to swear, but Aethelu was saved her reaction by another contraction. There was no way she could do this for another ten minutes, let alone hours.

"How are things over there?" asked Jennifer.

"We've barricaded the door well. It will take a lot for Andrew to get through that door. Alex is looking for something to use as a weapon in case he manages it. It's all quiet down there, though. I've not heard any more gunshots since we got up here. He's not tried to get into the attic yet."

"Let's hope he doesn't. You can't hurry a baby along."

'What then?' wondered Anais.

The second hand on the grandfather clock moved extremely slowly it seemed to Anais, and yet, each second counted down to another contraction. The pain was intolerable and endless. After each contraction, she asked if she was ready for the pushing stage only to be greeted with a chuckle and a 'not yet' from Judith. At that moment, she'd have happily put a bullet through Judith's head herself. She mentally berated herself for thinking bad thoughts, but as yet another contraction took over her body, she only thought it more. In an effort to think about anything but pain, she concentrated on Judith's eyebrows. They looked weird. They were as white as her hair, as were her eyelashes. They were oddly beautiful, weird, but beautiful. They contrasted perfectly with her black eyes and dark skin.

The clock ticked and Jennifer sang. At midnight, the clock chimed twelve and still she was told that baby was still hours away. The agony was too much for her to bear. Even the short time between contractions was painful as her mouth was dry from all the panting. She needed a drink desperately. She felt so dehydrated.

"Drink!" she managed to croak.

"We don't have anything. Can anyone see anything to drink?" asked Aethelu, desperate to relieve any of the suffering of her wife.

After a fifteen-minute search of the attic, it was apparent that there wasn't any liquid up there.

"There's nothing. There's no plumbing up here." Alex shrugged his shoulders.

"This is not happening!" cried Aethelu. Suddenly she kissed Anais hand and ran to one of the huge windows. She opened it and crawled out before disappearing over the edge.

"Aethelu!" shouted Anais but couldn't say anything else as the pain was too much.

"Right," said Judith after she had examined her again. "Things are progressing. Very soon, you are going to feel the need to push. Don't."

"What do you mean, don't?" squealed Anais.

"Just wait for me to tell you when to push. If you push too soon, you could cause damage to yourself. It's going to take all your willpower not to follow your body's instructions, but I don't have any medical facilities if anything goes wrong. We have to slow it down to keep you and baby safe."

"Slow it down? I need it to speed up!"

"Just do as I say and you will be alright," smiled Judith.

Anais didn't like her advice, but she was right about wanting to push. It wasn't long before the urge to push overwhelmed her.

"I need to push," screamed Anais.

"No. No. Hold off, just a couple more contractions."

"I can't hold off. I need to push."

"Anais, look at me. Look at me. This baby is ready to come out. In an hour, she will be lying in your arms. She can only do that if you keep yourself strong and help her. In two minutes, I will let you push. Until then, you have to hold off."

Anais gritted her teeth and squeezed her eyes closed tight. It took everything she had to ignore what her body was telling her. She could feel Autumn's head pushing down. Now the pain changed. It wasn't daggers anymore. Her whole body now felt like it was being stretched to its limit.

"Right, Anais, this is it. On the next contraction, I want you to push. Push as hard as you can."

Anais took a deep breath and waited. As she felt the pressure of another contraction build up, she waited until it felt right, then she pushed with all her might. She had Jennifer's hand in hers on one side and Alex's on the other. Both were being squeezed tightly by Anais.

"Good," said Judith, "You did beautifully. Baby is right where we need her to be. Keep up pushing like that and she'll be out in no time."

On the next contraction, Anais pushed again. It was a

strange sensation. Apart from the pain, she could actually feel the baby moving down. Lower and lower until...

"Oh, my god. I can see her head." Alex grinned and then fainted. Anais ignored him, as did everyone else.

"Ok, Anais," began Judith, totally ignoring Alex on the floor beside her. "This is the one. On the next contraction, I want you to push as hard as you can and get ready to meet your baby."

She gave one big push and felt something slip out. Judith caught the baby and quickly cut the cord with a pair of scissors that someone had found earlier.

Anais looked at her daughter for the first time. A rush of love like she had never felt before overcame her and she started to cry. Judith placed her on Anais' chest and covered them both with a blanket to keep warm.

"She is healthy. Well done, mommy. You did a fine job." She had a huge smile on her face as well as an expression of complete exhaustion.

Anais looked down at the pink wriggling little girl in her arms. She was perfect. Beautiful. Even though she had only just been born, she had her eyes open and looked up at her mother. She seemed totally content in the warmth of Anais' arms. Judith began to clean up the resulting mess, along with Jennifer, although Anais hardly noticed. She was absorbed by this little creature in her arms. This tiny thing who was only a matter of minutes old, but who had already stolen her heart.

It was only when she heard a scream that she tore her eyes away from her little sweetheart. It had come from Aethelu who had just climbed in through the window, arms full of bottles of water and a bag with more in it. Seeing what was in Anais' arms, she dropped the bottles, which rolled all over the floor and ran straight over to them.

"Oh, she's so precious. I can't believe I missed it." She burst into tears.

"Well, you are here now. Do you want to hold your daughter?"

Anais passed Autumn over to a terrified-looking Aethelu.

"She's so small. What if I break her?"

"You won't break her," smiled Anais. "I really could do with a drink, though."

Alex, who had been woken up by Aethelu's scream, bounded over and picked up the bottles, passing one to Anais. Jennifer took another bottle and wetted a piece of cloth. She used the wet cloth to wash Anais' face and arms before passing the bottle and cloth to Judith.

"She really is beautiful. I think she looks like me," said Alex.

"Don't say horrible things about my daughter's looks," laughed Aethelu. "She's the spitting image of Anais. Look, she's even got a wisp of dark hair."

"I think you are right. She is a mini-Anais."

"I don't want to interrupt, but we still have a problem. We are still stuck up here with no way out and no food," said Jennifer.

"Aethelu got out. How did you do it?" asked Alex.

I climbed down the side of the house. I found a drain-pipe to shimmy down and then let myself into the kitchen. I packed a bag with food and drink and climbed back up."

"Did you see Andrew?" asked Jennifer, wide-eyed.

"No. I didn't see anyone. I don't know where anyone is or how they all are."

"Do you feel in a fit state to shimmy down a drainpipe?" Alex asked Anais only half-joking.

"She won't be going anywhere for the next few hours let alone down a drainpipe," replied Judith.

"Couldn't we tie all these old blankets together and somehow winch Anais and Autumn to the ground?"

"It's not that easy, though, is it?" replied Anais. "If it was just a matter of escaping, any one of us could have walked out of the front door at any point in the last few months. We didn't, though, did we?"

"Well, no, but Andrew was planning to unleash the virus."

"Exactly!"

"So why hasn't he done that now? He thinks Judith is dead. There's no reason to keep any of us alive anymore," wondered Aethelu out loud.

"I don't know," answered Alex.

"Oh, goodness me, she is so gorgeous," sighed Aethelu, looking down at her little girl and changing the subject. It was so hard to be worried about anything when a new life was in your arms. The danger was very real, though.

"Pass her over to her Uncle Alex. I want to talk to her."

Aethelu passed Autumn over to Alex. She'd fallen asleep and was now making gentle snuffling noises.

"Now, Autumn..." Alex began with a mock stern look on his face. "If ever either of your two mommies is being mean to you or won't let you have chocolate, then I'm your man."

"You, share chocolate? That would be a first!" Aethelu threw a teddy bear that someone had found at him.

"Careful! You nearly hit Autumn. See, baby, your mommy is already being mean to you." He stuck his tongue out at his sister, then stood up and took Autumn for a walk around the attic.

"Actually, that reminds me. I put some food in the bag for us. I couldn't fit a lot in, but I've got bread, meat, and fruit. I was going to put milk in for Autumn, but I don't think babies can have cow's milk can they?"

"No," replied Judith. "She needs special baby formula."

"Which we don't have. Even if we did, we don't have any bottles for her. Aren't you supposed to sterilise them before each feed?"

"Didn't you read the baby book I gave you?" asked an irritated Anais. She couldn't blame her. They were woefully unprepared. They didn't have the right baby equipment and the few bits they did have were downstairs in a room they couldn't get to.

"I don't even have diapers!" Anais burst into tears. She felt like a total failure as a mother and she'd only been one for half an hour.

Judith moved to her side. "Hush, now. You are doing fine. You can feed baby yourself, there are a lot of clothes up here that we can rip up and use for nappies. We have blankets to keep her warm. That is all she needs. You, on the other hand, need rest. It has been a long night and the dawn will be here soon. None of us knows what that will bring. I'll ask Alex to bring her back and you can have a go at feeding her.

"I'll sort out a bed for you both." Aethelu gave Anais a kiss. I love you. You are the most amazing woman I've ever met. I can't believe we have a daughter. Thank you."

Anais smiled. She felt more exhausted than she ever had in her life.

Alex came back and passed Autumn to Anais. He then disappeared to the end of the attic with Aethelu and Jennifer, presumably to find bedding.

"What if she doesn't want my milk?"

"She will, you will be fine. Just relax and keep hydrated."

Anais brought Autumn's mouth down to her breast where she latched on immediately."

"Told you," smiled Judith.

"Thank you, Judith. Thank you for everything. How are you feeling?"

"My head hurts, but it is strange. I feel really strong. I feel like I could lift a mountain. Is this what you all feel like all the time?"

Anais thought about it. "I can't honestly say that I've ever felt like I could move mountains, but I was born with The Light. I've never known any different. How is your head, though, apart from it hurting, I mean?"

"I can feel where the bullet went through, the path it took. It feels like a scar running right through my brain. I feel like things have been lost in my memory, but somehow my mind feels bigger than it ever has. I can remember things from my childhood that I had completely forgotten, not just events in general, but in detail, including colours and smells. I can even remember the words my grandmother said to me on my fourth birthday. It is amazing!"

"What did she say?"

"She told me not to eat any more cake or I'd be sick."

Anais laughed so abruptly that she made Autumn jump.

"Oh, sorry, darling."

"There is a big part of my memory that is hazy. My childhood, I recall with such clarity. I remember coming here. I remember being with Rafe. I don't remember anything else. Why did Andrew shoot me? Was he jealous of Rafe?"

"Just a bit," Anais sighed. Judith still didn't know Rafe was dead. Andrew had screamed it at her just before he shot her, but did she remember? Anais told her the full story, right from the start when Judith arrived in England to be with Andrew. She told her how she had fallen in love with Rafe and left Andrew and that Andrew had threatened to kill everyone. She told her about the virus and the time in

Egypt of which Judith had vague recollections. She left out no detail up to the point where Andrew shot her and Alex carried her up to the attic.

"So my beloved is dead." She spoke quietly but didn't cry. Anais admired her strength.

"I'm sorry."

"Do not be. This was not your fault. I always knew there was something dark in Andrew. Oh, he said the right words, did the right things. I really loved him when I came over to this country. For the first few weeks, I was so happy, but then, well, he changed. I can't put my finger on it, but he got secretive. He kept disappearing, leaving me alone for hours. He'd never tell me where he was."

"That was probably around the time he'd decided to blackmail us into making The Light. He wanted you to be immortal. I guess he got his wish."

"I never wanted to be immortal. I told him that. He said that if I loved him, I would want to be with him forever. Forever scared me. For me, immortality is in your children, and your children's children, not in a magic potion. Rafe understood. He respected my decision."

"Is that why you left Andrew for Rafe?"

"No, not at all, Andrew was acting very strangely. One night I told him I was going for a walk. He told me he was busy, so I went alone. It started to rain, so I changed my mind. When I came back to his room, he was just going into some kind of secret room. When he saw me, he got angry. Told me he'd kill me if I ever mentioned it. I fled the room and ran to the library. Rafe was there. I didn't tell him why I was upset. I think he thought I was homesick. He comforted me. After that, I was scared. Andrew started to treat me very badly. He accused me of having an affair with Rafe."

"Were you?"

"No, I wasn't. I'd only seen him that one time in the library. He gave me a hug and a shoulder to cry on, nothing more."

"Andrew has cameras all over the house. He probably saw you hugging Rafe and jumped to the wrong conclusion. Hang on a minute. Did you say that Andrew had a secret room?"

"Yes. I only saw it once. There is a secret door that goes from his bedroom."

"What was in there?"

"I don't really know. I didn't see in it."

"So what happened next?"

I made plans to fly home. I told Andrew that I didn't want to be here anymore. By that point, I didn't feel safe. He kept telling me that he was doing it for me, but he kept threatening me. I'd already booked my tickets when I bumped into Rafe one night in the kitchen. I told him I was going home. He convinced me to stay. He listened to me. I guess I fell in love with him then. I was lonely and afraid. Rafe was there," she paused. "And now he's gone."

"Look what we found!" Alex came back carrying an old-fashioned cot with Aethelu at the other end. "I don't know who it belonged to because we never had any babies here, but it seems in good condition. It looks like it has never been used.

"It never was used. I think it was bought when one of us got pregnant, but as you know, women of The Light can't have children."

"Us?" enquired Anais.

"Well not me, obviously. I dunno, Mamma, Ava, Audsley, whoever."

"I think that particular curse has been broken now though, hasn't it?" Alex chipped in.

"It was Andrew though wasn't it. It wasn't a curse at all."

"Shh, Alex, I just heard something."

"What?"

"Shhh!" They all quieted down. Suddenly the noise came again. It was a key turning in the lock at the bottom of the stairs. Anais had to strain to hear, but she was sure she had heard it.

"Andrew!"

"What are we going to do?" Anais suddenly felt fear like never before. She had been through a lot in the last couple of years, but now she had Autumn to consider. She was not scared of her own death or suffering, but if anything ever happened to Autumn, she didn't think she could bear it.

"Ok, don't panic," said Sabine "We piled a lot of furniture behind that door. There is no way he can get in." She didn't look too sure of that fact herself.

The door made a sound as if being pushed from the other side but then stopped. The sheer amount of furniture had stopped Andrew from being able to move it more than a couple of millimetres. They all waited to see, or rather hear what Andrew would do next. He rattled the door a few times and then went silent.

They all looked at each other, not knowing what was going to happen next.

"Has he gone?" whispered Jennifer.

Nobody answered. There was not a noise to be heard. Suddenly the door started to rattle again, this time with more ferocity. There followed a loud bang, then another.

"He's trying to break the door down," Aethelu said hastily. She picked up Autumn and sat down close to Anais. Anais held her hand. She was shivering slightly.

Fear rippled through Anais. It was obvious that Andrew wouldn't be able to get past the furniture, but she was scared all the same. She could hear him screaming in a rage at the unmoving door below. Even though she was sure he wouldn't be able to get to them, there was nothing to stop him setting off one of his traps, if, indeed, he had one set up in the attic. They still had the threat of his Jagovirus to deal with, and what with them being stuck up in the attic, there was little chance of them being able to sort out that particular problem. Worst of all, she had no idea if the others, downstairs, were ok.

The banging stopped as abruptly as it had started. The waited for a few minutes, but Andrew had obviously given up.

None of the group spoke for a good few minutes until Alex piped up. "Do you think he's gone?"

"We've not heard the end of him. In fact, his being quiet is much more terrifying to me than him banging on the attic door. At least then, I know where he is and what he's doing," replied Anais.

"Well he's quiet now, at least, yawned Alex. It's been a long, long, night. I don't know about any of you, but I'm exhausted. I can barely keep my eyes open. We can't fight the madman on no sleep. Why don't we all catch some sleep and take it in turns to stay on guard; wake the others if he tries anything else?"

"I'll take first watch," said Anais quickly.

"Don't be silly," replied Aethelu. "You'll be the most exhausted out of all of us. If anyone needs rest, it's you."

"She is right," interjected Judith. You have had a difficult night. Your body needs its rest to be strong for your baby. I understand that you will not want to part with her in these circumstances, but we will look after her well and she will not leave your side unless she cries."

Anais understood that everyone meant well, and she

was more worn-out than she had ever been in her life, but she just wanted to hold her little girl a few moments longer. She wanted her all to herself, to look into her tiny perfect sleeping face, to gaze down at innocence. She didn't want to give that up, not even for a second.

"I am tired, but I can't sleep just yet. How about I take the first watch, just for an hour?"

Aethelu looked like she was about to argue, but then, she just wrapped her arm around Anais, gave Autumn a light kiss on the forehead and spoke.

"I agree. Let Anais have her time with Autumn."

Anais was surprised at this but grateful when the others found bits of old bedding and made themselves as comfortable as possible on the hardwood floor. Within minutes, the sounds of heavy breathing and soft snoring filled the air. Aethelu lay next to her, not sleeping but gazing down at her newborn daughter.

"I thought you were going to sleep?" whispered Anais.

"And miss this? Not a chance! This is our first day as a family. I want to treasure every moment."

"I wonder if it will be our last?"

"Shhh. We are going to watch our beauty here grow up. I'm going to walk her down the aisle at her wedding!"

Anais smiled. She wished she had the confidence that Aethelu had. Anais wasn't even sure there was going to be a tomorrow let alone a date so distant in the future. She looked down at her child. A small plump fist waved in the air slightly before coming back to rest. Autumn had not even woken up. Her mouth made little sucking motions as if she was having baby dreams about drinking milk. Anais hoped Aethelu was right. Neither girl spoke for the longest time. They just gazed at their daughter sleeping. Eventually, Aethelu took Autumn out of Anais' arms.

"It's been two hours and you promised you'd sleep after one hour. I'm watching her. You need to sleep. I'll wake you when it's feeding time."

Anais couldn't argue. Her eyelids had never felt so heavy. She gratefully closed her eyes and drifted off to sleep.

Sabine woke her a few hours later. She must have swapped watch duty with Aethelu at some point as Aethelu was snoring lightly beside her.

"Sorry to wake you, but I think she is hungry."

Indeed, Autumn was wailing and flailing her little fists around. She looked pretty angry with the world for not feeding her soon enough.

"I tried to soothe her by walking her around, but she wouldn't go back to sleep."

"Thanks, Sabine. I'll take her. Get some sleep."

"Thank you!" Sabine looked relieved to be passing the screaming infant back. "No news from Andrew. It's been pretty quiet. Jennifer is doing the next watch."

Anais walked Autumn over to the far side of the room, trying not to disturb the others. She found an old wooden chair and sat in it. Autumn latched on immediately and suckled happily. Anais was grateful that her daughter was so good at feeding. The last thing she needed was a fussy baby. With Autumn settled, she looked over at the magnificent model of The Manor and its grounds that Andrew had made many years before. It really was the most intricate, beautiful piece of work. She could see the switch that turned the lights on just under the table. She wouldn't be able to reach it with her hand without disturbing Autumn, but with her bare foot, if she stretched a little, she might just be able to reach it. Using her sock covered big toe she flicked the switch, which brought the little model to life. She knew that the roof lifted off and each floor came apart, but at the moment, the model was in one piece She could see the cottage at the end of the drive with the miniature August and a dog in the garden. She felt a momentary pang of sadness and wiped away a tear. The other tiny inhabitants of the house were all inside the main building apart from Alex who was outside against a car. She cast her eyes around the rest of the model. It covered the land around the manor. Thousands of tiny trees covered the huge table, and even some of the surrounding houses were represented. It really was the most amazing model. Each tree had been lovingly painted and placed around the house. As she looked closer, she could see the red of the tramway she had once travelled on with Aethelu. That was before Andrew had killed Mike, the man who had run the tramway. Despite Aethelu promising to take her on the tram again, it had never happened. As she watched, the little model trams moved towards each other and then passed each other. Anais had never seen the little trams moving before, but they were so small between the thousands of trees that they were not too easy to spot. She wondered if she had missed anything else on the model. She stood up, careful not to dislodge Autumn. She walked slowly around the table with the model on. Even the little nearby houses had tiny lights in their windows. A road that led to the manor, Anais recognised as the road from the nearby village. A few little houses at the corner of the table were enough to see that Andrew had started modelling the village, even if he had run out of space. She even recognised the houses. Tiny curtains hung in each little window. The detail was really quite spectacular. What a waste of his talent. It was really quite strange that the creator of this wonderful piece of artwork was somewhere in the house below them, plotting their deaths no doubt. Suddenly she felt a hand on her shoulder. She jumped, making Autumn cry for a couple of seconds before she calmed down and closed her eyes.

"Oh, sorry!" It was Aethelu. "I didn't mean to startle you...sorry, Autumn!" she added to the baby in a soft voice.

"Don't worry. I think she is full now anyway. Look, she's gone right back to sleep."

"Which you should be doing. I'll take the little princess."

"Oh, don't call her that. What if she's a tomboy?"

"She'll be my tomboy princess then," laughed Aethelu as Anais handed her over.

"I was just looking at the model and thinking it's such a shame Andrew turned out like he did. He has such amazing talent. I mean look at these little houses on the end of the village. He didn't have to add them, but I suppose he wanted everything perfectly correct and to scale."

"He always was a bit OCD like that. Everything had to be just so with him. Mind you, he's made a mistake here." She pointed to a patch of land just in front of the first house.

"What do you mean?"

"Well, this is the entrance to the village. You can see he's only managed to fit a few of the houses on, but in front of this one, in the real village is a small bit of land with a bench and some flowers in it. I sometimes sat there when I walked into the village."

"Why did he leave it out?"

"Actually, I don't think he did. I remember it being on there the last time I looked. He'd filled it with the tiniest daffodils and tulips. Look, you can see right through to the board underneath. It must have fallen off."

Anais looked at the small square of board. It was only about two centimetres square, but something caught her eye. She peered closer. The bit of model that had come away had been forcibly pulled up. It had damaged the table underneath.

"Is it just a garden? Is there anything else there?"

"There's nothing else there, just a bench...oh, and a stone. You know, one of those old village marker stones that they used to have in olden days. I think they found it about twenty years ago in someone's yard and decided to bring it back to the village. It had one of those plaques on the side telling the story. Why?"

"It's just weird that it's been pulled off the board."

"It could have fallen off."

"I don't think so. Someone's pulled it off, and if you look clearly they've put a small x with a marker pen in its place."

Aethelu looked down at where Anais was pointing, being careful not to bang Autumn's head on the side of the table. "What are you thinking?"

"It's just a silly idea, but what if Andrew ripped this off. Think about it. If you were planning on hiding lots of small objects but wanted to remember where they were, or plan where to hide them, what better way than to mark them on a map."

"Or a scale model. Oh my goodness, you are a genius. Andrew said that he'd hidden one of those vials in the village. I bet you're right. Quick, lift the top of the house off to check if he's marked where the others are."

Anais carefully lifted the roof off and placed it on the floor. She then removed the attic level, the second floor, and the first floor. The ground floor was now on the same level as the table. (The kitchen and cellar were built into the underside of the table.) She peered into the library and moved the miniature copy of the painting that covered the safe. Andrew hadn't bothered to build a little safe into his model but there, on the model wall was an unmistakeable x inked in black.

"I don't believe it!" exclaimed Aethelu. "Quick, check the painting in the hallway."

Anais moved the miniature portrait of Alex and Rafe. Behind it was another x.

"We have to check this whole model to find the others!"

"Not now," yawned Anais. "It's going to take hours to find all the crosses and we've barely had any sleep. Let's leave everyone sleeping and go through it tomorrow when there is more light."

"Good idea. You need to rest. I'll watch Tomboy Princess here and wake you when she's hungry again." Aethelu kissed Anais on the cheek and walked with her to where the others were sleeping. Anais lay down and was out like a light.

The next morning, it wasn't Autumn screaming for milk that woke her, but the excited voices of the others crowded around the model. Alex sat on the floor examining the top floor of the house, Sabine had the second and first floors, Judith had the ground floor, and Aethelu had somehow managed to dismantle the lower floors and was examining them. Jennifer sat near to Anais, singing softly to Autumn, who was contentedly looking up at her.

"I have changed her. I had to put the soiled clothes over in the corner, as there is nowhere else to put them. I did my best to clean her up without running water."

"She certainly seems happy right now. Thank you for looking after her."

"It is no problem. She is a pleasure."

Anais took Autumn and gave her a swift kiss on the cheek. Autumn responded by burping loudly and then crying.

"Charming!" smiled Anais. She took her over to one of the large windows and fed her daughter. She was beginning to feel hungry herself. Once Autumn had had her fill, she placed her on a bundle of clothes nearby where she promptly fell asleep. Anais took a look in the bag that Aethelu had brought up the day before. There wasn't much there. Probably enough for them all to eat today, but no more. She grabbed a small bottle of water, a bread roll, and a couple of slices of meat, which she hastily made into a sandwich. She gobbled it down quickly and then, when she still felt hungry, wished she had slowed down a bit. She couldn't eat anymore. It wouldn't be fair to anyone else. She contented herself by opening the water and sipping on that instead.

There was a loud cheer from the other side of the room.

"We've found another. There's an x in Andrew's bedroom!" yelled Alex across to her.

They had found nine vials in their earlier hunts. The x in Andrew's room meant that they had found the hiding place of another vial. Those and the one in the village gave them a grand total of eleven vials, eleven out of twenty-one. They still had ten to find. That is, if they were correct in the assumption that Andrew had marked all his hiding spots on the model. It certainly seemed that way. It took them most of the day searching the model to find the other crosses. There was one in the cellar. It took so long to find because it was underneath the tiny model of the computer. One in the parlour, one at the end of the driveway near the main gate and four in the attic, two of which they had already accounted for. They also found the crosses for the vials they had already found. That only gave them a total of fourteen vials in the house and grounds, fifteen including the one in the village.

Anais spent the day changing and feeding Autumn, so she didn't help in the hunt, but there were so many of them peering over the model that she would have just been in the way. The only other person who not searching the model was Aethelu. She repeated her expedition to the kitchens, despite Anais' protestations. She came back with more food than she had the day before, once again, seeing no one on her travels.

Eventually, at the end of the day, they conceded defeat. They had looked over every inch of the model and only come up with those three more crosses. That meant they still had four to find. Even if they did find them, they still had to find a way to disable the mechanisms that would break them.

"Alex? Didn't you already find two vials in the Attic? This model shows there are another two up here."

"I'm on it." He got up and began to search one end of the attic. The others followed his lead and between them they covered the whole attic.

"It's spooky," murmured Aethelu, between mouthfuls of food that she ate as she searched. "The kitchen looks the same as it always did. It's almost like Mama has just nipped out for a second."

The others were eager for information from her foray into the house downstairs, but they didn't give up in looking for the vials. Instead, they had a shouted conversation whilst they searched.

"Does it look like anyone else has been in the kitchen?" shouted Alex, obviously worrying about the rest of his family. They still didn't know if the others had escaped or if they were trapped in another part of the house.

"There were some food wrappers on the table which I'm certain weren't there yesterday, but they could have been left there by Andrew. I wanted to go to the other parts of the house, but I was too scared to. Andrew could be anywhere."

"Don't worry. The last thing we need right now is you getting caught. We'd not have this food if you had been." Anais held out her hand to Aethelu.

"I got one," came a scream from the far end of the Attic. Anais looked around and saw Judith with a vial in her hand. It had been hidden in an old chest of drawers, thankfully, one that hadn't been thrown down the stairs to barricade the door.

"This is just the one we found earlier," exclaimed Alex. Sorry, I guess I should have told you where it was.

Anais and Aethelu both rolled their eyes at him.

The others ran over to her and examined it. It was strange to see it up close. The vial contained a liquid that swirled as it moved. It looked the way oil would look if it was poured on water. Two separate densities of liquid swirled together, one red and one blue. They didn't mix to form a purple colour but rather danced around each other a little like a lava lamp. The mechanism looked pretty simple, but there were two wires attached from a battery pack to the vial.

"Which one do we pull out?" asked Judith fearfully.

"Both?"

"Isn't it always the red one in movies?"

"Give it here," demanded Alex. Judith was only too happy to pass the vial over.

He opened the battery pack and pulled two normal household batteries out. The little light that had shown it was operational flickered out.

"Idiot!" shouted Aethelu, whilst hitting him on the arm. "That could have set the mechanism off. You can't just go taking the batteries out!"

"You are the one that is dangerously close to knocking it out of my hands and smashing it. Besides, it worked didn't it?"

They all peered at the vial. The blue and red still swirled around aimlessly.

Alex wrapped up the vial as carefully as he could and set it down at the end of the attic. He then got the second one that had been found earlier and put it with the first. After another half hour of searching, Jennifer found the third vial located in the attic inside the dummy that held Arcadia's dress.

Alex removed the batteries from this one and put it with the other two.

The last one was accidentally found by Anais. She'd given up searching, as Autumn had started screaming for milk, and had sat on the windowsill so she could look out over the garden. It was actually a little red light that she noticed first. Andrew had opened the window and attached the vial to the outside. She called Alex over. He deftly opened the window and reached out for the vial.

At this rate, we should be able to find all the vials," she said to Alex.

"It's not safe to carry on like this, though," he replied. We can't stay up here indefinitely. Aethelu will get caught getting food from the kitchen sooner or later. We need to escape!" He stood up like a man on a mission. "We have the same problem as we did before. If we leave, Andrew breaks open the vials, everyone dies." Sabine smiled at him as he sat back down.

"We know where most of the vials are now, though. There is nothing to stop us climbing down the way Aethelu did and finding them all. We can do what August did and bury them somewhere deep in the woods where no one will ever find them."

"What about Andrew?" asked Judith.

"We kill him. He has nothing on us now. There are five of us here. We could easily overpower him."

"Don't underestimate him," cautioned Anais. "How many times have we said it would be easy to overpower him only for him to find a way to hurt us first? I don't care that there are five of us to his one. He'll have something up his sleeve. He's not stupid."

"Four," said Aethelu.

"Four?"

"Four against one, I'm not letting you come into the main house. Autumn needs you. You can stay up here to look after her whilst we go down."

"I can't let you go down without me."

"Aethelu is right," said Judith "You only gave birth twenty-four hours ago. Your body needs to recuperate."

Anais had to admit defeat. The truth was that she was afraid to be left alone up in the attic with Autumn. What if none of them came back? It would be just her and the baby. Aethelu seemed to know what she was thinking.

"Don't worry. We'll kill him and then come back for you. There's no way I'm leaving my girls any longer than I have to." She hugged Anais tightly.

'It felt nice being wrapped up in the warmth of Aethelu, soft and warm, like home. It made her eyelids droop. She closed them for a second...

When she opened them, she found herself lying with her head on Aethelu, using her as a pillow. Aethelu was asleep on the hard floor beside her. She sat up confused. Looking around her, she saw the others all asleep on the floor. Jennifer was stirring. Why were they all asleep?

Suddenly a fear gripped her. Autumn! She ran over to the pile of clothes where she had left her daughter sleeping. Autumn wasn't there. She ran to the old cot in the hope that one of the others had moved the baby there. It was empty.

"Aethelu! Alex!" she screamed. Her heart pounded so hard that she could hear the blood pumping in her ears and she could barely breathe. The others woke, stretched, and yawned. They had the same look of confusion on their faces that Anais had felt moments earlier.

"Andrew's taken Autumn. He must have piped sleeping gas into the attic and taken her when we were all asleep."

The others jumped up. Jennifer immediately began to search the room looking for Autumn. Judith followed her lead and searched the opposite side of the attic. Aethelu ran over to Anais and hugged her, both girls sobbing.

"How did he get in?" asked Sabine. They all looked to the entrance of the attic. It was still piled high with furniture. There was no way anyone could have got through it.

"He must have seen me climbing through the window and followed suit. Oh, Anais, I'm so sorry!"

Anais stroked her head. "It's not your fault. We need to get her back."

"Bastard!" yelled Alex. His face reddened with rage. He ran to the window Aethelu had used to climb out. He opened it and stepped out onto the ledge.

"Wait!" shouted Judith. "We need a plan. We cannot just go out there."

"Oh, I have a plan. I plan to rip Andrew's head from his body and then burn it." He grabbed the drainpipe and started to shimmy down it.

"Sounds good to me." Aethelu followed her brother out of the window. Anais was right behind her.

"You are not strong enough to do this. You have not long

since given birth." Judith came up behind her and put her hand on Anais' shoulder.

"If you think I'm going to wait up here whilst..."

Judith interrupted her, "I wouldn't dream of telling you to stay up here. I merely wanted to help you climb down. Here take my hand and I'll lower you to Aethelu."

Anais smiled a small smile through her tear-stained face.

Jennifer was the last to climb down. She wasn't as strong or as quick as the others, and it took her a long time to navigate the difficult path down the side of the building. At a few points, Anais was sure she was going to fall although she quickly grew impatient waiting for her, knowing that Andrew had her baby. Eventually, Jennifer made the last few steps and jumped to the ground.

"I went in through the kitchen before." They were close to the kitchen door so it made sense to get in that way. They jumped over the courtyard wall, not bothering to run to the gate, and Alex grabbed the kitchen door handle and turned.

"It's locked."

"What? Wait, it can't be." Aethelu pushed him out of the way and grabbed the handle herself. She rattled it and pulled it, but the door wouldn't budge. In frustration, she kicked the door. "It wasn't locked before."

"Andrew must know we'd come after Autumn. He's not going to make it easy for us," Anais said.

"Let's try the front door," Jennifer suggested. Anais knew it would be locked, too, but what choice did they have? They ran around to the front of the house only for Anais' suspicions to be confirmed. The front doors were locked, probably bolted on the inside, too.

"What now? This is the only other way in," said Judith.

"There's the tunnel from Augusts cottage. We could try that."

Alex ran down the front steps and Anais was just about to follow him until she saw that he was not heading to the cottage. Instead, he'd run into the middle of the lawn. He picked up the stone birdbath, slopping water all down his back, which he seemed not to notice. He threw it as hard as he could at the nearest window. There was a loud smash and the tinkle of falling glass as the birdbath sailed right through the window of the dining room. Anais and the others ran down the big stone steps and joined Alex as he climbed in through the hole left by the birdbath.

Anais was the next to climb through the hole, followed by Aethelu, Judith, then Jennifer with Sabine bringing up the rear.

The dining room was carnage. The body of the priest still lay on the floor where he had fallen, the blood from his head now a dried puddle on the floor beneath him. The food on the plates had not been taken away and now lay in rotting piles. Flies hovered around the mess and between the priest's corpse and the food, the room smelled ghastly. Anais held her hand up to her nose and tried not to be sick.

"He's not in here. Let's go." They all had to step over the body of the priest to get through the door to the main hall. Anais looked behind her to see Judith picking up a clean napkin and placing it on the dead priests face.

"Sorry," Judith whispered as she caught Anais looking at her.

Once inside the main hall, they stopped in a small group. The hall itself looked like it always had. The early morning light shone through the stained glass windows leaving colourful shadows across the walls. There was no sign of any struggle except one of the little side cabinets now lay on its side with the vase that it had been holding, smashed to pieces on the floor.

"What now? We split up?"

"No!" said Sabine, "Staying together keeps us strong. If we split up, it weakens us. You know he has cameras everywhere. He knows where we are."

"Well, watch this Andrew!" shouted Aethelu to nowhere in particular. She ran across the hall and ripped the painting of Alex and Rafe off the wall, exposing the vial behind it. Two wires were connected it to a small box, which Anais assumed to be a battery box and some kind of remote sensor. A little red light blinked from it. The wires were both black.

Anais watched her struggling for a second with the battery pack.

"What's taking so long? Just take the batteries out."

"I can't! This is different from the ones in the attic."

Alex picked up a shard of the broken vase and ran over to his sister. "Just cut the wires then."

"It's not like the movies. There's no choice between a red and a black wire. Which wire do I cut?"

"Let me see." Alex moved next to his sister and studied the box closely. He seemed to take an age to Anais, who didn't care about the box or vials at all at that moment. He only concern was for her daughter.

"Hurry up," she shouted unhelpfully.

"If we cut the wrong one, we could set off the mechanism," hissed Alex.

Jennifer solved the problem. She squeezed herself between Aethelu and Alex and pulled the whole thing off the wall; vial, wires, box, and all. She pulled a small cloth bag from her pocket, unfolded it and placed the vials and box into it.

Everyone stared at her.

"We'll bury it later, just like August did."

"You genius!"

Jennifer grinned shyly.

"Ok, great. We've got one of the vials. We need to find Autumn."

"Yes we do!" agreed Alex.

"We have to remember that even though we have some of the vials, Andrew still has the remote control over them, and he can see everything we are doing."

"Oh, damn!" none of them had thought of that. Anais, quite frankly, didn't care. Let Andrew do what he wanted. If she didn't find Autumn, nothing mattered anyway.

"He won't be able to do anything when I find him!" she yelled as she ran up the huge staircase. She could hear the others following behind her. At the top, she was in such a rush that she tripped over something that wasn't there before. She heard someone behind her scream. Picking herself off the floor, she turned to see what it was that had tripped her. It was Ava, or what was left of her. Her body was ripped to shreds. It was so bad that she was barely recognisable. Holes punctuated her body uniformly in a line, marked by red blotches of blood. Something had gone right through her, perforated the entire length of her small body.

"What the hell happened to her?" screamed Aethelu.

"I don't know, but it got Alfred, too, look."

Anais looked a little way down the corridor in the direction of Alex's bedroom and saw Alfred's body reaching out to his wife. He, too, had the strange holes running through his body.

Sabine ran towards him, but something happened before she got to his body. There was a flash of light and a strange noise and Sabine was on the floor screaming.

"Sabine!" Alex started to run towards her, but Anais grabbed him just in time and pulled him back. The flash of light and a metallic sound happened again. This time, they all saw what it was. A column of sharp skewer-like metallic rods came out of the wall and disappeared back in so quickly that they were difficult to see. Anais looked closely and could see where they had left little holes punctured in the wallpaper.

"Sabine, are you alright?" asked Anais.

The sharp points had just scratched down Sabine's back but seemed to have missed her vital organs. The blood that had been pouring out of the wounds was already beginning to clot thanks to her Light blood. Her leg had got the worst of it. Three of the skewers had gone right through her leg.

"I think so. I can't stand, though. My leg bone has been shattered. You have to go on without me."

"Like hell!" argued Alex.

"Alex. What can you do for me here? If you try to come near me, you'll end up with holes right down your body. Leave me here, find Andrew, then turn this mechanism off. Then you can save me."

"Andrew has planned this for a long time," interjected Judith. When was this hallway last decorated?

Alex gave her a strange look, but Aethelu answered her. "About twenty years ago, I think. Why?"

"Because these swords have cut through the wallpaper. They have been in this wall since before it was decorated. He's been planning this for at least as long as this wallpaper has been up."

"Since he fell in love with my mother. This was always about her."

"Go!" yelled Sabine "stare al sicuro, il mio amore. Uccidilo per me."

"Ti amo con tutto il cuore," answered Alex in Sabine's native Italian. "Tornerò per te." He blew her a kiss and turned away from her, towards the next staircase up to the floor that had Andrew's bedroom on it.

Instead of running straight down the hallway, he moved cautiously with his arms in front of him in case of any more of Andrew's surprises.

They all reached the bottom of the next flight of stairs without anything happening. Alex carried on his slow pace all the way up the stairs and down the corridor which held Andrew's bedroom and the room in which Anais had been held captive for the first few weeks she was here. The door at the end of the corridor, the one that led to the attic was in pieces. Andrew had obviously attacked it in such a rage that it now hung off its hinges. It had been the sheer mass of furniture piled up behind it that had stopped him from entering the room. A small chest of drawers had tumbled out and emptied its contents all over the floor.

Alex ignored the mess and went straight for Andrew's door. To Anais' surprise, it opened without having to be forced. Alex strode straight in. Anais was just about to follow when there was a loud bang followed by Alex's body flying backwards into her and sending them both crashing into the corridor wall opposite. Anais fell to the floor with Alex on top of her. There was a distinct smell of burning.

"Bastard!" coughed Alex. "He's put some sort of electric field around his door." He wheezed and coughed again. "Sorry, Anais."

He pulled himself off her and turned to help her up. His hair was singed and his clothes were smoking, but he was standing and strong enough to pull her up.

"Are you ok?" she asked him. His face was also blackened.

"I'll survive," he spluttered. He picked up the nearby chest of drawers, spilling the small amount it still contained and repeated his earlier trick. He threw the drawers through the door at Andrews computer. It crashed to the floor taking the monitor with it. The resulting spark set the drawers alight but the electric field had been disengaged.

"Judith, how did he open his secret room?" asked Anais hurriedly. The fire was already spreading to the curtains. She needed to get to Autumn fast if indeed her baby was in the secret room.

"I don't know. The wall over there was open, but I only saw it the one time. I don't know how he operated it."

Anais ran over to the wall and beat her fists ineffectually against it. Nothing happened. She could feel the heat building to one side of her. Aethelu, Judith and Jennifer started pressing everything they could see in the hope it was a secret button or lever to open up the wall. Alex ran against the wall next to where Anais was standing in the hope of knocking the wall down. It didn't work. The fire had engulfed the whole of the curtains and was now licking its way across the floor, sending the carpet up in flames.

"We have to get out of here," yelled Jennifer. Anais knew she must have been remembering the last time the both of them had been caught up in a burning room.

"I can't leave my baby!"

"We will die in here if we don't leave!" The fire had now flown across the ceiling. The heat was making Anais sweat. There was no way she was going to leave this room without Autumn. She was just about to say something to that effect when there was a whoosh and the wall opened.

"Found it!" yelled Judith over the roar of the fire.

The room behind the secret door was very small, about eight feet by six feet. There was a table covered with all kinds of strange looking instruments, some shelves with all kinds of computer parts on it and what looked like a row of computer screens although they were all turned off. It was very apparent that there was no Andrew and, more importantly, no Autumn.

"Where is she?" wailed Anais. Aethelu grabbed her arm and pulled her back through the fire to the corridor. They closed the door behind them, but smoke continued to billow out from under the door.

"We need to search the house. Get everyone out. There's no telling how much of the building this fire will destroy," shouted Alex.

"There's nobody up in the attic. Where does that door lead?" asked Jennifer.

"It's my old bedroom," replied Anais. It was doubtful that Andrew would have taken Autumn in there, but she had to check. She opened the door. It was exactly as it had been the last time she had seen it.

"No one here. What about the other side of the steps."

"Whose bedrooms are over there?" asked Judith.

"Well, Alfred and Ava were in one of the rooms. Audsley was in another," replied Alex.

They ran down the corridor, past the staircase to the doors. The first one on the left was Ava and Alfred's room. It was empty, as they had left it. Aethelu checked Audsley's room, whilst Anais checked the en-suite. Jennifer checked in the little shower room, whilst Alex looked behind the other doors, which were used as cupboards and storage.

"Anything?" asked Judith when they all congregated back in the corridor. Smoke was beginning to creep down the corridor, although Anais could see no flames yet.

"Nothing, come on, let's go." They ran back towards the fire. Anais couldn't believe she had to deal with fire again.

She had turned to the stairs to descend when suddenly there was a beep and it began to rain on her head. At first, she thought it was another of Andrew's tricks, but then she realised it was just sprinklers. The heat must have set them off. Andrew must have had them installed. At least it meant that the fire would be extinguished. She was sopping wet but rather that than burnt to death. The sprinklers must have been localised, because once they were down on the first floor, it was dry. Sabine sat up as they approached.

"Did you find her?" she asked expectantly, but then her face dropped as it became apparent they hadn't. "Why are you all so wet?"

"Fire upstairs. My fault. How are you?"

"Still in pain. I'm afraid I can't stand up. I think there's someone down this corridor, though. I'm sure I heard voices earlier."

"Did it sound like Andrew? Did you hear a baby?"

"No, it was a woman's voice. I think it might have been your Mother."

"We need to get to her." Alex put his hand out in front of him and waved it slightly until the movement hit the sensor, then he drew it back quickly before the skewers went right through his hand. They flew out and back in the blink of an eye. Alfred and Ava wouldn't have stood a chance against them.

"We need to get past these. How can we do it? Do you think I'll be quick enough to run through?" he asked to no one in particular.

"Is it worth risking your life to try it? Sabine was going through pretty fast, but it still managed to get her. Besides, you can't get much of a run up because there are some behind us, too. There must be, what else would have skewered Ava?" pointed out Aethelu.

"What then?"

"You are really quick, Alex." said Anais.

"I know. I honestly think I could make it, even though there's not much space to get a run-up."

"No, that's not what I meant. I agree with Aethelu. I wouldn't want you to risk running through them."

"What then?"

"Do what you just did. Activate the sensor. They only look sharp on the end. They are cylindrical down the whole shaft of them. When they come out, try to grab one. Then if you can catch it before it goes back in you can hold it back. They will all be attached to each other. If you can hold one back, they all stay back. Then we can squeeze past them."

"Ok, I'll give it a go." He motioned the sensor, and again, the spikes flew out and back in.

"Wow. It's really fast!" exclaimed Alex.

"You can do it! You were always the fastest when we were kids," Aethelu cheered him on.

He set the sensor again and attempted to grab them as they came out. He missed by quite a bit.

"Try again."

He tried again. The same thing happened.

"I think I was closer that time."

Anais held her breath. 'Please do it, please do it' she whispered to herself.

And this time he did. He caught the very end. He grabbed a higher spike to get a better grip and held it back.

"Yes!" Aethelu squeezed past and over to Sabine.

Judith went next. "I hope you are holding them tightly" she grinned as she edged her way past, followed by Anais and Jennifer.

Alex did a complicated manoeuvre where he swapped

hands and sidled past the spikes. He let them go and they disappeared back into the wall.

"You guys go on ahead. I'll stay with Sabine." He knelt down to her side.

Anais, Judith, and Jennifer rushed down the corridor.

Winnie and Aldrich's room was locked. Aethelu banged on it.

"Mama? Daddy?"

"Aethelu? Is that you?"

"Yes, Mama, we are all here. Open the door."

There was the sound of a key being turned and Winnie opened the door. She looked worn. Aethelu put her arms around her mother. Winnie burst into tears.

"I thought you were all dead. I didn't know what had happened to you. Come in."

She ushered them all into the huge bedroom. Alex followed the girls with Sabine in his arms.

"Are Audsley and Arcadia with you?"

"No, are they not here?"

"No. I don't know what happened to them. I didn't know what had happened to you. Oh, Sabine, love," exclaimed Winnie. What happened? Quick Alex, put her down on this rug. I'll get some bandages. I'm afraid there's no space on the bed."

Anais looked over. Both Aldrich and James were bloodied and unconscious laid out on the bed. Winnie disappeared into what Anais took to be an en-suite and re-emerged a few seconds later with some ointment and some bandages.

"The spikes! I suppose you saw that they killed Ava and Freddie. They got your father and James, too, but just grazed them. I was lucky enough to get past before Andrew activated them, so they didn't get me."

"If they only grazed Dad and James, why are they both laid on the bed?"

"The tips of the spikes are poisoned. Andrew left nothing to chance. They were both fine for a while, but they've been unconscious for the past couple of days. Whatever the poison is, it's not killed them. I'm sorry, but Sabine will be unconscious within the hour. I can bandage her up, but really, it's not the bleeding that's the problem."

Alex burst into tears. Sabine stroked his face. "Don't worry. I trust that we'll get out of this. Go find the baby." She closed her eyes, which made Alex cry even more.

"Baby?" asked Winnie, as she looked toward Anais. Her eyes grew wide.

"She was born a couple of nights ago. Oh, Mama, she's perfect, beautiful."

"I'm a grandma?" Winnie sobbed. "Where is she?"

"Andrew took her in the night. We think he pumped sleeping gas into the attic where we were hiding and stole her."

"Oh!" A look of shock spread over Winnie's face. "Oh, darlings." She enveloped both Aethelu and Anais into a huge hug. "She came early. She must be so tiny. Is she healthy?"

"She was born healthy. She is small, but she will need feeding soon or she won't stay that way," Anais replied.

"Oh, the poor little mite. How are you doing?" she asked Anais.

"I'm fine, Winnie, but we have to find her."

"Of course, we do. I can't leave Aldrich and James here alone, though."

"I'll stay. That way I can look after Sabine, too," replied Alex.

"We need you to get through the Spikes. You are the only one fast enough to stop them."

"I can't leave her," he cried.

"I'll stay." Jennifer knelt down beside Alex. "I'll look after her."

"Come on then. He gently kissed Sabine's cheek and softly rested her head on the rug."

They followed him out down the corridor. They checked the other bedrooms on this side of the house, which were all empty. They had to walk slowly with their arms out in front of them just in case there were any more sets of spikes. It seemed that Andrew had only put a set on the corridor at each side of the grand stairs, though. Alex caught the first set on his second attempt this time. They were just about to run down the stairs when they heard a shout from the other corridor. It was Audsley. She was peeking out of Arcadia's bedroom.

"Audsley!" shouted Aethelu. Is Arcadia with you?"

"She is. She needs help, though. Be careful. There are some spikes there. They killed Mum and Dad. They got Arcadia, too. We need help."

Alex set the motion sensor off on the second set of spikes and reached out to catch one. He mistimed it, and the spike went straight through his hand. He swore with the pain.

It did not stop him, though. He set the sensor off again and this time caught one of the spikes with his left hand. Judith squeezed past followed by Aethelu. They both ran down the corridor toward Audsley. Anais was just about to follow when she heard a baby's cry. It came from downstairs. She looked at Alex.

"I have to go find her, I'm sorry." She turned away from

him and ran as quick as she could down the stairs. Seconds later Alex caught up with her.

"What are you doing?" she asked him.

"You can't come down here alone. Andrew is down here."

"Alex. You know that poison from the spike will be slowly moving up your arm and through your body. You'll be unconscious soon. You won't be able to help me and now the others are trapped upstairs."

"Come on." He grabbed her hand with his left hand and pulled her down the stairs. In the hallway, they stopped and listened. At first, there was nothing and then came the crying again.

"She's in the kitchen." They both ran down the spiral staircase to the kitchen but it was empty.

"I heard her. I know I heard her," cried Anais.

"I heard her, too. She must be in the cellar."

They ran over to the larder door and opened it. The lift mechanism was not there, but there was a ladder disappearing into the darkness. Anais turned the lights on and stepped out onto the first rung. She quickly descended and jumped the last few rungs. Alex followed behind her, although he was slower due to his poisoned hand. She ran to the door and entered the code 2103. She then put her thumb on the thumb pad, but nothing happened.

"We need a key fob."

"I haven't seen mine since we were up in the attic. Where is yours?"

Anais tried to remember. It had been so long since she had last needed to use it. It was no use. It could have been anywhere.

"I have an idea." Alex climbed back up the ladder. "Someone might have left one in their coat pocket. There are quite a few coats hung up behind the kitchen door. I'll try there.

Anais waited as patiently as she could, but she could hear Autumn crying behind the door.

"Alex, hurry up!"

"I'm trying." She heard him should back distantly. He already sounded exhausted. The poison was beginning to overcome him. She only hoped he'd find the key fob in time.

"Found one. It was in August's pocket. She heard the jangle of metal fall next to her and realised that Alex had thrown August's keys down. She scrabbled around in the low light until she found them and pressed the key fob to the sensor. The first red light changed to green, but she'd waited so long that she needed to input the number and use the thumb pad again. Behind her, she could hear Alex climbing down the ladder. She entered the numbers 2103 and pressed her thumb to the thumb pad. The other two lights turned green, but nothing happened. The door didn't move.

She tried all three again this time in a different order. Still, nothing happened. What was wrong? All the lights were going green.

"It's not working!" she cried. She turned around to find Alex unconscious on the floor next to her.

"Alex!" She quickly dropped to his side, but she knew there was nothing she could do. Probably the only one who could save Alex now was Aldrich and he was unconscious himself upstairs. Anais had never felt more hopeless or alone. Her baby was on the other side of a thick steel door-- A thick steel door that refused to open. She sat on the dusty floor, put her head in her hands and wept.

She could hear Autumn crying on the other side of the door. A fierce rage built up inside her, a rage that she never would have imagined she could muster. She stood up and screamed as she ran with all her might into the steel door. She balled her fists and hammered the door as hard as she could. She'd heard that when a child is in peril, mothers have been known to lift cars. She was already stronger than most mothers. She punched and banged on the door hard. When she pulled her hand away, she looked at the door. Nothing. Not even a dent. Frustration bubbled up and she screamed again, this time kicking the door.

"You knocked?" The door opened and Andrew stood there with a smirk on his face. He'd operated the doors mechanism from the inside.

Anais ran past him and followed the sound of the baby's cries. Autumn was wrapped in a soft blanket and laid on the sofa. Andrew had put a pillow to one side of her to stop her rolling off. Anais scooped her up and held her close. The relief she felt knowing her baby was alive and safe was soon overshadowed by the fact that Andrew was standing between her and the only exit.

"Let us go, Andrew."

"Why would I want to do that?"

"What is the point of keeping us here or killing us? You aren't going to get Judith back. She doesn't love you. You must have heard her on your screens." She pointed to the CCTV monitors on the wall that showed most of the house.

"Yes, I heard. It was most unpleasant. Never mind, she will be dead soon. Just as you all will."

"She did love you, you know. If you'd just treated her well, she'd have continued to love you. Instead, you played a dangerous game with her and lost. Love isn't about trapping someone and making them unable to leave. It's about making a choice to be with that person and treating them well."

"As I said, I don't really care anymore. I have a new plan and it doesn't involve her." He spat onto the floor as he spoke

Anais didn't want to hear his plan, whatever it was. She just wanted to get out of there safely. She couldn't see a way round him and he was blocking the door so she just stood and listened to him whilst she tried to formulate a plan in her head.

"I'm keeping the baby. I think I'll call her Margaret. What do you think? Little Maggie?" He walked over to her and looked down at the baby causing Anais to take a step back.

"She's called Autumn." Anais didn't know why she felt the need to correct him. It just seemed important to her somehow, as if keeping her name meant keeping her safe.

"I don't think so. Margaret was my mother's name and I think it suits her. Give her to me."

"No!" she held Autumn closely.

Andrew pulled a knife out of his pocket. "I'll repeat myself once only. Give her to me."

Anais frantically tried to think of something, anything, to get away from him. If she tried to run for the door, she'd never make it up the ladder with Anais. She had no choice. Andrew grabbed Autumn from her arms.

"Don't hurt her," she begged.

"Silly, silly, silly!" He sat on the sofa and held Autumn. Anais didn't know what to do. The doorway was now clear, but Andrew still had Autumn. There was no one to help her. Alex was unconscious and the others were upstairs, trapped behind the spikes. There was the possibility of them somehow getting out but then what? The only thing Anais could do was listen.

"I'm not going to hurt her. I'm going to marry her."

Anais looked at him in astonishment.

"Don't worry. I know she's a little young at the moment, but I have all the time in the world. In another eighteen years or so, she will become my wife. We will live together in this house and perhaps have children of our own. Until then, she can cook and clean for me. I'll teach her to obey me. It will be perfect."

"You are not using my child as your slave and then your wife. I won't let you."

"I'm afraid you have no choice. I'm going to kill you. Then I'm going to kill the others. It's been fun playing with you all this past year, but now Margaret is here, I really have no need for any of you."

Anais began to panic. Where were the others? Surely, they would be down here soon! She tried to think of something to say to Andrew to stall him.

"What about your plan to unleash the Jagovirus into the world?"

"I've not decided yet. The way things are at the moment, I have no need to kill everyone. To be honest, I'm not sure I ever planned to kill everyone. I was just using it as a way to get what I wanted. Of course, that didn't turn out how I planned. First Sarah, then Judith, you women are all the same. They tell you what you want to hear so you think they love you, and then, they move on to the next guy. Well, not this time. Margaret will adore me. I'll be her king and she will be my queen. Of course, there is no point being king if you have no one to worship you. Therefore, I will probably let the human race live. I may change my mind in the future. Who knows? Unfortunately, for you, I don't include you in that statement. He grabbed hold of the handle of the knife and threw it at her. She saw the arc of the knife as if it was in slow motion, but shock had her rooted to the spot. It hit her right through her neck. Blood spurted out. Red droplets spattered the sofa, Andrew, and Autumn.

Anais fell to the floor.

A red puddle formed around her where she lay. She couldn't breathe. Blood clogged up her throat and the knife, still stuck in there, obstructed her airway.

She could see Andrew laughing at her, but he was beginning to get fuzzy. His laughing was distant and muffled.

Everything was turning black. The last thing she saw before she fell into oblivion was Alex coming up behind Andrew with a chain and putting it around his neck. At that point, she knew she was hallucinating because Alex was unconscious in the entryway behind her. There was no way he would have been able to get past her without being seen. It was a comforting thought even though it wasn't real. And then, everything was black.

14

"Anais, Anais."

Anais could hear someone calling her name. She ignored it.

"Anais, wake up."

It came again. This time, she recognised it and she then knew that she was dead.

It was Rafe's voice.

He was calling her onwards. She'd better open her eyes and pay attention

"Is this heaven?" She opened her eyes. It hurt. Everything was foggy. She closed her eyes again. Was her head supposed to hurt this much if she was dead? A cry broke through her thoughts, a baby's cry!

Autumn!

Anais opened her eyes again and sat up quickly. Her head spun for a minute and she felt as though she would pass out again. It was only the sound of her baby crying that kept her conscious. Then there it was, the warmth of her child in her arms. Autumn was ok. She looked up, expecting to see Alex, to thank him, but there in front of her stood Rafe.

"You're dead?"

"Is that a question? Because I think we can both assume that I'm not. How is your throat?"

"Er?" she felt the place where the knife had been. It was sticky but felt ok. "It's ok, I think. What happened?"

"Andrew has kept me down here for quite an age. He's had me drugged up to the eyeballs. I can't really remember. I just know that whatever he's been giving me is less effective now, or perhaps he forgot to dose me up. I've been drifting in and out of consciousness for hours. At least I think it's been hours, it could have been days or weeks. It's hard to tell. Anyway, after hearing the commotion down here I knew that someone else had managed to get in. It took all the strength I had to get out of that bed, but I managed it. Andrew hadn't shackled me to the bed. He was relying on his drugs to keep me under control. When I saw you, and then the baby, I knew that my chance had finally come to get him. I saw a bit of chain on the floor and strangled Andrew with it."

So it wasn't Alex she had seen, it was his twin.

"Is he dead?"

"Nope, it will take a lot more than a bit of strangling to kill him, as you are probably aware. He's unconscious and chained to the sofa."

Anais looked up. Rafe was telling the truth. Andrew was chained in the same shackles they had used to enchain James when they thought he was Jago.

"What are we going to do with him?"

"I don't know. Where are the others?"

"Alex is just outside the door. Andrew poisoned him using a booby-trap. Some of the others have been poisoned too. They are all upstairs. Everyone thinks you are dead."

"Alex is outside?" Rafe ran to the open door and fell down beside his brother.

"Alex?" He shouted and when there was no response, he cradled his head. "He's still breathing. Did you say he'd been poisoned?"

"Yes, his hand got pierced by a poisoned spear."

"If it's the same stuff that Andrew got me with, then it should wear off in a few days. Unfortunately, we need to decide what to do with Andrew now."

Anais stood up with Autumn in her arms and walked over to the sleeping Andrew. His long white blond hair covered up the majority of his face. She made sure to keep some distance between them. He could wake up any moment and she didn't know how long the chains holding him were.

How could one person be so evil, so calculating and cold and keep it secret so that no one knew for so long? It defied belief. He had lived amongst these people for hundreds of years, been their friend. But this was not a whim, a casual act of anger. He'd been planning this for years. At least, since he murdered her mother and her father. The grandparents that Autumn would never know. Her other grandparents trapped in their room, fearing for their lives. He'd murdered the first woman he professed to love and tried to murder the second. It was only a miracle that any of them had survived the ordeal he had put them through. She looked down at her child. Her little girl, only a couple of days old. Innocence in her arms. Andrew would kill her, too. The second she did anything to displease him, he would kill her as easily as he had the others. Anger and hatred bubbled up through her. She was not going to let that happen. This man would not hurt her child or any of them again. She passed Autumn to Rafe, who was still with Alex and turned back towards the monster who had time and time again abused them all and caused them untold pain. She picked up the bloody knife that Rafe had pulled out of her throat and casually dropped to the floor.

With as great a force that she could muster, she ran towards him the knife held in front of her. She plunged the blade into his heart as hard as she could. The force of the impact woke Andrew with a start. He screamed out in pain.

"Oh, you're awake. I thought stabbing you in the heart would kill you, but I guess The Light in you is working to my advantage."

"Your advantage?" he snarled at her, but she wasn't scared. She only had space left for anger.

"That's right. I want to see you suffer, just the way you've made us suffer. I want you to feel every cut of this blade. I want you to hurt."

"Kill me if you like." He spat out the blood that was beginning to form in his mouth and trickle down his chin "But don't think you are going to win. I will be triumphant."

Something beeped behind her.

"I don't think so." She raised the blade high over her head and brought it down with such force that she heard his ribs break.

"Anais, no!" Rafe ran to her side just as she brought the blade down again, and again. Tears coursed down her face, not of anger or fear but of relief. They were finally free.

Rafe pulled the knife out of her hand and held her tight. She could barely breathe, he was holding her that tight, but it made her feel safe. Her body, covered in Andrew's blood and her own, racked with sobs whilst Rafe stroked her head.

"It's over."

Anais, soothed by his words began to calm down and he finally released his tight grip on her.

"Autumn?" she asked, suddenly fearful.

"She's just over there by Alex. I laid her down carefully next to him when I saw what you were doing."

"You tried to stop me. Why?"

"Didn't you hear the beep? He must have had some kind of remote control in his hand that he pressed just before you killed him. I don't know what he's set off, but I think we can assume it's not good."

Anais looked at the screens that lined the wall. She could see the rest of the house. James, Aldrich, Arcadia, and Alex were still unconscious; the others were where she had left them. She scanned the rest of the monitors for something happening, but the rest of the house was quiet and still. There were still a few wafts of smoke emanating from Andrews room, but there was no other movement.

"What now?"

"I say we round up the others, find the rest of those vials, and get out of here. Before we go anywhere, I'm finishing this once and for all."

"What do you mean?"

"I'm going to cut his head off. You might want to step outside."

"Why? His chest has been pulverised. I killed him. He's dead."

"Think back to fifteen minutes ago. I pulled this very knife out of your throat. That should have killed you, but here you stand. Andrew's blood is twice as strong as yours. Don't underestimate what The Light can do."

"But I can see right through his chest."

"If that's true then you are not seeing what I'm seeing. Come closer and look again."

She didn't want to, but she looked at where she'd ripped his chest to pieces. When she saw what Rafe, was getting at, she nearly fainted. Andrew's heart was still pumping, slowly but noticeably. She could see his lungs moving as he quietly inhaled. Blood seeped out of them mixed with little bubbles of air. As she watched, she could see them healing. Every cut she had made was noticeably smaller.

"He's still alive. How is that even possible?"

"You saw for yourself that it was possible when you watched Jasmine cut out Abel's heart. If we left him like this, his body would be completely healed within hours. I have to cut off his head to make sure he is really dead."

The whole thing was beginning to make Anais feel nauseous. She had to take a few deep breaths to stop from being sick on the floor. Deciding to leave him to it, she moved back to Alex and picked up her daughter who was now snoozing quite happily in the nook of Alex's arm. She sang softly to her, a lullaby her own mother had sung to her when she was little. It wasn't to soothe Autumn, who was already asleep, it was to block out the sounds of Rafe decapitating Andrew in the next room. When he had finally finished, he came out to her.

"It's done."

Anais could only nod her head in silence.

"We need to get out of here. We need to get the others and find the rest of those vials. We should probably both get a wash too."

Anais couldn't disagree, they were both covered in blood. "There's a vial down here."

"How do you know?"

She told him about how they had found where Andrew had hidden all the vials as he had marked them on the model house.

"How about we get everyone together and then decide where to go from here? We can come back down, once we have a plan of action. Do you think you'll be able to carry the baby up the ladder?"

"Yes, I think so."

"Ok. You go first and I'll follow with Alex." He heaved his brother up onto his shoulders in a kind of fireman's lift.

Anais soon realised that it was impossible to hold a baby and climb a ladder safely. In the end, she used her sweater as a kind of a sling and tied Autumn to her so she could use both hands for climbing. Once in the main hall, Rafe laid Alex on the floor and ordered Anais to stay with him.

"I'm going to get the others and bring them down. Wait here."

"Watch out for the spikes. They come out of the wall at either side at the top of the stairs. You should see the holes in the wall where they come out. I don't think you'll be able to get past them.

"You did."

"Yes, but only because Alex had stopped them for me."

"I'll figure it out. You just stay here and wait for me to come back."

Anais was too tired to argue. She sat and cradled Autumn. Seeing her next to Alex, it was obvious that they were father and daughter. They had the same curve of the mouth and long eyelashes. Anais smiled despite their situation. She knew that at any moment one of Andrew's traps could appear out of nowhere and kill them all, but as she could not do anything about it, she sat and played with the fine wisps of hair on her daughter's head. A noise above jolted her, but it was only Rafe with Aldrich slumped over his shoulders. Behind him, Winnie carried Sabine, who was now unconscious and Jennifer carried James. Anais put Autumn down and ran to help.

"How did you get past the spikes?" she asked, as Sabine, James, and Aldrich were lowered next to Alex.

"I put a sturdy piece of furniture in the way of the spikes. Where is everyone else, Arcadia's room?"

"Yes, Judith is up there too."

"I know, I'll go back up and bring them down." He raced back up the stairs, slightly quicker than he had before.

"Watch out for the spikes on the other side," she shouted up after him.

Winnie ran straight over to Autumn and picked her up. "Oh, darling. Oh, my little darling. You are so beautiful. I can't believe it." She stroked Autumn's head as the tears splashed down on the baby's face.

No one said anything else until Rafe appeared back with Arcadia, Audsley, Aethelu, and Judith. He laid Arcadia down carefully. Judith rushed into his arms.

"I thought you were dead. My angel, this is a miracle. I thought I'd lost you."

"Never!" He stroked her head. "What happened to your forehead? It has blood on it."

"Andrew shot me."

"He shot you? How did you survive being shot in the head?"

Judith lowered her eyes.

"He gave you The Light, didn't he? Father and James finished it and he gave it to you. I told him over and over again that you didn't want it." Rafe's anger was obvious in his voice. "If I hadn't already killed him, I'd gladly do it again.

"I do not mind now. I..." but Audsley cut her off.

"You killed Andrew?"

"I chopped the bastard's head right off. He's dead."

Aethelu and Audsley cheered before they realised that no one else was.

"What's the matter? We are free. We won," said Aethelu.

"Not quite," replied Anais. We still have to get the vials before the mechanism breaks them open, and we think Andrew set something by remote control before he died. The whole house is probably booby-trapped. Andrew was never going to let us get off that easily. Besides, we only have four hours to find them. Correction, we had four hours from the point Andrew last inputted the code. Does anyone know when that was?"

Everyone looked at each other. Nobody knew.

"We thought that he might input the code through his phone when he went out. Perhaps if we find his phone we can find the code and maybe input it ourselves."

"His phone will be in his pocket. I'll get it." Rafe rushed downstairs only to appear a moment later with the phone.

"It's password protected. Does anyone have any clues?"

"Alex thought that Andrew would booby-trap the phone somehow if we put in the wrong code."

"I don't think we have much of a choice now," replied Rafe with the phone in his hand.

"Try Judith," said Aethelu.

"I don't think he would have used my name. He despised me at the end," replied Judith.

"Try it anyway," Aethelu urged.

Rafe typed 'Judith' into the phone's keypad. It made a funny noise.

"Son of a..." said Rafe

"What?"

Rafe held up the phone so they could all see. On the

screen was a message. It read 'Nice try. Get it wrong three times and I'll blow up. Two tries left."

"Sarah! Try Sarah. He was in love with Anais' mum." Aethelu shouted urgently.

Rafe typed the name 'Sarah' carefully.

The phone repeated the funny noise.

"Nope! Last guess. If we make a wrong move, I'll be standing here with no hand. Any suggestions? No pressure."

"Could it be his birthday do you think?" asked Winnie.

"It could be. Are you willing to bet my hand on it?"

"This is a stupid idea. It could be anything. Let's just leave the phone and try and find the vials as quickly as we can," said Audsley.

"But we could only have a few minutes left. We need to stop the countdown," argued Aethelu.

"Well, perhaps we should just leave and get away from this place," countered Audsley.

Anais suddenly had a thought. She ran right through the arguing cousins towards Rafe, grabbed the phone, and then ran to the other side of the huge hallway. Before anyone had registered what she had done, she inputted 'Margaret' into the phone. She braced herself as she pressed enter. The screen cleared and Andrew's phone unlocked. A countdown now appeared on the screen.

It read 52.03.

"Fifty-two minutes to go."

"Input the code to extend the time." Someone yelled.

"Ok," replied Anais. "What's the code?" she looked up into the dumbstruck faces of the others. No one knew.

Aethelu ran over to her and hit her lightly on the arm. "Don't do that again. Haven't you nearly died enough times in the past few months? You are a mother now."

Anais felt momentarily ashamed. Aethelu was right. She had her baby to look after.

"We need to get Autumn out of this place before we do anything. I'm not letting anyone do anything in this house until my granddaughter is safely away from it!"

Anais and Aethelu looked at Winnie and the look of indignation on her face made them both break out laughing.

"You're right. Someone needs to volunteer to leave with Autumn. I volunteer Anais. That's it, case closed."

"I'm not leaving. We need to find the vials and I remember where they are, well, the ones we found on the model."

"We all remember where the vials are. We saw the model too," argued Aethelu.

"I'm not leaving without the vials!"

"I'll go with the baby," shouted Winnie over them.

"But Mama, you can't drive!" shouted an exasperated Aethelu.

"Fine," replied Anais. "I'll drive her in August's car to the village. I can get the vial that's in the public garden there. I'll take Alex, James, Arcadia, Sabine, and Aldrich. There's no point in them being here."

"Deal!" agreed Aethelu. "We'll stay here and find the other vials."

The front door was remarkably easy to open thanks to Rafe having August's keys. It also meant that they could start his Range Rover. Between Rafe and the girls, they managed to squeeze Alex, James, Aldrich, Sabine, and Arcadia into the back seat. They strapped the men in and kind of draped Arcadia over their knees. Poor Sabine had to go in the storage space at the back. Winnie got in the front passenger seat with Autumn and Anais took the driver's seat. Aethelu kissed her on the lips and waved as they drove off down the tree-lined entranceway. Once they got to the gate, their first problem became apparent. The gates were closed. Anais was willing to bet that the key fob wouldn't work. She tried it anyway but was unsurprised that the gates stayed shut.

"Get out, Winnie."

"Sorry?"

"I'm going to ram the gates with the car and I don't want you or Autumn in here when I do."

"Oh, ok, what about Arcadia and Sabine? They're not strapped in."

"They are asleep. They won't feel a thing."

Winnie looked worried but stepped out of the car. Anais backed the car up slightly then put her foot down on the pedal as hard as she could. The car raced forward and took out the gates with such force that one came right off its hinges. She parked, and whilst she waited for Winnie to catch up on foot, she checked on Arcadia. She was still laid across the laps of the others and unconscious. She seemed fine. She hoped Sabine had fared as well in the back. Winnie fussed all the way to the village, so much so, that Anais was quite glad when she could get out of the car. She parked as close to the little community garden as possible on double yellow lines and jumped out.

The garden was little more than a few flowerbeds, a bench with a plaque on it, and the big stone village marker in the centre of the garden.

She walked all around it to find a crevice in which the vial might be hidden. The whole thing was stone. It was smooth with no holes or dents. She walked around it, knocking it with her knuckles to see if any of it was hollow, but it was not. There was nowhere to hide a vial or anything else for that matter on the tall stone. In a fit of desperation, she ran around the rest of the garden, pulling up flowers in case Andrew had buried the vial somewhere. After ten minutes, she gave up and sat on the bench. A jogger ran past and cheerfully waved at her before his face fell into one of horror and he picked up his pace. She couldn't blame him. She was still covered in blood, and now with dirt as well, and half the garden had been pulled up and was strewn around her feet. She knew she'd have to leave soon. The jogger was, no doubt, running to the nearest police station to report her. She stood up and looked at the bench behind her. The plaque read

'In memory of Harry Purton, who loved this place.'

She'd never heard of Harry Purton, but something about the plaque caught her eye. Someone had scratched a tiny cross onto its surface.

Anais whipped out August's keys and found a Swiss army knife key ring. She opened the tiny screwdriver tool and unscrewed the screws from the four corners of the plaque. It fell off and hit the bench with a metallic ting sound. Where it had been was a small hollowed out area with the vial in it. It fit snugly along with the mechanism for breaking the glass. She carefully pulled it out and ripped the batteries from it. A noise behind her alerted her to the fact that the vial was booby-trapped, but it was too late. The noise that she had heard was the sound of the huge stone tumbling towards her. She moved, but the stone came down, crushing her and pinning her to the ground next to the bench. She barely managed to keep the vial from falling out of her hand and smashing on the ground. However, she was pinned to the ground and didn't have enough strength to move the stone. 'What a stupid position to be in' she thought to herself and mentally cursed herself for not thinking of traps.

Winnie had seen what had happened and raced out of the car. Anais placed the vial carefully on the ground and between them they managed to lift the stone a fraction of an inch, just enough for Anais to squeeze out.

Her legs were in agony and her stomach severely bruised, but she knew she would heal quickly. She picked up the vial and with Winnie's help, she managed to hobble back to the car.

"I have to get back to the house. I don't have time to find a hotel for you all, you'll have to stay in the car." She looked at her watch. It had been fifteen minutes since they left the house, factor in another couple of minutes or so strapping the others into the car and another five minutes driving home, they only had about thirty minutes left. She turned the car around in a skid and raced back to The Manor breaking the speed limit the whole way. She parked on the road outside the gates.

"Winnie, there is a vial hidden here by the gates somewhere. You need to find it. Andrew will have taped it underneath something or behind something. It's probably on one of the gateposts or along the wall. When you find it, just take the batteries out. If you can't do that, detach it from the battery pack by pulling the wires out. It's important you find it in the next twenty minutes."

"Righto."

Anais kissed Winnie and Autumn and ran as fast as her bruised legs would carry her up to the house. She was much slower than usual and so by the time she got back to the front door, they only had twenty minutes left. The whole house seemed in chaos. It was in a much worse state than when she had left less than half an hour before.

Furniture had been upturned and there was noise coming from all over the house. She remembered where some of the vials were hidden but had no idea which of them had already been found. She still had the one from the public garden in her pocket. She carefully pulled it out and laid it on the only piece of furniture still standing the right way up, a side table. The last thing she needed was to smash the glass tube whilst running around the house.

"Hello?" she called out. She could hear the others but couldn't see anyone.

"Anais?" Rafe emerged from the cupboard under the stairs, which Anais knew held the concealed entrance to the hidden games room.

"Rafe! I got the vial. How many have you found here?"

"I don't know. I've got a couple. I think there was a problem with the one in the safe in the library. No one knew the code. Aethelu said that you knew it."

"I do. I'll go get it now."

She had turned to race toward the library when Rafe called after her.

"Wait."

"What?"

"Leave the one in the safe until last. We know where that one is. We need to tally up and see how many we have yet to find. We are running out of time.

"Ok, good thinking. Where are the others?"

"I don't know. We all separated."

"Ok, you go look for them upstairs. I'll search this floor and downstairs. We'll meet back down here in five minutes.

"Two, two minutes. We are running out of time."

He turned and ran up the stairs, taking them two at a time. Anais ran to the kitchen door and shouted out as loud as she could to see if there was already anyone down there. She waited for an answer but heard nothing. The last thing she wanted to do was go back into the cellar and see

Andrew's body, but with no sign of anyone else, she knew she would have to. She wished she'd have asked if anyone had searched the cellar for vials yet, but with very little time left, she ran down the stairs. Winnie had already searched the kitchen before so there was no point spending time looking there. She passed the big oak table and ran straight for the larder door. She flung the door open and jabbed the button that activated the elevator mechanism. Nothing happened. She then remembered that it wasn't working and she'd have to climb down the ladder again. Thankfully, this time she didn't have a baby strapped to her. Finally, she hit the ground and ran. She remembered that Andrew had drawn a cross under the computer in the cellar. She called out in the hope that someone was there already searching the cellar. It would mean she wouldn't have to go in. The cellar door was open, which was a promising sign, but no one answered. She would have to go in. Slowly she put her head around the corner. The sight before her caused her to inhale rapidly. Andrew's blood still coated the sofa and the floor, mingled with her own. That was not what had caused her alarm. It was the absence of Andrew's body.

She began to hyperventilate before she remembered that Rafe had cut off his head. The Light worked miracles, but survival from decapitation was impossible even with the Light running through your veins. Rafe must have moved the body somewhere. She couldn't imagine why, but it was the only explanation. Even so, she still felt nervous as she walked across the floor to the computer. Purposely stepping around the pool of dried blood, she skirted the sofa and reached Andrew's computer. It had been turned off. The giant screens on the wall in front of her were blank. Not bothering to be gentle, she pushed the whole computer and monitor to the floor. The screen smashed as it hit the floor and then Anais realised her mistake. She'd thought that the vial would somehow be hidden in the desk under the computer, but as she heard the sound of breaking glass, she realised that the vial could have easily been hidden in the computer itself. Looking at the bare expanse of desk in front of her, she saw that there was no hidden compartment. She bent down and searched under the desk, and then as a last resort, under the chair. Nothing. Either the vial was in the computer itself, or it wasn't there at all.

She looked down at the mess of broken glass and metal beside the desk and mentally cursed herself. The computer box was still in one piece but had a dent in the side where it had landed. She soon realised that she would need a screwdriver to open it up.

"Damn!" Where would she find a screwdriver? She couldn't recall seeing one at all in all her time here. The best bet would be in Andrew's room or in the Cottage, both of which were too far away to get to in time. She opened the desk drawer again. It was immaculately neat. Pens lined up in neat little rows, a ruler, some pencils, an eraser, a carving of Judith, and a chocolate bar. No screwdriver. She slammed the drawer closed and moved to the next drawer down. The wooden desk only had two drawers so she said a quick prayer as she opened it. This one was filled with books, the top one being a book on computer programming. She pulled it out and threw it to the floor along with the three or four books beneath it. A slight noise from behind her made her jump. Turning around quickly, she scanned the cellar. Nobody was there. Perhaps it was an echo of the books hitting the floor. Turning back to the drawer, she grabbed another handful of books and flung them onto the pile on the floor. On her third handful, she noticed something hiding at the back of the drawer. It was a Swiss Army Knife. She pulled it out and opened the screwdriver on it.

She looked at her watch. The minutes were ticking down fast. She hoped that the others had found all of the other vials or they would run out of time. It had already been three minutes since she had left Rafe upstairs.

It seemed to take an eternity to unscrew the computer box. It didn't help that she was sure she could hear something in the cellar with her.

Once again, she scanned the cellar, trying not to wonder where Andrew's body was. The hairs on the back of her neck started to prickle and as she unscrewed the last screw, she almost unconsciously flipped the screwdriver on the Swiss Army Knife in and exchanged it for the biggest blade.

Taking a last look around the cellar, she removed the top of the computer box. There it was--the vial. She spotted it almost immediately. She could see the liquid contents swirling around. Thankfully, the fall to the floor hadn't damaged it. Putting the Swiss Army Knife in her pocket, she pulled the vial out and disconnected it carefully from its wires.

A huge rush of relief overcame her and she breathed out.

Unfortunately, she couldn't breathe in again. Something was restricting her airway. The vial dropped to the floor. She brought her hands up to her throat and felt something around it. She grabbed hold of whatever it was and pulled it away from her neck in a quick motion. As the pressure immediately released from her neck, she felt a blow to the back of the head. She turned around. For the briefest of seconds, she thought that there was nothing there but when she lowered her eyes a fraction, the thing she did see made her scream in terror.

It was the most horrendous thing she had ever seen.

Andrew's body had been holding a length of rope, which accounted for the thing that had been wrapped around her neck. The reason that she had managed to unwrap it from her neck so easily was that Andrew's head was hanging in an unnatural position, flopping down over his neck. His eyes were almost upside down, but he still managed to look at her in such a way that made her blood run cold.

There was barely any neck there; however, his spinal cord was still intact. It was the only thing holding his head onto his neck. When Rafe had decapitated him, he'd somehow failed to cut completely through, instead, he'd left the tiniest bit of sinew and the spinal cord holding Andrew together. Not for the first time, Anais felt revulsion at what having The Light running through you meant. She tried to move back away from this creature, but the rope that had been around her neck was still in Andrew's hands and therefore still around her back. She was trapped in his arms.

Fighting the urge to throw up, she pushed him away. He moved back surprisingly easily, but the rope behind her pulled her with him, causing them both to fall over. Andrew hit the floor with Anais on top of him. His head made a sick slurping sound as it rolled in the opposite direction. It was disgusting, but at least it was the right way up. Almost immediately, where the severed ends touched, Anais could see that the unnaturally quick healing process was beginning to take place. His head was fixing itself. Only one side of his head was touching what was left of his neck so it was healing in the most unnatural position.

Something blew out at her and spattered her face. When she realised what it was, she immediately threw up. It was blood from Andrew's lungs, coming not from his mouth, which was still not connected with his lungs, but from the hole in his neck.

Andrew opened his mouth to talk, but no words came out. There was no way that they could. Anais could see a huge space where his vocal chords used to be, now just a gaping hole surrounded by bloody flesh.

She pulled back and when she felt the rope tightening around her back, once again, she punched Andrew in his sideways face.

The impact knocked his head into another direction and now he was looking at the wall. It was obvious he had no control over the direction his head fell although his arms seemed to be working perfectly. He let go of the rope and grabbed her arms, stopping her from being able to get up.

She desperately wanted to scream, but she could not get a sound out. This thing before her revolted her and repulsed her. How was it possible he was still alive? His eyes began to roll around in his head and his tongue hung out. Every time she tried to pull back away from him, his head rolled around. She wondered briefly if he could still understand. If his brain was still working or if the grip he had on her was just some kind of muscle spasm. Then she remembered the look he gave her. He still knew what was going on! The thought that he might be able to understand what was going on frightened her. The pain he must be in had to be horrific. Not that she felt sorry for him. It was an appropriate end, fitting, after all the pain he had put them through. Just thinking about it made her want to throw up again. She couldn't see her watch but she knew time would run out if she didn't hurry up and get away.

Andrew was strong, but his reactions were horribly slow, thanks to what had happened to him. That was how she had managed to get the rope from around her neck. Now, however, he had her arms and he wasn't letting go. His fingers dug into her arms and the more she moved, the more his head lolled around making her feel queasy. She pulled as hard as she could backwards which lifted his body slightly but the momentum toppled them both over, this time with Andrew on top of her. His head flopped to the side of her neck and she found herself looking right down his neck. She had to close her eyes just to keep from throwing up a second time. The downright disgusting situation was worse than the fear. He'd not managed to hurt her, but she was now pinned to the floor. Moist air dampened her face and she knew it was coming from his lungs. Repulsed, she tried once again to push him off her. She felt his face, heavy against hers as she pushed him away. Suddenly the grip on her arms slackened which caused her to open her eyes. The top of his head bobbled along her face and she ended up with a mouthful of his hair. She spat it out and quickly moved out from under him, grateful that his head was hanging down, and he couldn't see her fully. She pulled herself backwards along the floor until she was almost away from him, but then something happened that truly terrified her. He raised his head. The shock caused her to pause for the briefest of seconds, but it was all he needed to grab her feet.

How had he lifted his head? And then, she saw. The back and side of his neck had healed over. The front was still a gaping hole, but somehow The Light had managed to regenerate enough of his neck to make it strong enough to hold up. His eyes had regained focus, although his tongue still hung out of his mouth. He tried to speak again, but nothing came out of his mouth. His lungs were still not connected to his head. Anais wondered just how long the brain of someone with The Light in them would last without oxygen. She was about to learn the answer to that question, compliments of Andrew. He pulled her feet towards him, bringing the rest of her along. He let go so she kneed him in the stomach as hard as she could. It barely winded him, but it did seem to make him angry. He let go of her legs and brought his hands back to her throat. He squeezed tightly, stopping Anais' airflow.

She grabbed hold of his wrists and tried to pull them apart to no avail. He might have his neck held together with only a few inches of muscle and bone, but he had the full amount of Light in him compared to Anais, who only had half. He was by far the stronger of the two. Anais remembered the last time she had fought him like this. At that time, she only knew him as Jago. He wore a mask. Then, he'd managed to break her leg into a million pieces and nearly killed Aethelu. As Anais world turned dim due to lack of oxygen, she thought of all the others who had died at his hands and of the billions of others that would if she didn't find and destroy all the vials. A memory stirred just before she blinkered out. She put her hand down to her pocket and withdrew the Swiss army knife. Grabbing it as hard as she could she plunged it straight into his eye socket. He immediately let go of her and brought up his hand to his eye. She used the distraction to stand and move backward away from him.

He was in obvious pain, blood dripped from his right eye and his head, although upright, was healing at a strange angle and still not steady on his shoulders. Anais was in no doubt that if he was able to, he would be screaming now. She'd never seen anything more frightening in her life than this monster that flailed around in front of her. He now looked like the monster he always had been. Anais stole a quick glance behind her. The cellar's exit was still open behind her. She knew she could turn and run whilst Andrew was occupied with the pain of his eye. She could close the door and trap him in. The problem was, he was healing. He was healing extremely quickly. If she left him locked in, how long would it be until he healed completely and came after her? Probably, not that long. Besides, how could she lock him in? He knew the code to open the door and Anais had no clue how to change it. Another thought occurred to her. She still didn't have the vial. It had fallen out of her hands when Andrew had tried to strangle her with the rope. She looked down to where she had dropped it. It took her a couple of seconds, but then she saw it. It had rolled a couple of feet, but the vial had not cracked which was a small miracle. Unfortunately, it was on the floor behind Andrew.

She tried to estimate if she would be able to get to the vial before Andrew came to his senses. He was still flailing around in a horrific manner. Anais looked around for inspiration, anything she could use to kill him. There was nothing in the room besides the sofas, computer, and computer desk.

She briefly wondered if she could get a knife from the tiny kitchen that was attached to the cellar, but from memory, it held little more than coffee and mugs. She considered trying to get up to the main kitchen to get one of Winnie's butcher's knives, but a look at Andrew told her that she wouldn't have time. His neck was already half-healed, albeit at a strange angle. There was no telling if he was compos mentis but then again, he'd never shown much evidence of rational thought even with his head screwed on tightly. She had no choice but to run past Andrew and grab the vial. After that, she had no plan.

Pausing for a second to check if he was paying any attention to her, she ran past and grabbed the vial as quickly as she could, all the while, keeping an eye on the flailing Andrew. She thought she would make it back, but Andrew managed to pull the knife out of his bloody eye socket and had turned towards her. The only thing behind her was the wall. She knew she should try to run past Andrew, but he had always been faster than her, and now that she had his full attention again, there was every chance he would be able to catch her. She backed up slowly towards the wall, the vial in her hand while Andrew moved towards her.

She screamed for help. It was the only thing left to do. Unfortunately, the others were at least two floors above her and were unlikely to hear her. In the improbable event of one of them hearing her, there was not much of a chance of them getting down to the cellar in time to help her. She was truly on her own and backed into a corner with the monster that was Andrew, now mere inches away from her.

Then everything bubbled up inside of her. The hate of what this man had done to her, of what he'd destroyed just to make himself happy. He'd disregarded everyone else's happiness and destroyed everyone in an incredibly selfish attempt to make himself happy. These were the people who had loved him the most--his family. If only he could have seen that he already had everything he'd ever wanted and didn't need to travel down this road of destruction. Anais almost felt sorry for him. Where had it gotten him? Despite it all, he was alone. He could have lived, surrounded by the people who had loved him the most, but instead, he chose this.

Anais could barely comprehend it. She was damned if she was going to die at his hands and as a result of his choices. It was more out of overwhelming anger than fear or a desire to save herself that she did what she did next. As he came towards her, covered in blood, neck ripped open, she dropped to the floor and picked up the biggest shard of glass from the smashed screen. With a primal scream, she plunged the sharpest part into what was left of his neck. She withdrew it and repeated the action over and over again. Even as he was falling to the ground, she carried on. She was crying and screaming as she finally managed to sever his head completely.

It was only when she felt arms around her that she realised the others had heard her after all. Aethelu gently pried the glass shard out of her bloody hand and held her as she sobbed.

Rafe kicked Andrew's head clean across the cellar.

"Just to be sure!"

The shock that Andrew had still been alive was apparent on all their faces, but there was no time to stand around. There were still vials to find.

"How did you get on? Did you find any more vials?" She looked at her watch. Fighting Andrew had taken up a lot of precious time. They had barely twelve minutes left until the mechanism would break the vials.

"We've got all of them except for four. One is still in the library in the safe. That gives us just over ten minutes to find three more," Aethelu replied.

"Two." Anais held out the vial that she was still holding in her left hand. Actually, one, if Winnie has found the one by the gate."

"She did find it. She called me a minute ago. I already included that one. We still have two to find."

"Where can they be? Think!"

Anais thought back to all the places marked on the model of The Manor.

Attic, games room, studio... Anais assumed they'd found

all the ones that had been marked, or at least they had seen the marks for.

"Where could he have hidden them that we haven't already looked?"

"The tunnel between here and August's cottage?" offered Audsley.

"There are no hiding places there, though. It's just a tunnel."

"It's worth checking, though."

"Ok" replied Aethelu, you look there. "Where else?" she asked, as Audsley disappeared.

"The dining room, upstairs here - the little dormitory, any of the bathrooms?"

"He wouldn't have hidden anything in the bathrooms. They were the only rooms he didn't have cameras in and he'd have wanted to keep an eye on his vial," Rafe said. "I'll check the dormitory and get back to Judith and Jennifer. Aethelu, you try the dining room. Anais, you do the library. You know the passcode to the safe."

"Ok."

Aethelu took Anais' hand and they made their way back up through the kitchen.

"What happened to Judith and Jennifer?" asked Anais "are they ok?"

"Judith got caught by one of Andrew's traps. It got her leg pretty badly. We left Jennifer looking after her when we heard your screams. I think Jennifer was going to try to get her out of the house."

She paused for a moment.

"Actually, I've just had an idea where one of the vials might be."

"Where?"

"Could he have hidden a vial at the tramway?"

"Didn't you already find a load of the stuff in the building up there?"

"I didn't mean the building. I meant the tram stop itself."

"I don't know. Did he go on it much?"

"No. I loved the tramway, but he was never really interested."

"It seems a weird place to put it if he never really went there."

"Why? It's out of the way. It's close to where he was working. We'd never stumble upon the vial."

"We wouldn't, but a member of the public could have found it."

"Well, that would put his world domination plan into action sooner, wouldn't it?"

Anais wasn't convinced and with only just over fifteen minutes left, she didn't want to lose precious time. Aethelu could see her stalling.

"Please. If we run, we can be back in time to get the vial from the library."

"What about the dining room?"

"We both know there is no vial in the dining room. We've all been together in that room too many times for Andrew to hide it there."

Against Anais' better judgement, she let Aethelu pull her outside through the back door of the house.

They opened the courtyard gate and began a sprint down the little path that led through the woods. Aethelu was much quicker that Anais, and she was having trouble keeping up.

"Aethelu!" she called just before Aethelu disappeared out of sight. They'd almost made it to the wall that separated the Manor grounds from the public grounds. On the other side, was a pathway and then the little track that carried the two trams up and down the hillside.

Atop the wall was the electric fence. Anais hoped it had been shut down.

"What is it? We are running out of time," Aethelu shouted back irritably.

"I know. You go on ahead. I really don't think the vial is there, but you should check to make sure. I'm only slowing you down."

"I need you to help me look."

"You don't, you are much quicker than me. I'll get the vial from the library and then see if Rafe or Audsley have found the other one. I think we'd do this quicker if we split up."

"Ok." Aethelu turned and jumped over the fence. Thankfully, it had been disabled.

"Good luck!" Anais called after the blur that was now Aethelu at full speed.

Anais ran as fast as she could herself, in the opposite direction. When she passed the tomb where her father lay, something came back to her. The last time she had passed by this tomb was when Andrew had taken her for a walk to tell her of his plans to keep Autumn.

He'd not let her visit with her father. At the time, she thought that it was because he felt that he had more important things to do, but now she wasn't so sure. Had he not wanted her to go in there for an entirely different reason?

A thrill of excitement passed through her. The vial was in there! She was sure of it.

She opened the large wooden door and pulled the cord that switched on the light bulb.

It was scarier than she remembered. Cobwebs clung to the corners of the room. Her eyes flitted over to her father's stone tomb but rested there for only a brief second. She didn't have time to waste.

"Where would he have hidden it?" she whispered to herself aloud.

The only place she could think of was underneath the stone plinth that had been set aside for Andrew. One he'd never get to use. There was no way that his body would reside next to her father if she had anything to do with it. She was pretty sure the rest of the family would agree with her. She ran to the plinth with his name on it. Andrew John Shepherd. She'd never known his full name. He'd probably been just John Shepherd when he was born and adopted the name 'Andrew' when he'd consumed The Light, later to become Jago.

She lowered her head, but before she'd even managed to see the underside of the plinth, she knew she was in the right place. She could see a tiny light flashing. She grabbed it and pulled the wires out.

Just one vial left to find! She didn't have time to go searching for it. The one in the safe still needed retrieving. She prayed that either Aethelu, Audsley, or Rafe would stumble upon the last vial.

Leaving the tomb door open, she fled down the dark path back to the house and to the library to get the vial from the safe.

The library was remarkably tidy compared to the carnage in the rest of the house. All the books were still shelved in their correct places. Anais threw the painting that covered the safe to one side where it crashed to the floor and broke. Anais said a mental 'sorry' to Aethelu, whom she knew had painted it and turned her attention to the safe. She turned the dial as she had seen Andrew do in the film she had made on the little portable camera. Holding her breath as she dialled the last number, she pulled. The safe door opened. As soon as the safe opened, she saw what she was looking for. The little red light flashing on the mechanism helped her find it straight away. She put her hand in to grab it. As her hand curled around the tube, something happened that made Anais scream out in shock. She'd tripped a mechanism, set off another of Andrew's booby-traps. A sheet of metal with a semi-circle cut out had dropped from the top of the safe. Another one had risen up and locked in the middle. Anais was lucky that her arm had been placed in the centre of the safe or it would probably have cut her hand off. As it was, her hand was trapped in the hole the two semi-circles. She let go of the vial and tried to pull her hand free. Some internal mechanism had sealed around her wrist making it a tight fit. There was no way she would be able to pull her arm out. Even so, she tried. She made her hand as thin as she could by stretching it out and pulled back. All that she managed to do was make her hand hurt. When would she ever learn? She'd already set off one of Andrews booby traps today and now she'd set off another. She opened her mouth to shout to Rafe when she heard a scream from somewhere else in the house. It was impossible to tell who it was or where they were. Andrew was still beating them from the grave. She looked at her watch, which thankfully was on the other wrist. Just twelve minutes left until the vials were broken and the Jagovirus would be released into the air.

"Rafe!" She prayed that he was still in the house and could hear her.

No one came. She listened. There were noises all over the house. She could hear footsteps running, somewhere above her and people shouting. It seemed that all hell had broken loose. Rafe was probably caught up in whatever was happening upstairs. She hoped that whoever had screamed was ok. It looked as though she was on her own for now, though. She turned her attention once again to her trapped hand. There was no way she was going to get her hand out by pulling it. She wondered if it would be possible to somehow lever the two parts of the locking apparatus open. The join between the two was barely visible so tightly they were shut. She skimmed her eyed over the surrounding area to see if she could find anything to help her. The only thing she could see that had any chance of working was an old-fashioned fire stoker. She reached out to find that she was at least two feet away and had no hope of reaching it. Kicking her shoe off, she manoeuvred herself around so she could grab it with her toes. She had to be careful. If she knocked it over or away from herself, she would never be able to get it. With great difficulty, she managed to grab the rod between her big toe and second toe. Slowly she pulled it toward herself. With her free hand, she grabbed the poker and let out a little cheer. She'd gotten it! She slipped her foot back into her shoe and turned to look at the safe. The end of the poker was pointed, although not sharp. It was obvious by just looking at it that she would not be able to fit it between the two parts of the device that had trapped her. Still, she tried, to no avail. It very soon became apparent that she was getting nowhere. She looked at her watch. Nine minutes left. It had gone quiet outside the library.

"Help" she shouted once again. Still, nobody came. "Rafe? Anyone!"

It remained silent. Where were the others? Were they still upstairs? Had they left without her? For a brief second, she wondered if they had all died, but she pushed the thought to the back of her mind. They were still alive. She felt hopeless.

She held onto the poker tightly and struck the safe. A loud clanging sound filled the air and the poker reverberated in her hand. When Anais looked back at the safe, she saw that the poker hadn't made a mark. It hadn't even scratched the surface. The metal gleamed. Anger overcame her. She hit the safe as hard as she could, again and again and gave out a huge scream of frustration. The lock remained closed tightly around her wrist. Anais started to cry. Her watch told her what she already knew. Only five minutes left. There was no way that she would be able to open the safe and somehow detach the mechanism in five minutes. As she looked at her watch, the minute hand ticked, counting down to four minutes.

There was nothing she could do. The Jagovirus was going to escape. Millions of people were going to die. Perhaps the only ones left on the planet would be those that had consumed The Light Elixir. Anais tried to imagine a world so empty that only she and her family existed. Then she remembered Andrew's other little concoction, the second liquid in the vial that would kill anyone with The Light. That gave her a little over three minutes left to live. She thought about Autumn, asleep in Winnie's arms in the Range rover outside the gates.

Anais would never see her daughter again. She knew that now. She wished she'd had more time with her. What cruelty that she'd never see her take her first steps or hear her first word. She'd had a little over twenty-four hours with her baby.

Suddenly the door opened. Aethelu stuck her head through.

"Anais! There you are. I've been looking all over for you. We've found them all. The one in the safe is the last one. What are you doing?"

"I'm stuck. The safe was booby-trapped. I can't get my hand out."

"Oh!"

She ran over to Anais.

"Can you pull it out?"

Anais resisted the urge to shoot back a sarcastic reply.

"No, I've tried. It's stuck. Where is everybody else? They need to get out!"

"They are helping Judith get down the stairs."

"Why?"

"One of Andrews traps caught her leg and amputated it above the knee."

"Oh, God!"

"She's shaken up, but she'll survive. We need to get you out of here in the next five minutes before the vial gets broken."

Anais looked at her watch.

"Two minutes. I'm not going to be able to get out in time. You can, though. Get everybody out. The Range Rover is at the gate. If you run now, you will make it. Hopefully, if you get far enough away, you won't become infected. Perhaps we can contain this thing?"

Aethelu kissed her hard on the lips and then ran towards the door, disappearing through it.

So now, Anais was alone. She had just under two minutes left to live. She heard the main door to the house opening and closing. It was a long shot, but if they all ran quick enough, perhaps they wouldn't get infected. Perhaps nobody would. There was only herself that was anywhere near the vial. She'd already gotten the one from the village. Despite everything she'd been through, Anais smiled. They'd beaten Andrew. The others would be clever enough to set up some kind of exclusion zone around The Manor, a quarantine. After a while, the virus would simply die out with no host to infect. The only thing making her sad was the speed with which Aethelu said goodbye. Actually, she hadn't said goodbye. She'd just kissed her and gone. Anais knew that it was the only way to get everyone out in time. There just hadn't been enough time to say goodbye properly. Whatever was in that vial, she was ready for it. She closed her eyes and took a deep breath. Her mind began to wander and for some reason she thought back to the first time Aethelu had touched her. Just their fingertips had met and yet she'd felt more in that few seconds than she'd ever felt before in her whole life. Electricity had pulsated through her body. A brief smile played on her lips before something tickled them, causing her to open her eyes in shock.

"Aethelu! What are you doing here?" Anais shouted, more in shock than anger.

"Do you think I would ever leave you?"

"But...but"

"The others escaped. I told them to drive as far away as they could. They know they will have to alert the authorities. Our secret will finally be out, but there is no other way. There needs to be an exclusion zone around here and the only ones of us that know anything about viruses are Andrew and Father. Andrew is dead and Father's unconscious. I'm afraid that Autumn's first few months of life will probably be spent being prodded and poked by scientists, but at least, she will survive.".

"But you will die." Anais looked at her watch. Twenty-five seconds remained.

"I couldn't leave you," she replied simply.

She put her arms around Anais and they held each other tight, counting down their final moments together.

Anais could feel the warmth of Aethelu and a small shudder told her that Aethelu was crying. Even though her watch was silent, she could almost hear the ticking, counting down the last few seconds of her life.

Tick...Tick...Tick.

And, then, it was over.

15

She felt the vial smash rather than heard it. A sliver of shattered glass pierced her skin. At the same time, the part of the safe that was holding her arm withdrew. Both girls looked towards Anais' hand. A blue ring of bruised skin circled her wrist where the safe had trapped her, but that was not what sent a shiver of fear through Anais. It was the sight of her hand. Tinged slightly blue, due to the lack of blood flow, and dripping with both the red and blue liquid that the vial had contained, her hand now started to bleed. Red blood mixed with the contents of the vial and dripped on the floor as she pulled her hand from the safe. Aethelu grabbed her hand and gently removed the shard of glass that was sticking out.

"We need to wash it," she said.

"Why? I'm covered with this virus. It's already entered my bloodstream."

"Look, we don't know what it will do yet. We know that our bodies can fight the Jagovirus. Perhaps we will be alright."

"I think we both know that's not the case. He told us that

he'd put something more potent in there just for us. To be honest, I'm amazed we are still standing."

"But we are still standing. Let's clean you up."

Anais let Aethelu lead her out of the library. It was easier than arguing. As Aethelu led her through the entrance hall, she took a good look at her. She was barely recognisable from the girl she'd met a year and a half ago. Her hair was patchy and her skin scarred, thanks to Andrews itching powder. Perhaps if they had lived longer, she would return to normal. She was still as pale as she had ever been, but her eyes had black circles under them and the diamond flecks in her pupils were long gone, dulled by pain and tragedy. And yet, she was still Aethelu. The beauty that was intrinsically her was still there.

"I love you." It seemed such a silly time to say it, but it also felt right. Besides, how long would they have left? How many more 'I love you's' would there be?"

"I love you, too." It was the last thing Anais heard before she fell to the floor.

At first, Anais thought she had somehow passed out and was dreaming, but looking up, she could see Aethelu looking down at her, concern filling her face.

She could hear Aethelu calling her name.

"Anais? Are you ok?"

Anais tried to answer, but no words came out. In fact, she couldn't make a sound at all. Suddenly, the full horror of it hit her. She was paralysed. She tried to move but couldn't. Yet she could still breathe, and see and hear.

So this is what Andrew had in store for them. He never intended to kill the Guardians, just paralyse them. But why? It made no sense. He'd shown that he didn't care whether they lived or died. Why not just kill them? Then Anais remembered all the other tricks he had played. He wanted to cause The Guardians pain. It wasn't enough that he kill them. He wanted to kill them in the most painful way he could think of. However, apart from being unable to move or communicate, she felt fine. She was in no pain and her breathing was normal. For a second, Anais' panic receded before she remembered what Andrew had said about his virus. It wasn't very contagious, but it worked extremely quickly. What had he said about it? It would paralyse a Guardian. Then what? Anais breathed in quickly as she remembered what came next. Extreme pain followed by her lungs failing then death.

"Anais?" Aethelu screamed.

Anais tried to move, if only a little, to communicate to Aethelu that she was ok, but it was impossible. She had no control over her body at all. She couldn't even bat her eyelashes. Anais knew that Aethelu, herself, would succumb to the same fate very soon. By the look of panic on Aethelu's face, she was thinking the same thing.

Anais wondered how long it would be before the pain would come. It was the next step toward death. At the moment, her body, although locked, was not in any pain, actually, quite the opposite. She couldn't really feel anything at all. Her body was numb.

Suddenly she smelled something that made her situation much worse—Fire! But surely, the fire from earlier had been put out by the sprinklers! She moved her eyes to the side. They were the only part of her body that she still had any control over. She could see the bright orange of flames licking across the ceiling at a rate that wasn't normal. The fire moved above her in an unnatural way. The sprinklers should have come on by now, but it seemed that someone had disabled the fire safety system. No prizes for guessing who did it. This was Andrew's final trick. He planned to paralyse them all then have the house set on fire knowing that they wouldn't be able to move. The sprinklers had worked earlier when Alex had accidentally set fire to Andrew's bedroom, so the sprinkler system must have been set to deactivate at the same time as the fire started. It all must have happened at the same time as the vials of Jagovirus were set to break.

Aethelu bent down and tried to pick Anais up, but it wasn't so simple. Not only had Anais lost control of her own body, but her muscles had seized up to such an extent that her body had locked in the position she had fallen. Aethelu struggled to find a way to carry her.

She ended up half-carrying her, half-dragging Anais to the door. She managed to get her halfway across the hallway when she, too, was overcome from the Jagovirus . She fell to the floor next to Anais, her arm and leg just draping over Anais' side.

Both of them were now incapable of moving. Anais couldn't see Aethelu next to her, but she could hear the sounds of her panicked breathing. The whole ceiling was now blanketed in bright orange flames. She could barely see anything else but fire in her line of vision. The heat that radiated out was beginning to hurt her skin, but the smoke was the real problem. The room was turning blacker and blacker with thick smoke, which was now beginning to invade her lungs. She desperately wanted to cough but couldn't because of the paralysis. The smoke was relatively thinner here in her position low to the floor, but she knew it wouldn't be long before the smoke would descend and she wouldn't be able to breathe at all. It was a toss-up whether the fire would kill them first or the smoke. As soon as she thought it, a huge cracking sound came from above her. She could barely see the huge chandelier as it fell through the smoke and came crashing down right next to her. The resulting sound of shattering crystals hurt her ears, but that was nothing compared to the pain of the chandelier landing on her arm.

The heat was really beginning to hurt now. Anais could feel her skin blistering. Aethelu's ragged breathing continued beside her, and Anais could tell she was struggling.

Then the realisation hit her. This is what Andrew meant. The Jagovirus would only paralyse them. Then, the fire he planned that would cause them pain, the smoke would smother their lungs, and then eventually cause their death.

It did little to help her now, though. All she could see was orange, and all she could feel was searing heat. There was no oxygen left for her to breathe. Her last thoughts before everything went black were of her daughter. At least, Autumn would survive this nightmare.

16

The funeral was a lovely service. There wasn't a dry eye in the little chapel. The family had suffered many losses in the last couple of years, but somehow this one was the saddest. Winnie sat at the front, tears streaming down her face. Alex, sitting at her side, passed her a tissue, with which she dabbed her eyes. Sabine held his hand as the priest said a few words. The body was to be laid to rest next to Anais' father in the family tomb. It was one of the few bits of The Manor still standing. The main building was almost entirely gone, wiped out by the fire. The surgery, Aethelu's studio, and the huge garage were still standing, but they had been deemed unsafe by the authorities due to some fire damage. Some of Aethelu's paintings had survived and the family were permitted to take them out as long as they promised to wear hard hats.

Winnie stood up and offered her own eulogy. The service ended and the family followed the coffin to the nearby hearse, which was to carry Aldrich on his final journey. Arcadia, Sabine, and James had come out of their coma eventually. James had lost the use of his legs although he was currently receiving physiotherapy to gain some control back. Arcadia and Sabine had come through with no ill effects, but Aldrich had never really recovered. He died just a few weeks after the final day in The Manor.

Anais thought back to that day. Her last memory had been the burning of her own flesh before she had passed out. What had happened next she had no recollection of, but she had since been told. The family had seen the flames and smoke pouring out of windows of The Manor. They knew Anais and Aethelu were trapped inside, but they still had the problem of being infected with the Jagovirus. It was Audsley, who had come up with a solution. She had found a long piece of rope in the back of the Range Rover, one that was there to tow other cars, if needed. She had run back to the house and opened the front door. At first, smoke had poured out around her, thick black smoke, causing her to cough and splutter. After a few seconds, she had seen the outlines of Anais and Aethelu on the floor of the main hall. Knowing that she couldn't go near them, she tied the rope into a lasso and used her years of cowboy training to throw it around Aethelu. She caught her leg on the first go. She pulled as fast as she could, dragging Aethelu's unconscious body through the doors of The Manor. She had to pull her down the stone steps, banging her head on each one. She knew she had to keep her at a distance, though, unless she also wanted to contract the virus. It was then that she realised that she wouldn't be able to unhook the lasso from Aethelu's leg without coming into contact with her. That would surely mean she would contract the Jagovirus. She tried a couple of times in vain. The lasso had tightened around Aethelu's leg and refused to come off. At first, Audsley was going to run back to the Range Rover to see if there was any more rope, but when she looked up, she realised she was too late. The Manor's huge doorway was just about to collapse. There wasn't time to find more rope. She ran with The Light in her veins as fast as she could. To any normal human being watching, she would have appeared as a blur. She ran into the burning building. The heat hit her and she sucked in her breath.. It was a mistake as thick black smoke entered her lungs. The air was too thick to see Anais so she had to feel about for her. Her right foot knocked against something. She didn't think, she just bent down and grabbed Anais and ran out of the building just in time as the whole ceiling collapsed behind her.

She laid Anais in the garden, far enough away from the burning house before turning back for Aethelu, who was still perilously close to The Manor.

The others stood down the driveway watching from a distance. When they saw Audsley bringing out the girls, they started to run towards them.

"Stay back!" yelled Audsley, "We all have contracted the Jagovirus."

It was the last thing she spoke before she too seized up and fell to the ground.

Anais had been told how the rest of the family had stood at a distance watching the house burn and the three girls lie on the grass for hours. Rain drizzled down, soaking the three girls, but it was not enough to save the house. Audsley had fallen in such a way that she watched the whole building burn until she felt arms grab her.

A team of men wearing white suits pulled her onto a stretcher and took her, Aethelu, and Anais to an isolation room in a hospital many miles away. It was there that Anais had woken up. She remembered the day in great detail. She relived it in her mind every day. She thought back now and like all the other times she daydreamed of it, it was almost as if she was still there.

She had awakened with a mask covering her face. She tried to move it away to speak, but she couldn't move. She managed to make a gurgling sound to attract someone's attention.

A good-looking man in a white suit came into her line of vision. For a second Anais wondered if she had been taken to the moon. All she could see was the white ceiling and this man in his suit. She could see his face through a window in the face of the suit.

"Hello." His voice was friendly. It put Anais at ease. "My name is Thomas, Dr Thomas Williams. You are in an isolation ward of a specialist hospital. We deal with highly contagious diseases. You have contracted something that we have not seen the likes of before. We are currently running a lot of tests, but with your unique blood, we are dealing within the realms of something we have no clue about."

Unique blood? They knew about The Light? The family must have told the authorities and given up the secret they had carried for centuries.

Dr Thomas continued, "You were pretty badly burned so we've bandaged you up as best we can. The last time we changed your bandages, you had healed in a miraculous way, unlike anything I've ever seen. I think that if your body keeps regenerating this way, you will be as good as new within a few days. Unfortunately, this Jagovirus is going to be harder to cure. We don't know how to deal with it."

Anais wanted to know if Aethelu was ok but had to be patient and wait for him to tell her. She didn't have to wait long.

"Now I know you will be wondering about your family. So far, Winnie, Raphael, Sabine and Jennifer are in another isolation ward. They are showing no signs of illness so we are just keeping them in as a precaution. Your little girl has been brought a cot and is being looked after on the same ward. I know you must be anxious to see her, but, right now, it's the safest option to have her grandmother look after her.

I'm afraid the others aren't so good." He looked through his notes to remember all the names of this large family.

"Judith is currently in theatre. She has sustained damage to her leg and it needs surgery. She has already lost half of it but the half she has left needs cleaning and sewing up. She is ok, though, and once the surgery is finished, she will join the others.

Aethelu and Audsley are in the beds next to you. Audsley has already heard this and as soon as Aethelu wakes up, I will repeat it to her, too.

Finally, we have Aldrich, James, Alex, and Arcadia. They are still in another ward. Again, just like you, we have no idea what is infecting them. All have been placed on ventilators and we are giving them round the clock care, but they have yet to regain consciousness.

Anais tried to take it all in. It seemed half the family were totally fine, including Autumn, and for that, she was grateful. However, the other half had various problems, all thanks to Andrew.

What followed were weeks of tests and procedures to try to get them all healthy. In the end, it took electric shocks to finally stimulate her muscles into working. This was followed by months of physiotherapy. Anais had only been out of bed for a couple of days when she heard that Aldrich had died. Alex, James, and Arcadia had been responding to treatment well, but Aldrich's old body had just given up and he had died in his sleep.

Of course, telling the authorities meant that they could

no longer live in secret. Their bodies were tested in so many ways and they all had to give various bodily fluids to be kept on file in the hospital. The hospital team had promised not to share with anyone else what they had discovered in this immortal family. It had taken rather a huge amount of money to obtain the silence of everyone involved, but it was worth it to protect their privacy. The contagious disease prevention team had also managed to eradicate any traces of the Jagovirus not wiped out by the fire. Once they were finished with what was left of the building and a safe amount of time had passed, the family had had the whole Manor razed to the ground.

LATER

Anais looked down into the eyes of the newborn baby in her arms. Beautiful brown eyes stared back at her. A tiny little button nose atop perfect bow lips. The baby looked just like his namesake, Uncle August. Baby August chose just that moment to spit up.

"Oh, I'm sorry." Sabine ran up to Anais with a baby wipe.

"Don't worry." Anais smiled as she took the wipe from Sabine and expertly wiped his mouth. "Do you want him back because I think Granddad James is next in line for a cuddle.

"Did someone say my name?" James wheeled himself over in his wheelchair, held out his arms, and Anais passed him his grandson.

"He looks just like your mother, Sabine," he said for the hundredth time that day. "Come on August, my boy. Let's go and look at the boats." He lovingly placed Baby August safely on his knees and wheeled to the end of the patio to look at the boats in the harbour in the distance.

"He really is gorgeous," Anais said to Sabine as she

watched her own daughter toddle towards James and the baby to get another look at her cousin.

"Thank you. It seems he has a little fan there in Autumn." She loves him. Won't stop chattering on about him. I guess she'll have another little playmate to play with soon, too, if Judith gets a wriggle on."

"She's only overdue by a couple of days," replied Anais.

Anais looked over the beautiful French garden to where Judith was relaxing on a sun lounger. She had such a cute, neat, bump compared to the size Anais had been when she had been pregnant. Even though she had lost her leg and was overdue with her first baby, she still managed to pull off elegance effortlessly.

Arcadia and Audsley occupied the loungers next to her. Arcadia, much to her relief, had grown back her beautiful white blonde hair and only the smallest of scars remained visible on her skin.

Rafe, Alex and Aethelu sat at a little table playing cards and drinking beer, although Anais could see that Rafe had barely touched his, not wanting to drink too much in case he had to rush to the hospital with Judith.

They were all staying at Arcadia's villa in the south of France. Sabine, James, and Alex had flown over from Florence a couple of months before, as Winnie wanted to be nearby for the birth of her first grandson. The house was big enough to accommodate them all, but Arcadia had generously given Anais and Aethelu a part of her garden to build their own little house on. It was coming along nicely and in a couple of months, they would be able to move in. It was small, but the views were amazing.

The only noticeable absences from the group were Jennifer, who had flown back to her home in Egypt almost as soon as their ordeal was over. She'd sent a card of congratulations on the birth of August and a promise that she'd visit soon.

Anais had not seen her for over a year, not since they had left the hospital and gone back to The Manor for the last time for Aldrich's funeral. She wondered how she was getting on. The last she had heard was that she had reopened the hostel but under a different name.

Anais was snapped out of her reverie by Winnie, who appeared with a giant plate of chocolate chip cookies and a huge grin on her face.

"Cookies, anyone? They've just come out of the oven."

Aethelu ran up to her mother, kissed her cheek, and grabbed a handful of cookies. She took one to Autumn, who grabbed it in her little hands and stuffed it into her mouth greedily.

She brought one over to Anais.

As she passed the cookie over, her hand brushed Anais' hand.

Anais jumped as the electric shock of The Light ran up her arm.

It had been over a year since she had felt it. She looked up at Aethelu and smiled. The future ahead of them was bright and sunny.

EPILOGUE

T essa Gibson from the local village loved walking her dog through the local woodland by the tramway. For as long as she'd known it, it had belonged to a mysterious family, but the big house had burnt down last year, followed by the comings and goings of a lot of strange men in white suits. It had kept the village in gossip for months, but no one really had gotten to the bottom of what was going on. Even Mrs Smithson didn't have a clue, and she'd worked there for years. The family had all disappeared as mysteriously as they had lived. Tessa, always up for a bit of gossip, was delighted when the woodland had been opened up to the public. There was no fanfare about it, but the gates had been removed letting anyone in. The ruins of the ornate building were still there. There wasn't much left, but there were plenty of intricate stones strewn around the woodland where the great house had once stood. A little mosaic flooring still existed although the weeds were beginning to take over. You could even see a little way into the cellars if you knew where to look. The only bit still standing was a tomb which presumably belonged to the family. Today, however, it was locked and Tessa had no particular interest in it anyway. She just enjoyed walking with her dog, Nipper. Just then, she saw him digging in the ground. Something had caught his attention. A rabbit hole?

"Nipper. Nipper." He ignored her, so she had to go to him.

"What's that boy?" Nipper placed the unearthed item in her hands. It was the strangest thing she had ever seen, some kind of small glass vessel. Inside it, curious red and blue liquids swirled around each other.

Tessa looked down at her dog.

"What ever do you think this could be..."

THE MANOR

The Manor.

Even though the Guardians of The Light books are entirely fictional, there is one aspect that is real. At the bottom end of Baildon Village there really is a ruined manor and I've tried to describe the ruins how they look now as accurately as I can although it was a much grander building than the manor I've described when it was still standing. The place is called Milner's Field if you care to look it up. It was once owned by The Salt family and they had enough tragedy of their own to produce rumours about the house being haunted or cursed.

The tramway and the old building at the top are also real although I don't think there is anyone there with a secret laboratory planning the downfall of the world. Then again, Who knows? Maybe there is!

ABOUT THE AUTHOR

J.A lives in a total fantasy world (because reality is boring right?) When she's not writing all the crazy fun in her head, she can be found eating cake, designing pretty pictures and hanging upside down from the tallest climbing frame in the local playground while her children look on in embarrassment. She's travelled the world working as everything from a banana picker in Australia to a Pantomime clown, has climbed to the top of Mount Kilimanjaro and the bottom of the Grand Canyon and once gave birth to a surrogate baby for a friend of hers.

She spends way too much time gossiping on facebook and if you want to be part of her Reading Army, where you'll get lots of freebies, exclusive sneak peeks and super secret sales, join up here

Somehow she finds time to write.